LADY WU

BOOKS BY LIN YUTANG

KAIMING ENGLISH BOOKS (3 vols.)

KAIMING ENGLISH GRAMMAR

THE LITTLE CRITIC (2 vols.)

CONFUCIUS SAW NANCY
AND ESSAYS ABOUT NOTHING

A NUN OF TAISHAN

A HISTORY OF THE PRESS AND
PUBLIC OPINION IN CHINA

MY COUNTRY AND MY PEOPLE

THE IMPORTANCE OF LIVING

WISDOM OF CONFUCIUS

MOMENT IN PEKING

WITH LOVE AND IRONY

A LEAF IN THE STORM

WISDOM OF CHINA AND INDIA

BETWEEN TEARS AND LAUGHTER

THE VIGIL OF A NATION

THE GAY GENIUS

CHINATOWN FAMILY

WISDOM OF LAOTSE

ON THE WISDOM OF AMERICA

WIDOW, NUN AND COURTESAN

FAMOUS CHINESE SHORT STORIES

VERMILION GATE

LOOKING BEYOND

THE SECRET NAME

THE CHINESE WAY OF LIFE

FROM PAGAN TO CHRISTIAN

THE IMPORTANCE OF UNDERSTANDING

THE RED PEONY

IMPERIAL PEKING

PLEASURES OF A NONCONFORMIST

JUNIPER LOA

THE FLIGHT OF THE INNOCENTS

LADY WU

LADY WU

A NOVEL BY

Lin Yutang

G. P. Putnam's Sons   New York

C. 3

Library of Congress Catalog
Card: 65-13293

PRINTED IN THE UNITED STATES OF AMERICA

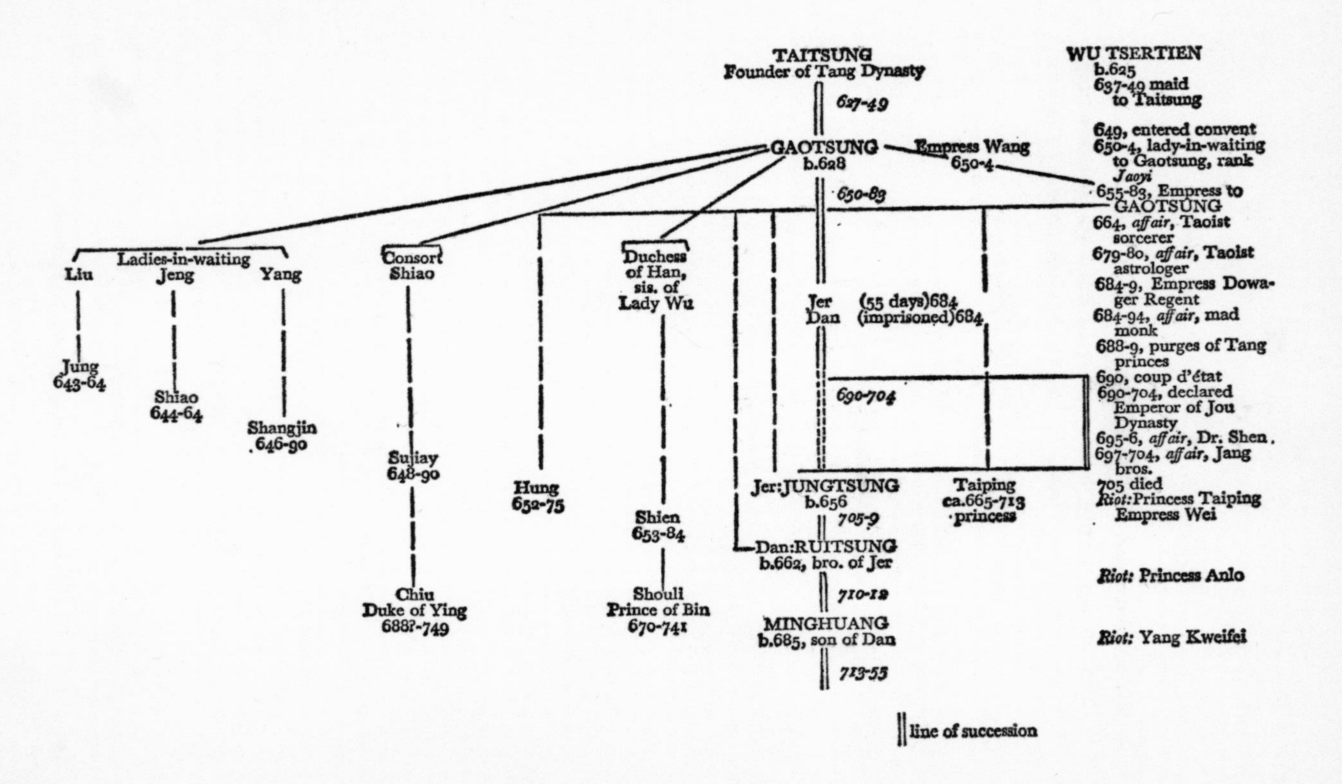
TAITSUNG
Founder of Tang Dynasty
627-49
GAOTSUNG
b.628
650-83
Empress Wang
650-4
WU TSERTIEN
b.625
637-49 maid to Taitsung
649, entered convent
650-4, lady-in-waiting to Gaotsung, rank *Jaoyi*
655-83, Empress to GAOTSUNG
664, *affair*, Taoist sorcerer
679-80, *affair*, Taoist astrologer
684-9, Empress Dowager Regent
684-94, *affair*, mad monk
688-9, purges of Tang princes
690, coup d'état
690-704, declared Emperor of Jou Dynasty
695-6, *affair*, Dr. Shen.
697-704, *affair*, Jang bros.
705 died
Riot: Princess Taiping Empress Wei
Riot: Princess Anlo
Riot: Yang Kweifei
Ladies-in-waiting
Liu
Jeng
Yang
Jung
643-64
Shiao
644-64
Shangjin
646-90
Consort Shiao
Sujiay
648-90
Chiu
Duke of Ying
688?-749
Hung
652-75
Duchess of Han, sis. of Lady Wu
Shien
653-84
Shouli
Prince of Bin
670-741
Jer
Dan
(55 days)684
(imprisoned)684
690-704
Jer:JUNGTSUNG
b.656
705-9
Taiping
ca.665-713
princess
Dan:RUITSUNG
b.662, bro. of Jer
710-12
MINGHUANG
b.685, son of Dan
713-55
line of succession

PREFACE

In the spring of 1944 I visited Si-an, in the northwest of China. An archaeologist friend strongly suggested that I should visit the ruins of the tomb of Empress Wu's father. He mentioned the extraordinary bronze horses and animals there; it was his discovery and as the place was some forty miles outside the city, beyond the usual route of the tourists, it was practically unknown. Kung's enthusiasm was contagious, and we went off in a car. The plains northwest of Si-an are a vast stretch of mausoleums of kings of the past dynasties, from the Jou down, now dotting the landscape in mounds a hundred to two hundred feet high, completely abandoned and ignored by the local people and subject to the ravages of time—just a series of bare, loess hills, sometimes very close together, presenting the appearance of a desert, silent and immense.

I have no recollection of the exact route which took us to the tomb garden, but we must have been driving for two hours. When we arrived at the rectangular enclosure, about two hundred by one hundred yards, and saw the bronze animal figures, I was truly amazed. Empress Wu—for she *was* an empress, and if she would be contented with being an empress, there would be no trouble at all—Empress Wu, in an effort to found a dynasty of her own, had created her father "emperor" posthumously. The bronze horses standing on a pedestal were life-size, extremely well preserved. The surface was perfectly smooth and the gold and patina shimmered in the sunlight. Neither my friend nor I, being no specialists, could tell exactly what went into the composition of the statues, but of their unusual high quality and workmanship there was no question. Such lavish indifference to the treasures of antiquity was characteristic of Si-an, the Tang capital "Changan" in our story. This was my only indirect physical contact with the fabulous queen who dominated China in the second half of the seventh century.

Since 1955, ten years ago, I began to take notes on the history and doings of this extraordinary woman, unique in all history, ancient or modern. The first draft was completed in 1956. Her rascality and her superb intelligence charmed me. In the course of the last ten years, I have had occasion to review and re-evaluate the doings of this historic queen. They always frighten and amuse me by turns. I cannot find any parallels among the queens of western history.

To come close to the scene, I've let Shouli, Prince of Bin, tell the story from his point of view. He was the grandson of Emperor Gaotsung, but perhaps was not the grandchild of Lady Wu. At any rate he was privileged to grow up inside the Palace and know all that was going on. He was born around 670 and died in 741, in his seventies, and was a survivor of the bloodbath designed to exterminate the Tang Princes. When Lady Wu's projected Jou Dynasty collapsed and the royal Tang House was restored, he would have time to recollect and reflect on all that had happened. Incidentally, he had about sixty children with his many wives, all of them mediocre, according to history.

Because of the incredible and bizarre adventures of Lady Wu, it is necessary to state here that all the characters and incidents, even most of the dialogue, are strictly based on Tang history. The facts are based on the two official Tang histories, the *Old Tangshu* (10th century) and the *New Tangshu* (11th century). All other historical works dealing with the period go back after all to these primary sources. The latter is a revision of the former, but the *Old Tangshu* is really the more valuable for research; where the *New* is succinct, terse and elegant—the purpose of the revision—the *Old* has fuller details and more unedited dialogues, besides the many letters, memoranda and documents eliminated by the *New* for the sake of classic brevity; also the *Old* is based on several old shorter histories of the different periods, compiled by contemporaries. These dynastic histories contain one important feature: by far the greater part (150 vol. out of 200 in the *Old*, and 150 vol. out of 225 vol. in the *New*) consists of lives of the men of the period, with all the human drama, incidents and dialogues. From these "Lives," and from the genealogical tables and special sections on rituals and music, costumes and carriages, foreign tribes, geography, astronomy and astrology (the last recording every strange phenomenon from the appearance of comets to the birth of quadruplets) —from all this mass of data, it is possible to reconstruct a clear picture of the doings of this strange woman. Stories found in popular novels, such as her early affair with the mad monk, or her issuing an edict to command the flowers to blossom in winter, having no basis in historical records, are of course excluded. On the other hand, her cavorting with two handsome painted boys of her harem, the Jang brothers, is part of history, and was responsible for the crash of her dreams.

The spelling of Chinese names in this book is chosen for the reader's convenience, made so as not to be a tax on his memory. Thus Lai Jyunchen is shortened to Lai, and Changsun Wuji is shortened to Wuji, and this is kept consistent in the book. The first occurrence of such a name is given in full, with the omitted part in parentheses, for serious students who wish full identification; thus *Lai (Jyunchen)*, and *(Changsun) Wuji*. A few changes in Wade spelling are made, such as *sh* in place of *hs,* and *nay* in place of *nei,* for the reader's convenience. *Gao* in Gaotsung rhymes with *Mao* (read as *mow* in mowing machine). The *b–d–g, p–t–k* of the National Romantization system have replaced the *p–t–k, p'–t'–k'* of the Wade spelling, and are more likely to be pronounced correctly by Westerners. *J–ch* also replace *Ch–ch'*.

Book One

❋ I ❋

How can one write about one's grandmother, especially if she was a whore? There is a convention among the Royal House, His Majesty our present sovereign (Minghuang) included, that we must never speak disrespectfully of Grandmother, though we never mince words about her nephews, the Wus. There is a hush when her name creeps up accidentally in the conversation, for she was our grandmother after all, wasn't she? I am not quite able to share in this fiction and, in my case at least, there is considerable doubt as to whether she was my real grandmother; I am inclined to believe that my father was born of the Duchess of Han, and not of her, as I shall explain in the course of the story.

I, Shouli, Prince of Bin, have decided to write these memoirs of a woman who has made history and who attempted and almost succeeded in wiping out the Tang Royal House. My grandmother, if indeed she was my grandmother, was a woman most feline, predatory, cruel,—with a love for pomp, ceremony and splendor, who would stop at nothing—including murder—to attain what she desired. When we were children, His Majesty Minghuang and I used to tremble and our blood curdled when we heard her voice next door. It is so hard to describe such a woman—gracious and endearing when she chose to be; then suddenly, her sharp claws would be unsheathed to pounce and tear and destroy out of sheer malice and enjoyment of the power to kill. The curious fact was that she appeared almost always cool and correct; she looked every inch a queen before her courtiers, with an air of pontifical poise and dignity; but when her eyes narrowed and her lips compressed and she assumed a semi-divine look——Beware! She was always in the right, and not to be crossed. My sympathy goes out to my poor suffering grandfather, Emperor Gaotsung, who was married to this monstrous woman.

I must not give the impression that Lady Wu was just a spiteful, mean, domineering woman. She would not have been so dangerous if she were just that. Her exploits and her achievements were fantastic; she was driven by a will to rule that was superhuman. Her political showmanship was superb. Her religio-amorous extravaganzas were nothing short of spectacular. If she succeeded in her ambitions, it was because she was easily a match for all her ministers. We disapprove of her cruelty and wiles, but we cannot help admiring her political skill and brilliance. She was probably the most intelligent person of her generation, certainly the most outstanding, next only to Judge Di Renjiay. After all, it showed no mean ability to usurp the Royal House of her husband, found a dynasty of her own. It showed no mean ability for a sister of a convent to displace a crowned empress, or for a concubine of sorts of a dead emperor to marry her husband's son, without loss of public approval. She was always correct and never at a loss for a means of achieving her goals. And she was sometimes quite a moralist as is evidenced in her books, *Domestic Duties of Women* and *Lives of Model Women.* She was always serving the country and helping her cowed royal spouse to rule, to ferret out conspirators and nip rebellions. She stood for law and order. Even her barefaced debaucheries with the street wrestler "Baby Feng" took on a semireligious coloration. The wrestler was made an abbot and he sat in the Hall Celestial behind the Divine Temple of All Creatures where she received her courtiers.

Part child, part woman, and a merciless autocrat, she blazed such a path for herself as to make her the most powerful, the most unique, woman in all history.

Astute, with an intuitive political skill, she planned her moves, marked her victims and bided her time. This much must be said for her: she knew her men. When her new Jou Dynasty was established, all her executioners were killed within a year after having served their purpose during the terror; she remembered all the good men she had banished, and recalled them to power. She was able to rule the country in peace for fifteen years. There were no longer frame-ups; one heard no more of alarms of conspiracies and rebellions. Toward the end of her reign, law and justice recovered their ancient dignity. Ironically, it was in this very period of outspoken ministers and honest, courageous judges that the seeds of her ruin were sown.

How does one write of one's grandmother if she was a whore and a murderess? This question came up the other day when my Cousin Chiu, Duke of Ying, and I had a hunting dinner at the Tsuiwei Palace and I told him that I was starting these memoirs. Chiu is the son of Uncle Prince Suchiay; my father was Prince Shien, at one time co-regent. Both of us are among the fortunate survivors of Grandmother's bloodbaths. He lost his father as I lost mine in the same wave of persecution. He is a good man and has helped many of the orphans of the Royal House. Many of the princes and dukes today owe him his help. He, too, was left an orphan and knew fear, hunger and the utter loneliness of a child wandering in the jungles of subtropical Hainan in the South China Sea, feeling like a convict's son, with a taint on his name. His mother and nine of his brothers were murdered on the same day, while he and two of his youngest brothers were exiled. He and I often sit over a cup of wine and exchange notes about the person responsible for it all, our grandmother. He is as doggedly proud of his father as I am of mine. Both of them were real scholars. What difference does it make? His father was hanged and my father was forced to hang himself. But he and I often enjoy these talks, like sailors recounting their escape from a disaster at sea.

"By all means, write the story," said Chiu. "We owe it to grandfather, and to your father's memory and to that of mine. As for that Wu whore who wanted to destroy us, the Lis, you know very well that my father was not born of her, but of the ill-fated Queen Consort Shiaofei. My father often told me about the horrible tragedy of his mother and of the stupid Empress Wang whom Lady Wu displaced. As a matter of fact, I hardly remember seeing Lady Wu, but you practically grew up in the Palace with His Majesty Ruitsung and his children, including our present sovereign. You must have known many inside details that the public does not know."

"Indeed I do," said I. "I was shut up in the Palace with Uncle Tan [Ruitsung] and his children, and never saw the outside world until he was released, a total of eighteen years [680-698]. I grew up in the Palace from the age of ten. We saw a lot of things."

"What was she like?"

"I was shut up in the Palace when Grandfather Gaotsung was still living. His Majesty was already a physical ruin, bedridden, with a cloth around his head, always complaining of headaches. Grandmother was just inside of sixty, still going strong. She had made a wreck of him all right. She had a square forehead and heavy jaws, and very black eyebrows, but I imagine she was a beauty in her youth. I don't know what tonic she took—her mad monk lover must have given her secret medicines. Anyway, her life began at sixty, when Grandfather passed away and her whoring began. She'd had paramours before, chiefly sorcerers in nightly sessions, but it was never like that. What was frightening was when she became angry, the color of her eyes changed to green."

"I sometimes see that in Princess Taiping, too."

"She takes after her mother—almost a replica in temperament, sexual tastes, ability and facial contours. I imagine that was how Grandmother looked when she was young. Believe me, Taiping was quite slim then. In her thirties she suddenly began to put on some flesh and developed a gait like Grandmother's. Taiping was five years my senior. When she was seventeen or eighteen she was absolutely wild, often dressed as a boy. She was married then to her first husband, Shuay Shao, but no matter. A maid spoke to her about the physical prowess of the mad monk—then a street wrestler. He came in constantly to see her, and it was she who introduced the wrestler to her mother. They shared the bed—that was after Grandfather had passed away. That was why the street wrestler was given the family name of Shuay, as the adopted father of her husband, in order to justify the intimacies. His real name was Feng, nickname Shiaobao [*Baby Feng*]. What a baby! He was a massive chunk of a man, not really vulgar except in his speech—his wrestler's argot. He had brawny arms, a powerful neck resting on broad shoulders, and plenty of stiff black hair before they shaved his head to make him Abbot of the White Horse Temple. Quite a braggart, and he walked with a swagger. In those days, as a representative of the church, he had free access to the women's quarters. It was quite a sight. With a flying purple cassock, he would jump onto a horse from the imperial stables while the Wu nephews, Sanse and Yitsung, held his reins for him. Then he would swing his whip and dash off."

"Why was he called Baby?"

"You know why. It was a love-name. It was the *little precious* that the mother and daughter loved."

"Didn't he have a name?"

"We don't know. The *little precious* was his trademark, his entrée to the women's chambers. When they made him abbot, he assumed the name of *Huaiyi* [Embracing Righteousness]. A monk never uses a family name, but the name Shuay was tagged on for the reason I have mentioned."

"Why did Princess Taiping have him killed?"

"That was in the end. He got madder and madder. Grandmother had a new lover in Dr. Shen, a physician, and the abbot became insanely jealous. He set fire to the Hall Celestial and Grandmother had to cover up for him. But he had become insolent to Grandmother, and was intolerable. At this time, the affair with the mad monk had become known to the man in the street, for during the execution of Ho Shiangshien, the young man on his way to the execution ground spat, broke loose from the guards and delivered his dying speech. He didn't care; he didn't have long to live anyway. Out came the whole sordid story of the princess and her mother. The crowd listened, enthralled. After that, the prisoners were gagged on their way to the execution ground. But it was too late. You could cover up and hush a scandal about immorality in high places, but you could not prevent it from passing from mouth to mouth, and that is the fastest system of communication known. Wise counsel spreads slowly, but wicked gossip travels fast. Grandmother and the princess tricked him to the palace garden, and a dozen husky women ambushed him and felled him, tied him up with ropes and strangled him. Then Grandmother picked up the handsome Jang brothers. She was then already in her seventies. She grew a new wisdom tooth and later was reputed to have grown a secondary eyebrow, although I never saw it. A remarkable woman."

"Her new life began at sixty."

"And it continued on to eighty, what with the gland extracts, aphrodisiacs and the cheek and the flamboyance which Grandmother certainly had."

"I hear many stories that her affair with the wrestler began while she was a nun at the Ganyiay Convent."

"That isn't true. It couldn't be. There is so much gossip by people who do not know. The mad monk was in his thirties and Princess Taiping was eighteen when she discovered him. The mad monk was probably only a baby when Grandmother was a nun."

"That's all the more reason why you should write these memoirs. You know of things firsthand that the others don't. Does His Majesty know you are writing them?"

"No. I haven't told him yet. I am like his elder brother. He can't stop me. Heavens, no. This respect for Grandmother is a fiction which he, as the Emperor, must keep up —in public, at least. Don't forget that his own mother, Empress of Ruitsung, was murdered by that old woman. When he ascended the throne and wished to give his mother a reburial with imperial honors, he couldn't even find out where her remains were, or if she was in fact ever buried at all. She had just disappeared. Both the wives of Ruitsung had disappeared. She was ceremonially buried with a set of clothes without her body in the coffin. If he hears about my writing, I am going to tell him that I am writing about the feud between the Lis and the Wus. After all, it was he who started the *coup d'état* and put an end to the last of the Wus and forced Princess Taiping to commit suicide. I remember one day we children were let out of the palace to worship at the ancestral temple. The little Wu nephew, Yitsung, tried to stop us. Minghuang replied, 'We are going to worship *our* ancestors, the Lis. What has it to do with you?' How in his heart of hearts, he must have hated and despised Yitsung, Sanse and all the rest of them!"

So let this be. It will be the recollections of a man about a woman who happened to come into our lives. I am not a political diarist or journalist and have no intention of writing a proper history of the last three or four amazing decades. Some of the politics will come in inevitably. But primarily Grandmother fascinates me as a woman. And I am not a prude; I record, but do not condemn. I am far from a paragon of virtue myself. I have a weakness for women; the fact is quite well known. I have incurred debts to the tune of several hundred thousand dollars and spent the money on women. In my time I have served the Emperor, as Minister of Justice and general and all that. Heaven has sent us peace in the last two decades, and I am fortunately placed to live a prince's life of luxury and pleasures. Now living in retirement in my old age, it would seem ungrateful of me not to enjoy all the sights and sounds and all the ministerings of pleasure that surround me. While I live and my health permits I intend to enjoy every moment of it.

This leads me to a little reflection on women, and then I'll have done and will proceed with the story. I do not know about the life of the common people; it may be that there is politics in every common home. But for us princes who more or less cannot escape public duties, the intrusion of women into politics is a much more serious matter. Women are men's pleasure; their charm is their power, and he is an idiot who is insensible to them. We are as attractive to women as they are to us; they desire our affection, our attention, as much as we desire theirs; there is no escape from it as far as I can see. In the case of nymphomaniacs like Lady Wu, they are quite as susceptible to us as we are to them. But let us stop somewhere, draw the line somewhere, especially for those charged with governing a nation. Lady Wu has often been compared with Empress Lu, wife of the founder of the Han Dynasty. She was a licentious woman, like Grandmother. It is even recorded in official history that she "hunted the empire for men with enormous members and made Laowei her lover." But that was her private business and it did not influence politics to any appreciable extent. In the case of the mad monk, he had nothing to recommend himself except what recommended Laowei to the Han Empress. The love of bigness in Lady Wu was psychological, as we shall see. But it became a political scandal. Perhaps she had wanted to keep it strictly her private affair, too. Unfortunately, she allowed her grandiose fantasies to go wild, and propagated the legend that she was Buddha Maitreya incarnate, entitled to the services of the giant of a priest. In the end it was a mixture of sex and religion, of muck and glory —often more muck than glory.

Somewhere a line must be drawn about women in politics. I believe that when they are in power, their predatory instinct is much more fearful, more devastating, than men's. Have we not had enough examples of this in the reigns of the last three Emperors? Taitsung's Empress, as everybody knows, was indeed an immense help and a source of strength to the great Emperor. She was truly great because she was gentle and had compassion for her people. If she ever influenced her husband, it was when Taitsung flew into a temper and was inclined to be unjust to his ministers. She would remind him not to turn his back on his loyal supporters. But we have Lady Wu under Gaotsung, and we have Empress Wei who actually murdered her royal husband Jungtsung, and the riotous examples of Princesses Taiping and Anlo, who arrogated to themselves the power of promoting and degrading public ministers and generally turned the machinery of government upside down. The last, Anlo, was called "Princess of Diagonal Seal" because letters in her envelopes, diagonally sealed, appointing and dismissing public officials, could go out straight from the Palace without the due procedure of the ministries. Besides, I do not think there was a period of more licentiousness and adultery at court in the nation's history than during the reigns of Jungtsung and Ruitsung, a consequence, no doubt, of the example set by Grandmother. The *yin* had overcome the *yang.* I am all for women, but have the men all become idiots to permit this state of things to go on?

Grandmother was a clear, and rather extreme, example of the power of women. She was a match for all the kings and Tang princes and able ministers, in sagacity, in use of men for her tools, in timing of her actions, in sheer coolness. She blazed her own path to political glory, which was what primarily interested her. But still she was a woman in certain respects. Her vengeance against Empress Wang was close to the animal level. Her intolerance of other women was characteristic—she murdered all her four daughters-in-law. She loved sorcerers, astrologers and priests.* Her ruthlessness, based on political expediency, such as pushing the children and grandchildren of the princes to the bank and slaughtering them in the hundreds, has a touch of feminine ferocity which the masculine mind can try to explore but never quite comprehend. There was also a feminine touch in her capricious promotions and sublime disregard of the system of civil service examinations. Her making of a portrait of Buddha two hundred feet high suggests to me the fantasy of a girl playing with her doll. There is a child in every woman. But the whole bravado of the episodes with the mad monk and the Jang brothers in her old age and the mock-religious extravaganzas were things which the more rational minds of men could never conceive or understand. Certain restraints were lacking.

The *yim* and the *yang* must necessarily complement each

* Women and astrologers are inseparable within the last decades; we have the case of Princess Hopu and her several priests, both Buddhists and Taoists, one of whom could see ghosts, and the cases of Princess Taiping and Princess Jinshien. The priests all became powerful and wealthy.

other. When one overwhelms the other, life cannot go on. Hens should not cry cock-a-doodle-do.

I have this advice for princes. The women are out to get us. They have their fulfillment in us as we in them. It is so in nature. All creatures, male or female, have an urge to seek the other sex. As it is, we are the fish and they are the anglers; we are their legitimate preserves. The variety of lures and baits with which they try to catch us is limitless. It is an instinct primordial and goes beyond morality. They have certain ambitions, hopes and desires to seek their place in life and live in comfort and security, and they have no other means except through the men that interest them. Don't run away from them, but don't let them run away with us and get away with everything, either. Love the women, but keep them away from politics. This should be a principle in the training of a crown prince.

❋ 2 ❋

In the twenty-third year of Taitsung (649), the old Emperor, my great-grandfather, was lying on his deathbed in his beautiful retreat in the Jungnan Hills, surrounded by trees and a luxuriant vegetation. It was his summer resort, connected with the capital, Si-an, by a charming valley crossed by the Tsan, a clear, gurgling stream coming down from the hills and running to the southern suburbs where the villas thickened toward the Chujiang Lake. The hills ran on and became part of the great rugged Taipo Range beyond; but here, about a thousand feet above the city, was a plateau, secluded and a world of its own.

The Palace, the Hanfeng Hall, was simple and in the rustic style of summer houses, built out of the timber removed from another old palace. It was characteristic of the Emperor. Founder of the great Tang Dynasty, he never went in for grandeur and magnificence in buildings and edifices, and lived in the palaces inherited from the defeated Sui Emperor, contenting himself with minor repairs here and there. For he knew his people were poor, torn by decades of war in the preceding chaos, and grand buildings involved vast expenditures and labor from the people. He had indeed built the Lingyen Tower inside the Palace, but it was to commemorate his "Twenty-four Founding Knights" who had fought and labored by his side to found the new empire and bring peace to the country once more. Again, it was so like him to give recognition to his friends and his generals, his comrades in battle. These were his knights, and their portraits were a tribute to, and a celebration of, their meritorious service to himself and to the Empire.

The dysentery he had contracted had never been completely cured, though he had got better for a period. All strength seemed to have ebbed out of him and he was greatly emaciated and enfeebled. Stricken at the age of fifty-two, he felt his end was near. He had been a hale and hearty soldier with a good sense of camaraderie with his generals and able ministers. A natural leader of men, distinguished by his humanity and great charm of natural simplicity, he was forthright with his ministers about their mistakes and asked for equally forthright criticisms of his own. Around him had gathered a group of able men, men of courage and honor, who admired him as much as they loved him. He had known the smoke and dust of battle and had personally led the campaign in Korea; with his great generals he had smashed and broken up the Eastern Turkish Confederacy in the north and brought the western frontier to the outskirts of Turkestan near the Caspian Sea; other generals had invaded India from the north and compelled tribute from Nepal.

He had no side and no airs, and behind his fierce stiff whiskers "on which one could hang a bow," he was a man with a deep compassion for his people. It was this compassion for the people which was the key to the strength of the great and glorious Tang. He had won the hearts of the people, and it was their loyalty to the Tang House that spelled the eventual ruin of Lady Wu's dreams. I mention this in contrast to all that was to follow.

Taitsung was preparing for his end. Archduke Changsun Wuji was constantly by his side. Wuji was not only brother of the deceased good Empress; he was the first of the Twenty-four Knights of Lingyen Tower. For thirty years he had been by his side during the campaigns as his strategist and closest adviser.

"I want a few important words with you," said the Emperor. The guards took the hint and withdrew.

"I know I have not long to live. There are a few things on my mind—"

"Your Majesty, you are not feeling well today, but—"

"No, I know. Of course, my good Empress will be buried with me. First, I want to have stone sculptures of my eight warrior horses made and placed at the entrance to my mausoleum. You know them by name. I want this done more than anything else."

Wuji saw a smile on the Emperor's face.

"It will be done as Your Majesty wishes."

"Sometimes I think they love me and understand me more than many of my subjects. In the days to come, my poor Pheasant [Gaotsung] will need all the help you can give him. He is good-hearted—that is the principal thing in a ruler—but he is weak, sentimental, and so young. I am happy that his wife, Princess Wang, is from one of our own royal families, well-bred, modest, decent. I don't care for brilliant, scheming women. A ruler has enough troubles abroad; he does not want intrigues at home. But my mind is not completely at rest. Pheasant is young and you must protect him. Come here."

Wuji drew nearer and the sovereign and minister spoke almost in whispers.

"Li Chunfeng has warned me. At first I thought nothing of it. In the last two months while I have been here, I have noticed things. This girl Wu Meiniang worries me. She has served me well, is very able, very correct, and remembers all details. But things have been going on behind my back. Recently I saw a new look in Pheasant's eyes. Li Chunfeng's warning is not entirely without foundation. Remember Tawny Mane, the horse that no one could break? One night Wu Meiniang said to me, 'Your Majesty, I can.' I said 'How?' and she said, 'Give me an iron chain, an iron hammer, and a stiletto. If I could not break him with lashes from the iron chain, I would subdue him with a hammer, and if I couldn't do that, I would plunge the stiletto into his neck.' I do not know whether she said it in earnest, but it was frightening to hear such words from a young woman. It was no way to break a horse. But from the way she said it, she looked as if she could really do it."

"Has there been something between those two?" the Archduke asked cautiously.

"I think so."

"It would be easy to dismiss her from the Palace. Send her home without giving any reasons. We don't want scandals. Or, better still, you can send her into a convent. That will settle it."

As was the custom, ladies or palace maids who had received the favors of a king could not be touched by other men; but it was not a law. Many of them had in fact married after the king's demise. It would be commendable if they took religious vows, and many of them did.

Taitsung deliberated for a moment and said, "I didn't have the heart to have her killed as Li Chunfeng advised. He may be a better reader of the signs from heaven than of the minds of men. But this seems to be a good idea. I want to test her. Call her in."

While they were waiting for the maid to appear, Taitsung asked, "Has General Li Tsi set out for the northwest?"

"Yes. He left several days ago, as soon as he received the order."

"Good! He must have been puzzled over why I did this to him. That's the kind of implicit, unquestioning obedience I want."

Lady Wu was then one of the "ladies of the inner court" with the rank of *tsairen*. Her duty was to attend to the Emperor's wardrobe and baths, the work of a royal chambermaid. By court protocol, the ladies of the inner court consisted of 1 empress (*hou*), 4 queen consorts (*fei*), 9 ladies-in-waiting (*bin*), 4 graces (*meiren*), and 5 selects (*tsairen*). There were, besides, 27 of each of the two lower classes of palace maids whose access to the royal chambers was limited. Each of the ladies was entitled to receive the "favors" of the king, a term used when a royal person took a woman to bed. Records were kept in case one conceived.

Lady Wu was twenty-four and had been in the royal service for ten years. Her father had been a commander in one of Taitsung's campaigns, and when Taitsung visited her home in Shansi, he had taken her into the royal service as a favor. It had been rather frustrating, for after ten years of service, she had not risen above the lowest rank.

This was the end of May; the day was hot, but it was cool in the mountains. The young *tsairen* had attended to the sick Emperor this morning and had retired to her room, whose window looked out on the roofs and trees of the Crown Prince's residence on the east. The Emperor was dying, she knew. Across in the Crown Prince's court, surrounded by a wall, she knew the Crown Prince's quarters and all the ins and outs of the place, for she had made herself useful and offered her services to the Princess. Here she was, surrounded by all the splendors of the imperial court and given a deep sense of the imperial power. In her own room, she had her own maids. She was familiar with all the court forms and routines, and had an easy sense of competence inside the Palace. How stupid and mediocre the average man and woman were, she thought—the simple-minded Princess Wang, the doltish young Prince himself—honorable, affectionate, sometimes temperamental, but so easily pacified. He barely indulged in sports, preferring to sit around admiring the ladies whenever he could escape from the presence of the official tutors. Recently, a new prospect had opened. She had dared. A swift glance, a lingering look, a smile and an accidental touch of the body—and the Prince had come to her. It was all so easy. And Princess Wang had suspected nothing.

But her heart was heavy. The Emperor was passing away. What was going to happen to her? To her surprise, her maid came and told her that she had been sent for. Quickly she went to the kitchen, chopped an onion and squeezed the juice into her eyes until they hurt. She sat before her bronze mirror, saw that her eyes were moist and swollen, tidied her hair.

From her lowered head, she saw with surprise that Wuji was there. She looked at them both.

"You sent for me, Your Majesty?"

Wuji stood up, apparently having broken off a conversation. The Emperor's head was propped up in bed. His voice was weak and tired, but there was still that full powerful look in his eyes which all his ministers respected and admired.

"Come here," he said at last.

Lady Wu advanced and he took her hand, almost affectionately.

"You've been crying."

"Have I?" she answered, head still bent. The Emperor let his hand drop. "I am sorry. Are you feeling better now? Can I do something?"

The Emperor looked at her and said slowly, "Meiniang,

you have served me faithfully all these years. I know my days are numbered. What do you propose to do after I am gone? Do you want to go home?"

Meiniang sensed something was wrong. She observed Wuji's intent look at her. Did he know? Had he found out? She had not been able to make headway with these two men, Taitsung or Wuji. She said quickly, "Your Majesty, I have been honored to serve in your presence. You may do with me as you wish. But do not send me home. My body belongs to Your Majesty. As your royal servant, my only wish is to continue to serve you in the future life. That I would gladly do, if you would permit me to follow you into the grave. I would not want to live."

"That I forbid. I am against human sacrifices."

Meiniang's voice was brittle as she said with controlled emotion, "Once my body belongs to the royal Li family, I am a Li woman. Nothing can change that. . . . Is there a better way?"

A sudden silence. Both looked at Wuji.

"Your devotion to His Majesty is admirable," said the Archduke. "You can do better by staying alive and praying for his soul as a nun."

The solution had been apparent in the young woman's mind. It would be like this, she knew.

"I thank Your Majesty. If you so wish, I will cut off my hair and devote the rest of my life to prayers for Your Majesty's happiness."

"I am sure you will be well provided for at the Ganyiay Convent. Some of the other ladies may want to join you. So be it!"

Meiniang withdrew. As Taitsung saw the figure of the young woman, dressed in her silk dress covering her ankles, with a high coiffure of black hair, he breathed a sigh of relief.

"That's that. One worry off my mind. She made a pretty good show, as I had expected, don't you think?"

"Indeed she did."

"I think I've done right. Pheasant is a good and dutiful son, but perhaps too weak as a man to shoulder the responsibilities of the Empire. On your advice, I have chosen him, rather than Chengchien or Tai, my favorite, as my successor. It's up to you now to guide and protect him. Send for Suiliang immediately. I want to entrust the Crown Prince to the care of you two."

"I will send for the royal carriage immediately. He should be here this afternoon."

Wuji went to the door to deliver the order and walked back toward the bed.

"Meanwhile, send for Pheasant. I'll have some important words with him."

"Your Majesty should not tire yourself out, don't you think?"

"I am all right. I must have these things off my mind while I can still say what I want to say."

Gaotsung came in. Taitsung loved him. He was twenty-one, a good-natured young man, not brilliant and never very robust, like his father. The choice of the successor to the throne had given the father a lot of trouble. Taitsung had fourteen sons, of which three, born of the Empress, were entitled to succession. The eldest, Chengchien, had been made Crown Prince but had behaved abominably. He was known as a dissolute young man. Tai would be the ideal choice in character and ability. He looked like the father. Without actually changing the Crown Prince, Taitsung had been training Tai in the Eastern Palace, and it was generally assumed that Tai would soon be made the Crown Prince to replace the eldest. A bitter feud arose between the two brothers, and Chengchien, misguided by his advisers, actually started a rebellion in order to have Tai killed. Taitsung was thrown into a towering rage and despair. In his ministers' presence, he took a sword and threatened to kill himself if this went further. On the advice of Wuji and others, Gaotsung was chosen. They agreed that if either of the other two succeeded the throne, he would kill the other. This was the greatest crisis in the family. The edict was given, declaring that Gaotsung was henceforth the heir, and that the question of succession had been settled once and for all and anyone who brought up the question again would be summarily killed. That was six or seven years ago.

Gaotsung had now rushed in, with his usual preoccupied look, and greeted his good uncle and the Emperor familiarly. His hand fidgeted on his girdle and he looked unusually solemn, waiting for his father to speak.

"Pheasant, my boy, I have sent for you. It does not look as if I can tide over this crisis. I have been kind to my people and have given them peace. The burden of the Empire will fall upon your shoulders. Don't be afraid of the responsibilities. You'll have Uncle Wuji and others to assist you. You will learn, if you are humble to learn. Do you think your old father can give you some words of advice?"

"Your Majesty, the responsibilities are great but I am willing to learn."

"Good, then. These are simple words, but try to remember them always, especially in a crisis. The temptations of a king are to act on his own judgment. The most difficult thing is to learn to take criticism offered in good faith. Your mother taught me this. Remember Wei Jen? I didn't like his criticisms, but I took them on your mother's advice and saved myself many costly mistakes. Above all, you should listen to your uncle. He has built this empire with me. So long as you are willing to listen, you will grow. And second, power is a terrible thing. Your heart must be always with your subjects.

The throne is only a trust, a Mandate from Heaven. Remember the preceding Dynasty? It forfeited the Mandate from Heaven when the people's hearts were turned against it. Your mother didn't want to have an expensive mausoleum built for her because she wanted to spare the labor of the poor people. On her advice, I have refrained from building grand palaces and monuments for my own amusement. She knew our people had suffered enough in the last decades of war. That is the spirit of your good mother I don't want you ever to forget. You don't need fortresses; your own people's hearts and loyalty will be your fortresses. That is why my armies are invincible. There is no mystery about government, understand?"

"I am grateful for the advice," said the Crown Prince.

"There is another matter. General Li Tsi is a very good general, but a stubborn, self-opinionated, rather simple-minded man. He would go through fire and water for me. I have purposely sent him away to a frontier post. If he had dickered, I would have had him killed. I want you to recall him to power yourself when you are on the throne, and then he will serve you as loyally as he has served me."

"Is that why you did it? People were wondering why and what offense he had committed."

"You understand now?"

"Yes."

Of all the famous generals of the campaign, many had passed away and Li Tsi was now the most powerful one.

"And a further word. About women. You are happy with Princess Wang, I presume?"

"We are very happy."

"Good. You are a man, and as the king, you will have many ladies around you. How do you like the Shiao girl?"

"Very charming. She has borne me a son, as you know."

"What I mean to say is that a king may take his pleasure of

the women he likes. Princess Wang will make you a good empress and she will not grudge you your royal prerogatives. I understand your wife and this Wu Meiniang are great friends."

His voice suddenly sharpened and stopped.

Gaotsung blushed at the mention of Lady Wu. "Yes, they get on very well . . . very well . . . indeed. The Princess rather likes her; she's been so good and helpful in every way." Gaotsung managed to get through his sentence.

"Well, she has just offered to go into a convent after I am gone."

Gaotsung looked at his father, not knowing whether he had found him out.

"It's nothing important," said the father. "I just want you to know."

After Gaotsung had left, Taitsung said to Wuji, "We have done right. She will go into a convent."

That evening, Suiliang was ushered into the royal chamber, as soon as he arrived. Suiliang was an old minister of impeccable honesty and treated by Taitsung like his own sworn brother. Gaotsung and his wife had been sent for. This was to be a very special occasion. Archduke Wuji and Chu Suiliang were to receive the royal will, and as such (*guming dachen*), were executors of his trust.

The Emperor knew that he could trust these two.

Wuji, Suiliang, the crown prince and his wife were now in the royal chamber. Holding Suiliang's hand, Taitsung said:

"You two have served me faithfully all these years. I have sent for you to receive my last will. You know the Crown Prince is a gentle sort and has been a dutiful son to me. I commend him and his wife to your care. I have chosen her, you know. Guard them from harm and guide them to uphold the tradition I have set and maintain the future of the royal house. I shall leave the conduct of affairs in the hands of you two."

The Emperor turned to his son and daughter-in-law and asked them to kneel on one knee before the two ministers in acknowledgment of their new position.

"So long as Suiliang and Wuji are there to assist you, you do not have to worry," he said to his son.

Suiliang was then asked to take down his will. This done, he said to Suiliang, "Wuji has been my right hand from the very beginning. I have won the throne and established the Empire largely through his help. See that he is not made a victim of politics. If you do, you will have failed in your loyalty to me."

Suiliang promised solemnly, and the Emperor knew that he could depend on Suiliang's promise. He did not know that Suiliang had a woman to reckon with, now: in the very room where he was sitting—only a maid.

❋ 3 ❋

Taitsung died on May 26. Precautions were taken and the news was not announced until all security measures had been taken. The next day, Gaotsung set out under special guards and cavalry toward the capital. Four thousand royal guards were posted along the route of the imperial casket straight to the Anhua Gate, and Gaotsung returned to Hanfeng Hall. All preparations were ready for the return of the casket on the 29th. Taitsung's body lay in state at the Taiji Hall. All had gone on smoothly, and Gaotsung was proclaimed Emperor on June first, two days later. In August, Taitsung was buried at the great Jaoling Mausoleum.

A few days later, dozens of the ladies in the service of the deceased Emperor took their vows at the Ganyiay Convent, the twenty-four-year-old woman, Wu Meiniang, among them.

During the long nightly vigils, it had been Lady Wu's duty to attend upon the young Emperor. In the darkened hall where the royal remains lay in state, lighted by huge white candles and filled with the exotic incense from Cambodia, they had opportunities to be alone. Prayers were said and offerings were made at proper intervals, accompanied by the somber music of bells and horns. Periods of activity were followed by periods of complete silence. Everybody walked on tiptoe and talked in whispers. The young Gaotsung, as son of the deceased, had to stay by the coffin most of the time. Wu Meiniang would come at intervals, bringing him a cup of tea or offering to relieve him when he was too tired and exhausted. She had been indeed a great help to Gaotsung and the Princess during the ceremonies. People noticed her great presence of mind amidst all the ceremonial wailing. The young woman had a queenly dignity of her own.

Gaotsung seized an opportunity to speak to her when they were alone. The young woman was heartbroken.

"So you are really going to leave us?" asked the young king.

"I don't want to leave you. But what else can I do? Our ways lie apart. Why, I don't expect even to cross the threshold of the Palace after I leave. But my heart shall never change, in a convent or elsewhere. I shall never change."

"You don't really want to go, do you?"

"Who does? I only wish that it had been different, that I could be near you, and help you. But it is foolishness even to think of it. I shall be grateful if you do not forget me entirely. . . ."

"Forget you? Impossible!"

"I know you wouldn't. Come now and then to the temple, so that I can see you again, will you? As for me, my life is ended as far as the world is concerned."

"Don't say that. You are so young."

"What's the use of youth to me shut up in a convent?"

"Is it so hopeless?"

"Isn't it?"

Gaotsung was silent. The young woman eyed him for a moment. "Even though you are the Son of Heaven, you can't do anything about it."

"Oh, can't I? I can do anything I wish."

"Don't do anything foolish. I only ask that if you think of me, come to the temple. I must see you again."

"I promise."

That was their last chance for a long private talk. During the following days Gaotsung was closely surrounded all the time by the courtiers and attendants, going through the crushing duties of a bereaved son at the funeral.

The young Wu Meiniang already showed a remarkable resourcefulness. Any other young woman sent by royal order to a monastery would probably bemoan her fate, and nothing more. But clearly the unique instinct which led her to rise to power was already there. She knew she needed a strong ally, and must keep up a good connection with the Palace.

Before her departure, Wu Meiniang packed up her things and distributed them among the maids, jewels and gold and silver ornaments. To her own maid, Lan-erh, she gave a giant ruby ring, a coat of sable, and three trunkloads of silks and brocades. To Princess Wang she gave a jade ring of unusual size and luster.

"Take this, your Royal Highness, as a sign of devotion to you and a souvenir of the good days I enjoyed in your company."

"You really shouldn't do this. Keep it."

"What use do I have for jewelry now? You have been so kind and I want you to think of it as something very special from me."

"What are you giving to Lady Shiao?"

"Nothing. My devotion is only to you."

"And I shall never see you again?"

"Come and visit the temple when you feel like it. I can't come to see you, but you can come to see me. And I have this request to make of you." Pointing to her maid, she said, "Lan-erh has been a most devoted servant to me. Why don't you take her? She is absolutely loyal and I have always relied on her. If you want someone reliable and discreet, I can honestly recommend her."

In the days that followed, Lan-erh was able to come and visit her at the temple and bring greetings, gifts from Princess Wang, and above all, news of the Palace.

With Lan-erh's help, Sister Wu had been able to learn all that was going on in the Palace. The Princess, who was now Empress Wang, was in trouble. She had borne the king no son, and on the advice of her maternal uncle, Liu Shy, and with the consensus of opinion of all the elderly ministers, a seven-year-old son of Gaotsung, named Jung and born of a lady of a lower class, was adopted as her son and made the Crown Prince. Wuji, guardian of the Emperor when he was a prince, was now head of the government, Lord Secretary of the Imperial Secretariat and Lord Chancellor as well. But Gaotsung was spending his days and nights with Lady Shiao, now a queen consort of the first rank. The king had been bewitched by this gay, witty and very clever young woman. She was slim and vivacious and very amusing. In looks, the Empress knew she was no match for Lady Shiao. And there are many things which a decent well-bred woman could not do, or even say. Lady Shiao was gloating in triumph when they met, and the Empress was at a loss for words to reply. Both began to complain about each other to Gaotsung. For the first time, Gaotsung realized what it was to live with two women by his side, move continuously between their jealousy and hatred, and keep both pacified. The Empress sensed clearly that Gaotsung was growing cold toward her.

On the anniversary of Taitsung's death, a big mass was held at the Ganyiay temple. The Empress persuaded Gaotsung to go with her to the temple. The latter was delighted at the suggestion. They brought Lan-erh along and all the way the Empress said nothing.

The royal visit had been announced and had created a great excitement among the sisters. Clad in dark maroon, they were lined up in the hall to receive the royal visitors. In spite of their monastic attire, many of them were young and pretty women. Gaotsung had known many of them in the Palace. He told them to get up from their knees and granted them permission to sit down.

Lan-erh rushed ahead to meet Sister Wu, and then the Empress, followed by the Emperor, came up to speak to her. Sister Wu smiled through her tears.

"You have not forgotten me?"

"Of course not," said Gaotsung cheerily.

While Their Majesties went around to chat with the abbess and other old acquaintances, Lan-erh pulled Sister Wu aside and informed her what the Empress was planning to do. She would like to get Sister Wu back into the Palace for her own good reasons. Gaotsung was yet unaware of her purpose in fighting a snake with a snake. The young Empress needed a charmer to break the charm of her rival Shiao. Wu Meiniang would be more than a match for Lady Shiao.

Special seats were provided for the royal couple. The hall was sumptuously furnished; the half-closed serene eyes of the gilt Buddha Sakyamuni looked out from behind pointed embroidered white strips of brocade, his forehead hidden in the half shadow of the niche. The Buddha was seated on a giant gilt lotus studded with jewels, with Buddha Ananda on his right, and Buddha Manjusri on his left. The nuns were seated on straw cushions on both sides, each holding a white candle in her hands. The chants were sung to the beat of the wooden fish, and the prayers were long.

After the prayers, the royal couple was invited to visit the grounds. A fine vegetarian dinner was served in the Emperor's honor. By special invitation, Sister Wu was asked to sit at the royal table. The Empress was the vivacious one today; she did all the talking. Sister Wu looked her demurest and did not speak much at the table. She had learned the news and looked as if she were not there, as if her spirit had already left the temple. She did offer a toast to the king, and their eyes met for a brief second.

Before their departure, the Empress whispered to Wu Meiniang that she should await good news in a couple of days.

While in the carriage on the way back, the Empress said, "Meiniang is very unhappy. I want to do something for her. And I want her company, too. I want to get her out of the convent to live with me."

Gaotsung was incredulous. "Do you mean it?"

"Of course I do."

"We could send a carriage for her and do not have to say anything. Just say that her spiritual services are needed at the Palace."

Gaotsung could barely conceal his joy. It was his fervent wish, and he didn't believe the Empress would make it so easy for him to have this wish fulfilled, to have Wu Meiniang daily at his side again. "My good Empress, it's marvelous of you to think of this. I will send for her tomorrow." He had an unaccountable sense that something unexpected, but momentous, was happening to his life. She was his destiny. He could hardly wait for the morrow.

"Are you happy?" the Empress asked.

"Very happy indeed. You won't be jealous?"

"I know I shan't be."

That night, Empress Wang confirmed what she thought to do. "You think I am jealous because of Lady Shiao. No, I am not. I am liberal. I shall be a good wife to you, and a king should have many queen consorts. But I do want harmony and peace at home. Wu Meiniang and I shall be happy together and we shall serve you faithfully in harmony. She has ever been faithful and respectful to me and I can trust her. After this, she will never forget what I have done for her.

What I cannot stand is this insolence and constant bickering with Lady Shiao."

Two days later, Lady Wu was smuggled into the Palace in the Empress's own carriage. Her position was that of a nun living at the Empress's court. Her identity was kept a close secret, as far as Lady Shiao was concerned. But it could not be kept for very long. What could not be so well concealed was the fact that not many months had passed before the nun had conceived. The time would be when even her ample cassock could not deceive the women's eyes. Lady Shiao found out early enough; the king was inclined to stay in the Empress's court most nights and visited her less and less. At last she forced a confession from the king's own mouth.

Lady Shiao could not believe that the Empress, who was so jealous of her and backbiting her, as she had learned from Gaotsung, would bring herself to tolerate such an arrangement.

It would be a scandal, and it would be regarded as incest.

Wu Meiniang, sure of his affections, now went to work on the romantic young king with all the feminine charms and wiles with which nature had endowed her. She was a woman three years the king's senior, and twice more mature. She made the young king completely happy. The weapon of sex she knew; what sophistications she needed she had learned at the convent from the other ladies, for the Ganyiay Convent was different from others, and the noble ladies who took vows went there not of their own accord. One and all, they were used to luxuries and licentious living. It was already on record that she was "flexible and brazen, to do the important business" (in bed). The king, a young man and an idealist, was an easy victim. The king's heart belonged to her and to nobody else. He began to neglect Lady Shiao, as the Empress had planned.

Lady Wu had charted her course, and now had hit the target. The course of her rise to power was clear.

❋ 4 ❋

Wu Meiniang was impatient for public recognition of her status as the king's favorite, since the king truly loved her. Gaotsung should not be ashamed of her. There should be no subterfuge, no concealment. When her son was born, she wanted him to be born a prince. She had let her hair grow again, and although it was still short, she would wear a wig arranged with all the artistry of a palace hairdresser. There would be no difficulty in that and she loved to see herself with the full glory of a high and fashionable bouffant. Now that Lady Shiao knew, she no longer cared; she would not care anyway since she was already so much in the king's favor.

What happened was unexpected. A few days after she had discarded her monastic clothing, there was a dinner at which the other ladies were present. It was a special party for Lady Wu. There was a lot of gaiety, and everybody was enjoying herself. Lady Shiao had come with her three-year-old boy, holding a candy monkey on a long stick, and the boy was playing by Wu Meiniang's side. His candy stick, intentionally or unintentionally, came near knocking at Lady Wu's hair-do several times. "You shouldn't do that," said Lady Shiao hastily, and in trying to push the candy stick, again intentionally or unintentionally, upset Lady Wu's wig, which almost toppled down, revealing her crop of short hair. Lady Wu flushed all over.

"Oh, I am so sorry," apologized Lady Shiao.

She shouted to her maid and asked her to take the boy away. The maids had rushed around and helped reset the wig on the nun's head. Lady Shiao herself came to reset it and give it a few final touches.

She whispered, "It's perfect now. Even Taitsung should be pleased to see how beautiful you look today."

The stab sank and Lady Wu blushed. She kept silent, but knew that one day she would have to pay heavily for this day.

Gaotsung spoke to Archduke Wuji. The latter had not even known of the re-entry of Wu Meiniang into the Palace. He had been too busy with his official duties, and Lady Wu had outplayed him. He did not know that while she was in the convent, she had kept in touch with the court politics through Lan-erh, her maid.

Gaotsung now informed the Archduke that Lady Wu had conceived and he wished to create a new queen consort post for her. The Empress was beyond rank, the *fei*—or queen consorts—were first rank, and the *bin* were of second rank.

This was a momentous decision to make for the Privy Council, as it involved a matter of court protocol, and moreover, it would be officially sanctioning a technically incestuous relationship. Ordinary decency forbade that. Lined up against this action were all the elderly statesmen, members of the Privy Council. There were, besides the Archduke, Suiliang, Han Yuan (the eldest of them all), Lai Tsi, Liu Shy and others. All regarded it as a sign of bad morals, a reprehensible conduct, a violation of the sacred tradition. Dynasties had always fallen when a king became licentious with women, the argument ran. The four *fei* posts were all occupied. They could not, and would not, break court protocol, especially when it involved a woman who had been in the service of the king's father.

The Archduke informed His Majesty that all the ministers had turned it down. As a result, Lady Wu was created *Jaoyi,* the first of the nine *bin* allowed a sovereign.

It was not what she had hoped for, but it was a rank which she had not been able to obtain under Taitsung.

Once the official status was given, Lady Wu never doubted but that this was only the beginning. She was installed in her own court. Outwardly, she was still an ally of the Empress. She was always respectful, and even affectionate to her sovereign. She had overcome the greatest obstacles to her rise to power—the monastic vow and the charge of incest. The rest should be easy for her.

In a short while, Lady Wu made herself master of the court and popular with the Palace servants. It was her business to know all that was happening in the Empress's court, as well as in Lady Shiao's. Whereas the Empress had neglected such details and her mother particularly had been haughty toward the servants, Lady Wu was steadily cultivating the goodwill of the maids. On occasions when the Emperor gave her gifts, she would distribute them, freely and generously, to the maids not only of her own court, but those of the others, especially those who hated the Empress and her insolent mother. She made sure that loyalty to her would be rewarded, but her informants should keep her posted of everything in the Palace and be willing to do her bidding. If she could not keep absolute control of what went on inside the Palace, only an area half a mile square, how was she ever to rule an empire?

This was in the year 651. When her child was born, it turned out to be a girl, to her great disappointment. Lady Shiao had a boy—she could never forget that. As for the Crown Prince, Jung, adopted by the Empress, she would not give it a thought if she had a boy of her own. What would she do with a girl?

It came to her like a brainstorm. Why, it was her best chance! The gods were kind to her; they could not have done better than send her a baby girl.

One day, when the baby was hardly ten days old, the Empress, who had no child of her own, came over to see the baby. She took her up in her breast, fondled her for a while, and laid her back in the cradle. Lady Wu had gone out for a stroll on purpose when the Empress's visit was announced. She came in after she left, strangled the baby and covered it under the quilt. She knew the Emperor would come and see her after court duties.

Gaotsung came. Lady Wu was the happy mother who could not help talking about her wonderful baby.

"Take the baby out for His Majesty to see. And wrap her up well," said the happy mother to one of her favorite maids.

Lan-erh came out with the baby, and the mother went to receive her in her arms. To her consternation, the baby didn't open her eyes, didn't move, didn't breathe. She crooned, she purred, but the baby didn't move. She was dead! Lady Wu was terrified, or looked as if she was. She was stunned, shocked into a moment of silence.

"What happened? She was well and lively this morning," she cried in utter despair, frantic, sobbing out loud at this sudden loss of her dear child.

"We thought she was quietly lying asleep," said the well-coached maid.

Drying her tears the mother, who had not quite broken down, asked, "Has anyone been in the room when I was away?"

"The Empress was here. She came to see the baby, fondled it for a while and put it back."

Lady Wu's and the Emperor's eyes met. It was incredible; such a heinous thing to do!

The Empress denied it of course. But to what avail? Why

hadn't she cultivated friendship with the maids? She was the only one who had touched the baby in the last hours.

Gaotsung, never very fond of his wife, was now completely disgusted with her. She was now as jealous of Lady Wu as she had been of Shiaofei. But this was beyond the bounds of decency for one who was supposed to be a model to all the wives and mothers of the land. And poor suffering Lady Wu, who only shed silent tears of mourning for her dead child—his heart warmed toward her.

"I have a mind to depose this despicable woman. She is no longer fit—no longer worthy—"

"Don't ever think of such a thing. What's done is done," replied Lady Wu with considerable magnanimity.

Lady Wu became more amorous than ever—luck was with her. The next year, she was blessed with a son, Hung, and the following year, with another son, Shien. She had waited long enough. The ridiculous thing was that she was still not in her rightful place, to be the Empress and assist the king to direct the government as she knew how.

Gaotsung the romantic idealist was gradually learning what it was to live with three women constantly pouring complaints against each other into his ears. But when he was tired and weary, Lady Wu comforted him; when he was hesitant and confused, she gave him good advice; when he was angry and upset, she calmed him down and reminded him of his powers. She wanted in every sense to be his support, his solace and his guide. And Gaotsung was pleased with her.

In the sixth year of Gaotsung's reign, the year 655, matters came to a head. Empress Wang had apparently attempted by sorcery and black magic to undo the Emperor, to cause shooting pains in his chest, and possibly to end his life. A wooden figurine had been discovered under the Empress's bed—again how careless she had been about her maids!—with the name, surname and horoscope of the Emperor inscribed on it and a nail driven through the heart of the wooden figure. The matter had been secretly reported to her husband indirectly by someone—not directly by Lady Wu, of course—and he had personally led the search.

The Empress was, as it were, caught red-handed. She was aghast, struck speechless. What could she say to clear herself, except deny and deny? She knelt down and pleaded her innocence. What reason had she to wish his doom? She guessed who had the figurine planted there, but all the evidence was against her. She realized now that she had driven away a snake in order to be bitten, this time mortally, by a scorpion. O woman! Why has thine species been created to play havoc with the hearts of men and with thine white arms encompass and shake the foundations of a royal ancestral house?

Rumor spread quickly throughout the Palace and at the court. The high ministers were shocked, and the younger secretaries speculated. Could it be that the Empress had used black magic to undo His Majesty, or was it a frame-up? Was it not more logical for her to use black magic to accomplish someone else's end—Lady Wu's, for instance? The whole affair sounded incredible. The Empress could not have done it herself; she must have had a sorceress do it for her, used an accomplice. What was the sorceress's name? Questions asked of the maids should easily establish the evidence or completely disprove the charge. Should she be deposed, and, if so, who was most likely to be promoted? Lady Wu had not been inactive; in the course of three years she had given the Emperor two sons and a daughter—the murdered one. All the more right to be crowned Empress.

The fight around Empress Wang started. The court was in an uproar. The Empress had tried to kill the Emperor, so it was alleged; and she was about to be deposed.

Suiliang and Wuji, entrusted with Taitsung's dying request to take care of the young Emperor and Empress, sensed what was coming. And the story was incredible from any viewpoint. Lady Wu knew it would not be easy, but she was not going to be balked.

One of the officials, Shyu (Jingtsung), saw in this crisis a chance for a quick rise to power by playing Lady Wu's game. A glib talker and court historian by profession, Shyu sprang into great activity. He was known to have tampered with historical facts, so low was his conception of a historian's duty, and on many an occasion officials were able to buy a place in history for some consideration, or have praise and blame for victory or defeat in battle better distributed to the buyer's liking. Shyu alone went about showing why Lady Wu should be raised to Empress's rank. He was the author of the famous saying, "Even a farmer sometimes takes a concubine when he has a big crop. Why shouldn't a monarch take the woman he likes?" This saying went the rounds of the court gossip. When he came up to Archduke Wuji, the Archduke quickly shut him up. Almost all the higher ministers knew what was boiling behind the palace walls, and they did not like the smell of it.

Suiliang and Wuji had since Taitsung's death done their best to keep up the fine tradition set by the late Taitsung. They had each day asked ten of the ministers to come in and tell them about the conditions and problems in the country, and suggest the policies to follow and the measures to put through. Confronted now with a challenge to their sacred trust—the dying Taitsung had expressly told them to look after both his son and daughter-in-law—they took this matter very seriously. An empress should not be deposed without sufficient reason and investigation. Furthermore, she was the daughter-in-law chosen by the father himself. A worse choice could not be made than to legitimize incest by permitting the Emperor to marry one of his father's women. Such a step would tend to discredit the throne and vitiate the whole atmosphere of the regime. Both for considerations of state and for their personal obligations and duties as executors of Taitsung's will, they were bound in honor to oppose such a possible catastrophe.

Lady Wu knew that, of all the personalities at the court, Wuji's weight counted most. As the first of the three archdukes of the nation, as field marshal, and as the Emperor's own uncle, he must be won over to her side. If Wuji approved, all the rest would be easy. She suggested to Gaotsung that he should personally pay the uncle a call at his home, and she would accompany him.

An emperor's descent to a subject's residence was an unusual honor, usually recorded in the official "journals" of a sovereign (*shihlu*). When the Emperor's arrival was announced, the Archduke suspected the purpose of the visit, and when he saw that Lady Wu was with him, he understood.

"Where is Aunt?" asked Lady Wu sweetly.

So it was to be a family visit. The royal guests were ushered in, and the Archduchess came out to receive them. Both Gaotsung and Lady Wu were extremely amiable, and Lady Wu particularly warm and gay and cordial. They tried to make conversation, but neither would mention the subject they had come to discuss. And they sat and they sat and they sat until it was the supper hour.

The Archduke naturally suggested that they stay for supper. The royal guests suddenly realized that it was so late; they hadn't realized; they had been having such a good time talking. Of course they would; they had nothing else to do. "Let's have the men and women sit together at the same table. It's all in the family," suggested Lady Wu.

Dinner was served and toasts were made to this happy occasion. Wuji's four sons had joined them. In the course of the dinner, the Emperor inquired what his boys were doing, one of them being of age, the others still in their teens. Wuji was a man of strict principles. In Taitsung's time he had originally disapproved of establishing hereditary ranks. His eldest was court librarian. Learning that the three younger sons had no honorary title, the Emperor there and then offered to confer upon them the honorary rank of *dafu*.

Wuji was embarrassed and declined out of courtesy.

"Why, Uncle," said Lady Wu, "you have done more for the country than anybody else. Please accept. Certainly the government should do something to show its appreciation. It is but your right."

Wuji could not refuse under the circumstances and ordered his young sons to leave the table and bow their thanks to the Emperor for this special favor.

More toasts were drunk. The atmosphere was easy and relaxed and everybody was happy. The Emperor summoned enough courage to mention the affair of the wooden figurine, and gently hinted that as the Empress had borne him no son, she should be deposed.

Lady Wu sat silently and watched. Wuji, like an experienced diplomat, hemmed and hawed and tried to evade a direct answer to the question. He would not say "Yes" and would not say "No." Such an important question, he thought, should be considered carefully. There was no hurry.

Gaotsung scented his uncle's disapproval and was none too pleased. The result of the evening's cordiality was a failure. Soon after, the royal guests took their departure.

The next day, Lady Wu sent over to the uncle's house in the Emperor's name ten cartloads of silks and gold and silver presents. Lady Wu's own mother, Madame Yang, personally brought them, to make sure that there was no doubt in their minds of Lady Wu's love and respect for the Emperor's uncle.

This gesture was too obvious to Wuji. The previous night

his sons were given honorary ranks, and now all this gold and silver. Did Lady Wu think he could be bought? He selected a few silks in token acceptance and sent the rest back to the Palace.

* 5 *

Lady Wu seemed to have run into a formidable opposition. The archdukes, the Lord Chancellor and Lord Secretary seemed solidly lined up against deposing Empress Wang in favor of Lady Wu. It was a contest between four men and one woman.

It may be useful here to give a brief outline of the administrative staff and their functions, in view of the references which will come up. The top of the government was divided into three departments: 1) *the Imperial Secretariat,* closest to the Emperor, which handled all reports to the Emperor and outgoing replies, orders and edicts; 2) *the Chancellory,* headed by the Lord Chancellor and two Vice-Chancellors, who were to assist and advise the Emperor in matters of government policy; and 3) *the Cabinet,* which had charge of the ministries. There was no real prime minister acting as one-man head of the government. Nominally, the President of the Cabinet was the prime minister, but in honor to Taitsung, who had occupied the office and responsibilities of Premier, the post was never filled. Heading the Cabinet were two Vice-Premiers of equal rank with the Lord Chancellor. Power was concentrated in the Emperor, with a flexible, ill-defined group equivalent to a privy council, which participated in all important deliberations and decisions. This group had no particular name, but members were appointed to it by cumbersome phrases like "equal to third rank," or "participating in government deliberations," etc. The term *shiang*, or royal assistant, was loosely used referring to one who belonged to this group.

Here is the government setup. Their relative ranks are indicated by the numbers (1), (2), (3), etc.:

3 Archdukes (1) and 3 Grand Masters (1), or high advisers: positions of the highest honor, filled by men of long standing and high prestige, with no particular duties.

Privy Councilors (3) the "group" (shiang): the highest deliberating body, usually consisting of the Lord Secretary and Vice-Secretaries, the Lord Chancellor and Vice-Chancellors, the first two Vice-Premiers, and anyone appointed to it by edict, with the clause "equal to the third rank."

Imperial Secretariat (Menshia):
- Lord Secretary (2)
- 2 Vice-Secretaries (3)

Chancellory (Jungshu):
- Lord Chancellor (2)
- 2 Vice-Chancellors (3)

Cabinet (Shangshu):
- Premier (2A)
- 2 Vice-Premiers (2B)
- Minister of Civil Service (3)
- Minister of the Interior (3)
- Minister of Rites and Ceremonies (3)
- Minister of War (3)
- Minister of Justice (3)
- Minister of Public Works (3)

Attorney General's Office, or Censorate (Yushy):
- Attorney General (3)
- 3 Assistant Attorney Generals (4)
- 6 Prosecutors, or Censors (6B)
- 9 Court Censors (7B)

15 Circuit Censors (8)
(Important cases which came up to the Central Government were handled jointly by the Censor's Office and first-class secretaries of the Imperial Secretariat and the Chancellory.)

Supreme Court (Dalishy):
Chief Judge (3B)
Assistant Chief (4B)

The Lord Secretary and Lord Chancellor were generally the top men. The Imperial Secretariat's routine duty was to go over an edict, make a copy of it, and hand it out to the Cabinet for execution. But it was more than that: the Lord Secretary and Vice-Secretaries had the right, and the duty, to resubmit an emperor's order for reconsideration or revision for any reason, or even to reject it. In the good old days of Taitsung, the Emperor once strongly reprimanded the Secretariat for automatically passing on his orders. "What's the use of you people? If I wanted you just to pass on the orders, I needed only clerks, not able men, for the job." The actual influence of the high advisers—the Archdukes and the Grand Masters—varies with the individuals. It could be nothing or everything. They didn't have to bother with government problems or policies, but they could with every problem and policy if they wanted to.

There was now a strong lineup of the ministers: Vice-Premier Suiliang, Field-Marshal Wuji, Lord Secretary Han Yuan, Lord Chancellor Lai Tsi. They were all for Empress Wang. There was General Li Tsi too, one of the few surviving veteran generals, a good, honest man but a simple soul, perhaps more naïve at a crisis.

The high ministers met in the side court, awaiting the bell to go in to audience. Wuji pulled Suiliang aside and informed him of the Emperor's visit to his house and the conversation. The other ministers stood around, tense as if expecting a storm. Someone had to speak first, naturally Wuji.

"No, let me do it," said the stout-hearted Suiliang. "It would be embarrassing for the Emperor to reprimand his own uncle."

"Lord Chancellor Lai Tsi, then."

"Again no. His position is far too important. If the Emperor's mind is made up, as it seems to be, it will mean a disaster, as I can foretell, for those who oppose Lady Wu's plans."

"But how about yourself?"

"Oh, I don't count. I rose from a humble family. To me it is just my line of duty. I received Taitsung's will. His daughter-in-law was entrusted to my care. If I don't, I shall not be able to face His late Majesty in the next world."

The ministers filed in when the bell struck. The Emperor was on the throne, and behind him, separated by a silk gauze curtain, sat Lady Wu, listening to this crucial conference which concerned her most.

Gaotsung opened by telling the ministers that the Empress had perpetrated black magic against his sacred person. The usual penalty was death. She had proved herself unworthy to be an example to all wives and mothers. It was his opinion that the Empress should be deposed.

Suiliang took a step forward and said, "Your Majesty, it is my duty to advise you against such a step. The Empress was chosen by your father. On his deathbed, he took my hand and said to me, 'I entrust my son and my good daughter to your care.' Your Majesty heard this yourself. The Empress has not been proved guilty of any crime and should not be deposed."

Gaotsung calmly produced the wooden figurine. "Take a look," he said and passed it around. A nail was driven through the heart of the carved figure, with the name and horoscope of the Emperor on it.

"Why not investigate?" said Suiliang. "Someone must have carved it. There must have been accomplices, and witnesses, and a sorcerer or sorceress who would be known to the maids. How do you know that the figurine might not have been placed there by someone who wishes her harm?"

The Emperor was silent.

Lord Secretary Han Yuan advanced and supported Suiliang's opinion. "I hope Your Majesty will forgive me for blunt speaking. It is not for the good of the country that the Empress should be lightly changed. I am afraid the court and the nation will be greatly disturbed by it. I agree with Vice-Premier Suiliang that the Empress was your father's choice and should not be cast aside."

As Wuji started to speak the Emperor shouted, "Get out!"

Suiliang and Han Yuan retired and the audience was abruptly terminated.

That night, some ministers held a private conference at Wuji's home, including Wuji's personal friends. They had received the news late that afternoon that Liu Shy had been dismissed. Liu Shy was Empress Wang's maternal uncle, and had once been Lord Chancellor. Lady Wu seemed to mean business.

"There goes Liu Shy!" said Wuji. "It looks bad. What are we going to do tomorrow?" he asked Suiliang.

"What shall we do? Why, stand our ground. My duty is clear. No compromise."

Bei (Shingjien), the metropolitan magistrate, was as enraged as the rest. He was a mathematician and a student of the philosophy of *yin* and *yang*. "If this is allowed to happen, it will be the beginning of the end," he said.

The atmosphere was tense at the next morning's court session. While awaiting the order to go in, they heard that Bei (who was later to become a great general) was cashiered. It was as fast as that. One Yuan (Gungyu), who was present at the night's party, had hurried off after the party to report Bei's words to Madame Yang, Lady Wu's mother.

"So there goes another one," remarked Suiliang sadly. Coolly and calmly, he told the rest that he was going to stop this, or resign; or he might be dismissed or exiled—he didn't care. He knew exactly what he was doing.

Once more the ministers filed in, wearing grave faces. Gaotsung opened by quoting Mencius: "Of all the sins of filial impiety, the greatest is to be without progeny. The Empress has given me no son. Lady Wu has. I have made up my mind."

Suiliang leisurely stepped forward, and knelt down before the throne. His hands were holding the ceremonial ivory tablet which all ministers had to hold at audience.

"It is my duty to remind Your Majesty of your father the late Taitsung's words. I cannot ignore my promise to your father. Nor should you. If Your Majesty's mind is already made up, I shall have nothing to say. I hereby return you the audience tablet. Pardon me, I have no choice."

He laid the ivory tablet before the throne and knocked his head on the floor aloud, as a form of vehement protest.

Gaotsung was quite taken aback. Suiliang's gesture was insolent, his tone brusque.

Suddenly a brittle, rasping voice was heard from behind the curtain: "Have the rascal slugged to death!" It was a feminine, yet not too feminine, voice, which could be heard across the hall.

Wuji spoke. "Suiliang is doing what he feels to be his duty. He should not be punished."

"Take him out!" commanded Gaotsung.

The audience ended as abruptly as the previous one.

Suiliang was dismissed from the Vice-Premiership and sent out as governor of a district in the mountains of Kweichow. It was the usual form of punishment for a minister who had crossed the sovereign's will. Suiliang went away, with a clear conscience and without regret, but also without knowledge of what was yet to come.

Gaotsung now acted with manly decision and single-minded purpose—with Lady Wu behind him. Dismissing and ignoring the ministers' advice, he just went ahead. Wasn't he the sovereign? Of course he was.

Gaotsung and Lady Wu had noticed that from the last audience General Li Tsi had absented himself. Perhaps he was more pliable. He had now the rank of an archduke. Gaotsung would certainly need an archduke for the coronation of an empress. He approached the old general and the latter replied, "This is your private business, it is not for your subjects to interfere."

The decision was made. An edict was issued. Empress Wang had perpetrated a crime and was deposed, to be confined inside the Palace. Lady Wu was to become Empress Wu. The dethronement of Empress Wang and the promotion of Lady Wu made sensational news and afforded the public a much relished subject for gossip. It was a scandal. The new Empress had been a mistress of the king's father. What was worse, she was a nun and should still be in the Ganyiay Convent. And what was still worse, she had a child by the king while still a nun. Clearly she was a "bitch." The nation's sense of decency was outraged. The teahouses buzzed with gossip. Wuji settled down and sulked at home.

The date for the coronation was set for November, only one month away. Lady Wu was not one to be crowned apologetically. Not Wu Tsertien! The coronation was to be a grand affair, celebrated with more pomp and pageantry than that of an emperor, in order that the world might know that

Lady Wu was rightfully the queen. And it must be said that lavish pomp and grandeur suited her well, were her very life. She knew the common people loved to be impressed. Shyu was of course the man to prepare all the details of the ceremony. A thousand things had to be done and the time was short—the coronation gown, the carriage, the new seal to be given the Empress, the songs and music and dancers and entertainers, the reception, and the preparations of all the Princes and Princesses and the members of the court and their wives for the great occasion.

The day came. The music of drums and bells was sounded. The hall was crowded with members of the court and officials of the highest ranks. Assisted by her maids, Lady Wu came in, her headdress glittering in gold and pearls, fully decked out in the formal *weiyi,* the formal gown of an empress worn on grand occasions such as the annual worship of Heaven and Earth. It was a navy blue satin, hand-painted with phoenixes on the wing in rainbow colors, with a broad red band coming down the center to the edge of the skirt, with gold-embroidered shoes and belt and hangings similar to those of the Emperor.

Calm and dignified, with a well-proportioned chin and large, bright eyes, she looked indeed every inch an empress. Probably on that day, during the coronation hour, the least flustered person was Lady Wu herself. The Empress's seal was formally handed to her in a jade box by Archduke Li Tsi—the man whose corpse was to be mutilated by her years later. She ascended the queen's throne. The imperial scroll was read, other congratulatory poems in pompous four-word lines were declaimed, the solemn classical music was played, and the formal ceremony ended.

It had been specially arranged that, breaking all precedents, the new Empress was to show herself to all her courtiers at the Shuyi gate tower west of the Palace. The big, long carriage, used by the Empress on such occasions, had been made ready. The body was blue and gold, with eight windows hung with purple sashes and curtains, the top and the rear wheels painted vermilion. At different points along the sides stood long pheasant plumes, symbolic of the queen, while the horses' accouterments glittered with gold. The carriage was preceded by guards on horseback, decked out in full uniform, and the usual complement of insignia-carriers in an imperial procession.

Arriving at the gate, she ascended the gate tower and stood at the balconied terrace. There, spread below her, bending on their knees in the square, were the princes and officials and representatives of the conquered races, all in their formal gowns. Those in front wearing purple, with gold and jade belts, were the Princes and the officials above the third rank; next and behind them, those in deep lavender with gold belts, the fourth; those in light lavender with gold belts, the fifth; green in two shades, with silver belts, the sixth and seventh ranks, etc.

Lady Wu smiled her gracious smile to acknowledge the homage of her subjects. Then she drove back to the Palace, where, as a novel measure, the wives of officials and foreign representatives were given a reception at an inner court. Everybody admired her dignity and self-possession and tried not to think of her origin. Some ladies noticed that her mouth was too wide, suggesting a voracious character; others were frightened by the line of her lips, or her hard, sharp glance, betokening a woman of great determination. Grandmother was never shy; she loved to see people, meet people, deal with people and receive their adulation. On this day she had already broken many precedents.

After the reception, a royal dinner was given for all the invited guests, with music and dances by the imperial troupes, and the usual acrobatic shows. The gaieties drew deep into the night. Grandfather was very tired that night.

❋ 6 ❋

Lady Wu was crowned Empress in November of 655, at the age of thirty. Her name was now Wu *Tsertien,* "Modeled after Heaven." We are not witnessing merely an ambitious woman who aspired to the highest position and honor of womanhood; we are witnessing a terrific will to power that was now only becoming manifest.

No man knows a woman until he has married her. In the case of Grandfather, the discovery came very early.

In December 655, only one month after her coronation, something strange happened. Gaotsung had now realized the caliber of the woman he had married. In a way he had a gratifying sense of having a queen who showed great competence in public and private affairs, a helpmeet, and not just a beautiful plaything like Lady Shiao. He could not help thinking of the latter and of the condemned empress now in distress, and was bitten with remorse. But he would never show Lady Wu that he was thinking of them.

One day he went to visit them when Lady Wu was on a visit to her relatives. Alone, he sauntered along to the back court, with a bad conscience and almost a feeling of guilt. It was a shock. He found the door securely locked, with only a hole on the side permitting servants to bring in food. A court lady falling under disfavor was usually relegated to a back court, neglected, but not even under house detention. This was real imprisonment.

He called through the hole, "Empress, Queen Consort, where are you?"

After a while, he heard shuffling feet and soft, faint, distressed voices from within.

"We have been disgraced. Why, you are addressing us by our former titles." Lady Shiao's voice was pleading and clear. "For old times' sake, let us out, we beg you. Just set us free, please. If you do, we shall call this place the Hall of Mercy."

Gaotsung was deeply touched. "Don't worry. I will do something about it."

Ruefully he found his way back, both distressed and humiliated at what he had seen.

The Emperor did not know his wife yet, that her spies would immediately report the visit to her. She knew Gaotsung's weakness too well. She had a network of spies to inform her of all that was going on in the various courts, to see, for instance, that no nun like herself should be smuggled into the precincts and replace her as she had replaced Wang.

When Lady Wu returned, the Emperor's stolen visit was reported accordingly. It was evidence that he was still thinking of those two women! She would take no chances.

Before the Emperor had the opportunity to speak to her, she spoke to him. He had been to see the two convicts, she was told. Was it true?

The Emperor quickly denied it.

"Oh, I'm glad you didn't."

Time and again, we are to see a decision reversed and the course of events changed by the confronting of a dull, nervous man and a determined, alert, forceful woman.

It was not in Lady Wu's nature to tolerate such deviations of the king's affection. She would put a stop to it, not only for these two confined rivals, but for the benefit of all ladies in court to know henceforth that they should watch their steps. It had to be a lesson, final, driven home and entirely educational. A woman herself, she knew how dangerous a woman could be.

Lady Wu gave orders to her servants to have the two women whipped a hundred lashes. Then she ordered that their hands and feet be cut off. After that, with their arms and legs crooked behind them, they were to be thrown into wine vats.

"Let these wenches' bones and marrow melt in drunken ecstasy," she said. The phrase was a reference to sexual pleasure.

After a couple of days, the two women died, as was to be expected. Their death was reported.

"Have their bones and marrow melted in drunken ecstasy?" she asked with an idle smile.

"Yes, they have, Your Majesty," answered the servant.

Lady Wu let Shyu complete the rest. Legally the murdered Empress was guilty of treason. Her uncle, Liu Shy, had already been dismissed a month before the coronation. She had, however, another uncle. These and the entire clans of the deceased Empress and Queen Consort were banished to Kwangtung in the remote south. The Empress's father, Wang Renyu, was dead, but his descendants had inherited ranks as children of a duke. Always subservient to Lady Wu's wish, Shyu argued that the Emperor had been too lenient to a traitoress, that the late Empress's father and his heirs should be deprived of all ranks and titles, and that the Duke's grave be opened and his corpse mutilated. Gaotsung found this too disgusting, but he did go so far as to deprive his father-in-law of all ranks posthumously—a sore trial for his soul—and thus carry her vengeance to the grave. All children and grandchildren of the family were degraded and exiled.

In her triumph, Lady Wu now turned into a merciless and

rather uncouth punster, with a wry sense of humor. She thought happily that the deceased Empress's name, *Wang,* rhymes with *mang* ("cobra"), and *Shiao* was homonym for "vulture." She decreed that henceforth the children of these two families should bear the clan names of "Cobra" and "Vulture" respectively. One chapter of her life was thus closed, or so she thought.

Lady Wu had a fine start—for it was only a start. She had ridden to success and power over the corpses of two women.

Surely Grandmother had a good body, good perfumed flesh. But what venom! Grandfather had taken the bait like a fish and now felt a piece of metal hook in his gorge which he could not spit out unless his whole entrails were torn open.

Gaotsung was grieved. He was moreover shocked by the unnecessary cruelty. Would not a merciful "grant for self-hanging" be enough? He reeled as if under a hammer blow, which was struck at himself as well as at the confined women. All this had been done behind his back. Was he a king, or a beggar? His spirit rebelled against this woman, but he said nothing. The fight of the sexes was on.

The enormity of the act was soon to become apparent. What Wu Tsertien wanted was a clean house—in other words, strict monogamy. How very unfair, as we shall see! The holy state of matrimony was to be purified. Too many women, Lady Wu decided, was enervating for the Emperor's health. There were no longer to be queen consorts, or graces, or selects. Imperial dignity required that he should have the back courts filled with a number of women; the Emperor must not live like a monk or a poor farmer, or the Princes would laugh at him. Their number would be reduced, however, and their functions better defined as female assistants to the Emperor's Virtue. For the sake of clean morality, a new system was created. The number was cut down. In place of the four *fei* and nine *bin,* there were two of the first rank, entitled "Assistants to Virtue," and four of the next rank, entitled "Monitors of Propriety." That these were not just high-sounding titles and that these several governesses all tried to monitor the king and dissuade him from straying off the narrow path of Virtue can well be believed.

The relationship of Gaotsung and Lady Wu had changed after this incident. Some men are born virtuous and some have virtue thrust upon them. Gaotsung was one of the latter. The curious effect of this moral injunction was that he withdrew into himself, became morose and unhappy. His love for Lady Wu had changed into a sense of positive revulsion, and gradually he thought of himself as having married a black panther. The image of the Black Panther constantly intruded into his dreams and he had wild, frightening nightmares. You could not have relations with a woman whom you feared and hated in your heart. To his surprise, at the age of twenty-eight, his wife could no longer arouse him and this further increased his shame and humiliation. The *yang* fires had been dampened when he was in her company. This explains the strange fact that after 656, Gaotsung, who had had one child almost every year since he was married at the age of fifteen, stopped having progeny either by her or by any other woman. Jer was born in 656. It was not till six years later that another son, Dan, was born. This also explained some of Wu Tsertien's extramarital exploits. The destructive tendencies of this unhappy marriage progressed as the years went by, until Gaotsung, a man in his late thirties, was a host to neuralgia, neuritis, spells of dizziness and a number of other aches and ailments which the imperial physicians were not able to diagnose. Then he grew white hair. He became increasingly shy and diffident, hated his official duties and left the Empress very much the freedom to run the government as she wished.

But we are anticipating. The history of the next twenty years—merely a preliminary to the exploits of Wu Tsertien when she was to be a widow and alone—was a story of one frustration after another for her husband; now his every wish was overruled.

Gaotsung's character underwent a change; this was inevitable for the man who married Wu Tsertien. He now had only one wish—to be left alone.

❋ 7 ❋

It was not in Wu Tsertien's nature to be merely a figure of public worship, to adorn a court with her graciousness and beauty, or to receive the glad homage and adulations of the courtiers on social occasions, as she did that day on the balcony. She now had visions of greatness—to be not just a queen, but a great queen. She had an ecstatic vision that she would do such remarkable things that the name of Wu Tsertien would be writ large in the annals of history. She would be Wu Tsertien the Great, the Unique, the Unclassifiable.

Her first and foremost business was now to unify the government. No government could function properly until there was one will, one law—absolute obedience to one person. Things were wrong, vastly wrong. She had not forgotten how those four men, Wuji, Suiliang, Han Yuan and Lai Tsi, had tried to thwart her will and block her way to the throne. Two months after her coronation, Jung was deposed and her eldest son, Hung, was made Crown Prince in his stead. Shyu, who had run a court campaign for her, was made secretary of the Imperial Secretary, in office nightly at the West Gate of the Palace to receive her orders. Shyu would do. An expert at law and statutes, he could be useful. She would use Shyu as a whip to whip the whole machinery into shape. Government was business and she would not allow sentiment to interfere.

Lady Wu proceeded with the task of unifying the government by purging elements who had opposed her. Suiliang was gone, but the old score with Wuji, Han Yuan and Lai

Tsi was not yet settled. She remembered, too, that there were others who had either opposed her coronation as Empress, or had been noncommittal, or held aloof. Wuji had, for instance, been holding aloof, keeping silent. He had not bothered himself with active administration, but had been compiling a history of the two preceding regimes, of Taitsung and Taitsung's father,* of which he himself was an important figure. Others had not fallen into line. Both Han Yuan and Lai Tsi were elderly statesmen who held their heads high and spoke straight, men who had not learned to cringe and fawn and hasten to agree with Her Majesty. To her, the court looked like a complete mess.

The time had now come to consolidate her power and to institute a regime firmly under her control.

Lord Secretary Han was to receive the first blow. How to remove Archduke Wuji was her real object, for he was the king's support, the most powerful personality, not easy to bring into her camp. It testifies to the great statecraft of Lady Wu that she did not tackle the Archduke first. Being the most respected, he should be left till the others were destroyed and he was left alone.

Han Yuan gave Lady Wu the first chance. He had the audacity to ask for Suiliang's pardon. Suiliang's banishment had hung upon his conscience. After waiting a year, he thought it his duty as a friend and as Lord Secretary to right the injustice done to a good man. Some of the fine spirit of men trained in the tradition of Taitsung still remained, men willing to stand their ground on matters of state policy, at the risk of offending the king and losing their position, if necessary.

In the course of his long memorandum begging for the par-

* Officially, Taitsung's father was the first Emperor of the Tang Dynasty, but Taitsung was the real founder who led the campaign to establish the Empire.

don of the banished Suiliang and allowing him to return to the capital, he outlined the fundamental principle of keeping honest, good men at the government, quoted historical examples of how a government deteriorated with the departure of good men, reminded the Emperor of Suiliang's record and concluded: "Even though he did offend Your Majesty, he has already suffered punishment for a year. Would not His Majesty be so gracious as to grant him pardon?"

Han Yuan might be unaware that Lady Wu was sitting behind a screen listening, or he didn't care. When he finished reading, the Emperor said: "I respect what you say. But I think you are making the case sound more serious than it is. I know that Suiliang is an honest man. But he was terribly rude to me. Was I wrong to punish him for his disrespect to the throne?"

Han Yuan replied firmly, "I am afraid I look at it otherwise. Any good government must be based first of all on selecting and keeping the good men. The question is whether Your Majesty wants lackeys or men. As we say, a fly can make stains on a white cloth. I do fear that the way may be open for self-seeking individuals to go on smearing and driving away the good men." Han Yuan forgot himself as he quoted example after example. "The *Book of Songs* says, 'A splendid house like the Jou was destroyed by Powse.' I do not wish to see the House of Tang destroyed."

The reference to the notorious Queen Powse, who ruined an empire, was undiplomatic and tactless. It amounted to an open insult to the Empress. Lady Wu did not utter a sound during the audience, but her silence was even more ominous. Han Yuan's fate was sealed.

"You may withdraw!" growled Gaotsung.

It will be remembered that there was the former Crown Prince Jung, who had been deposed at the age of thirteen, and who had nobody to defend him. He was born of a lady of low rank and his adopted mother, Empress Wang, was now dead. His case looked interesting to Lady Wu. He could be useful as a pretender to the throne, around whom she could build a conspiracy to destroy all who had disagreed with her. Anyone who disagreed with her, or stood in her way, was a member of the hideous Jungite gang. The politics of the next few years was to be built around the poor boy, still in his teens, hounded and living in constant fear of his life.

In the following year, Han Yuan and Lai Tsi were accused of treason, charged with consorting with Pretender Jung to raise a revolt. Han Yuan was banished to Hainan, an aboriginal island off the Canton coast, and Lai Tsi was sent in another direction to the coast of Chekiang to meditate on his errors of judgment.

Such banishments were at the pleasure of the king, and Shyu did not have to substantiate his charges. It was either true or untrue, and if true, Prince Jung should not have escaped with his life and the two ministers should have been decapitated. But it didn't really matter. With or without evidence, Shyu knew he had the Empress's full backing. Conveniently, Shyu stepped into the outgoing Lord Secretary's shoes.

Unfortunately, that was not the end. Shyu elaborated the case and finally alleged the conspiracy to have been planned to start—with Suiliang as leader—from Kweilin, and that was the reason why Han Yuan, while still Lord Secretary, had Suiliang sent to Kweilin. Suiliang was exiled still further, this time practically outside the pale of civilization, to Hanoi (in Indo-China). He wrote a pathetic, brief letter to Gaotsung, reminding him how the Emperor had fallen upon his neck crying at the moment of swearing-in, before

Taitsung's coffin, as Emperor. He was sorry for his offense and asked to be permitted to return to China. The letter went unanswered.

Suiliang died a year later and was buried in Hanoi. His two sons had been banished to the same place and died about the same time. The same is true of Liu Shy. So ended the life of an honest and brave man, whom posterity will always honor for his courage and loyalty to the Emperor.

Han Yuan, Suiliang and Lai Tsi had fallen, crumpled under the iron whip. Wuji was now alone. He sensed what was coming and continued to occupy himself with writing a history of the two previous regimes. It was in eighty volumes,* and at its completion he was awarded two thousand pieces of silk.

Next the ax fell on Archduke Wuji, Taitsung's closest assistant and First Founding Knight of the Tang Empire. The Empress also had a few persons to destroy and dismiss besides Wuji, men like General Yu Jening, of Taitsung's old gang, who had not fallen into line. It was always the shadowy story of a Jungite conspiracy, which Shyu went on pursuing with ever-widening fruitful results. In the following spring, 659, Shyu tried very hard to obtain a witness against Wuji for complicity in the plot. One of Wuji's friends, Wei (Jifang), was caught on a charge of corruption. Shyu, now Lord Chancellor, was concurrently Chief of Supreme Court, which was packed with his men. The Judge promised to let Wei off lightly if he would turn witness against the Archduke. Wei might have taken bribes, but to sell an honest man, no. Under the application of torture, he refused, and attempted to take his own life. He had cut himself at several places and was on the point of death. Unsuccessful in obtaining the testimony, but seeing that the man was dying

* A "volume," *jyuan,* is usually the length of two or three short English chapters.

soon anyway, Shyu reported that Wei had confessed and Wuji, rather than Suiliang, was the leader of the ring of rebels.

Gaotsung was shocked. He ordered another examination, under Shin, one of Shyu's men. The result was a confirmation, though the dying witness could not talk anymore.

"Shin is a fool," said Gaotsung. "My uncle would never do such a thing. Why should he?"

Shyu had a ready answer. His Majesty could see Wuji had been keeping aloof and staying behind; a disgruntled person. He had advocated making Jung crown heir in the first place. Now he found himself in a vulnerable position after Jung's displacement. Moreover, he had always stood against Empress Wu, and now, in fear of his position, he was plotting rebellion with Jung to keep himself in power.

Gaotsung was distressed. Dismissing Wuji was like cutting off his own right hand. He hesitated very much to sign his arrest. A sigh escaped. "I am ashamed. That this should happen in my family!"

However, Shyu insisted on having Wuji arrested at once. The Emperor was reminded that Wuji had a powerful following, at court and among the generals. Now that his plot had been discovered, he might be forced to take desperate action. No time was to be lost. Moreover, an emperor should put the law of the country above his personal feelings.

"Let me think it over," said Gaotsung. He had not the courage to ask for a direct interview with his uncle. That night, in the company of Lady Wu, he signed the order for the arrest of the Archduke and Field Marshal and his banishment to Jienchow (modern Kweichow).

Wuji was like an institution; his name was associated with Taitsung and the founding of the Empire. Gaotsung ordered that he be permitted to keep his rank and title and that on his way he should be received by officials with the courtesy due to a first-rank minister.

Once in disgrace and exile, it was easy to dispose of a person. The following year, Shyu sent out an assistant judge of the Supreme Court, the same Yuan Gungyu who had secretly reported to Lady Wu's mother after dinner at Wuji's home during the first fight around Empress Wang. Yuan was told to obtain confessions from Wuji implicating others. Wuji refused.

"Why don't you hang yourself?" said the Judge. "I will have your confessions signed anyway when you are dead."

Accepting the inevitable and helpless, Field Marshal Wuji, brother-in-law of Taitsung, hanged himself. As far as the Judge's report of Wuji's confessions was concerned, it was said that the Judge could have had the whole confession written out before he started out from the capital.

On the same journey, Yuan had been asked to look up Han Yuan and do the same thing as he had done to Wuji. Fortunately, Han Yuan had died. His coffin was opened and his body identified. Han Yuan's and Wuji's families were exiled to Kwangtung, to be turned into slaves.

The unfortunate Prince Jung, who was now a boy of eighteen, saw his name implicated in all these proceedings about a conspiracy of which he knew nothing. He was degraded as a commoner, banished and imprisoned in the same district where Wuji had met his end. Having seen all that had happened around him, even to Archduke Wuji, the nervous boy developed fears of persecution. He often dressed himself as a girl and changed his bed to elude his would-be assassins. These fears grew, and he often had frightening dreams which made him jump out of bed at night. He often consulted fortune tellers to interpret the meaning of his dreams. Then he languished, abandoned and friendless. Apparently Lady Wu, his stepmother, still thought his life useful, for nobody could start a revolt around a dead pretender to the throne!

At last, Archduke Wuji, Suiliang and Han Yuan were all

dead, within five years of Lady Wu's coming into power.* Lady Wu was in firm control of the government. The procedure had followed a pattern. The timing was perfect.

* Lai Tsi, disappointed and furious, had rushed forward in battle and got himself killed.

❋ 8 ❋

Gaotsung's wings were clipped. The Empress had not snatched the power away from him; it had merely slipped out of his hand into hers. More and more often she began to assist at the imperial audience with the courtiers. Then, too, her opinions were always clearly expressed, her decisions firm, and her reasons well given. She had indeed been a help in this respect. Underneath it all, Gaotsung knew that the ministers were more inclined to agree with her and do her bidding. There was now no one like Han Yuan or Lai Tsi who could serve as a deterrent, who, when the occasion came, might be expected to fight for his opinion. The government was running smoothly, too smoothly. The administration was "unified," with no dissenting voice, no intransigent opinion, no one to say "No" to Her Majesty. Shyu and Li (Yifu) and Yuan (Gungyu) and others worked as a well-organized unit. That these men were venal and corrupt and took other men's wives or lands, in no way directly affected the throne. Li's corruption was especially notorious. At his mother's funeral, the procession extended several miles long. What of it? The Empress wanted to see those who did her bidding wallow in power and glory, which was in her power to give or take away.

Grandmother was not too happy with her maiden family. She had not had a happy childhood, had been taken to the Palace at the age of fourteen and lived away from home for over a dozen years. Her father had two sons by his first wife before he married Lady Wu's own mother. There was no love lost between the two wives, or between the stepbrothers or sisters.

One day she gave a grand reception to the Wu relatives and clansmen, who were permitted to enter the inner courts. Her elder sister, of the same mother, a Madame Holan, was there with her young daughter. She was now a widow and was made Duchess of Han. There were her two stepbrothers, too, who were occupying posts at special bureaus close to the Palace.

These two stepbrothers, Yuanching and Yuanshuang, had been a sore in Lady Wu's eyes and in her mother's eyes. They had always been insolent. Lady Wu's mother, now living in the Palace, was known as Lady Yang,* and had been created a duchess.

She said, rather crudely, to her stepsons, "Remember the old days? How about it now?" She almost crowed.

"It is indeed a little embarrassing," replied the stepsons. "Our sister is now the Empress. People might misunderstand and say that we owe our positions to her and not to our father!"

The same old insolence! Lady Yang felt greatly angered, and told her daughter Lady Wu about it. She had her stepbrothers banished as magistrates in the remote provinces, "to show," as the edict says, "that the Empress is not partial to her own relatives."

This was one of her shrewdest moves. Yuanching died as soon as he reached Lungchow in the remote south. Yuanshuang refused to die so easily: he was further removed, implicated in some charge and condemned to death. The happenings over a thousand miles away in a remote semi-bar-

* In Chinese society, especially in official families where there are several wives to distinguish, a woman is addressed by her maiden name. Thus Lady Yang was Mrs. Wu, but came from a Yang family.

barous district did not even cause a perceptible ripple in the smooth life of elegance at the court.

Her husband was now temperamental. He began to chafe at his bit. He was often irritable and glum by starts. He lost his appetite, while Grandmother had very strong teeth and an unrivaled digestive system. He often sulked at dinner and watched his wife gorging herself with food.

"Aren't you eating?" Her Majesty asked.

"No."

Into his eyes crept a look of ambient distaste for everything and a cold, lurking hostility. Conversation was halting and forced, and sometimes Gaotsung adopted a tone of sarcasm which was unbearable. Lady Wu had written a tract on *Domestic Virtues* for good wives while she was *jaoyi* and had caused it to be circulated for her own promotion. Once Gaotsung said to her:

"I was enjoying reading it again last night. *The important thing in a woman is keeping her place at home. She should be neat and tidy, speak as little as possible, and attend to her needlework. She should regard her husband's wish as her law, and above all, should be good to her parents-in-law and all her husband's relations so that an atmosphere of peace and harmony in the home may exist. . . .* Quite beautiful sentiments, don't you think?"

Lady Wu found this irritating and answered it by silence. There were, however, subjects on which she was more touchy and now and then explosions were inevitable.

For Lady Wu was sensitive about two things, the mention of the deceased Empress and cats. She had been seeing ghosts of the murdered women and had developed a phobia for cats. These ghosts were, according to her, haunting the Palace. She had seen them appearing in the corridors at night coming at her, their hair disheveled and two bloody fingerless hands wheeling about and wanting to jab her. Or when she lay in bed at night she would often see a river stained with blood and on it were floating dead men's hands everywhere, bloody hands, hundreds of them. When Empress Wang and Shiaofei were tied with hands and feet chopped off and thrown into wine vats, the Empress had merely said, "It was my mistake. I had taken her for a loyal friend," but the spiteful Queen Consort Shiaofei swore, "When I die, grant that I may be born a cat; I will pounce on the neck of that harlot in bed, you bet." This had been reported to her. Cats were banished from the Palace; she would rather endure swarms of rats than the shadow of a cat.

Once Gaotsung threw it at her.

"I have been seeing a doctor," said Grandmother, "and asked him if he could do something for you. It's not right for a young man like you . . ."

"There is nothing wrong with me. Yes, I've been thinking about Lady Shiao and Empress Wang. It is not too pleasant, is it? You and your sweet friendship for the Empress! You used her as your stepping-stone, scheming against her in cold blood while frothing in your mouth with protestations of affection and love. She did you no harm. If she had not pulled you out of the convent, where would you be today? You and your harlotry. One Shiaofei is worth more than ten of you nuns—"

"Stop it! For heaven's sake, stop it! You are not a *man*. If you were, you would not be blaming others."

However, the phantoms appeared again and again. They disappeared when she went to Loyang. The ghosts did not bother her there. She was so pleased that she visited Loyang again and again and stayed there as long as possible. For instance, she took three trips to Loyang in the year 657, in January, then again in July and December. She was already thinking of making Loyang her Eastern capital.

In October, 660, about the time when Wuji was forced to

commit suicide in his place of exile, Gaotsung had his first stroke, and never quite recovered from spells of dizziness, pains in the bones and numbness in the limbs.

Lady Wu now had a new palace, the Penglai, built north of the haunted palace, ostensibly because the old palace, inherited from the preceding dynasty, was low and damp and full of rats, not good for the Emperor's health, but also because she hoped the apparitions of the murdered women would cease. Ever solicitous of her husband's welfare, she told everybody that her husband was suffering from rheumatic pains because the ground was too low and damp. It would cost some money of course, but after all, the Emperor's health and happiness came first. Behind the Palace was the great royal park, with hills coming down from the great range on the northwest. She selected a site just beyond the north city wall to the east of the Old Palace and connected with it by a strip of strictly private gardens running east and west. Thus the Old Palace was abandoned and the New Palace, the present Daming Hall, originally called Penglai Hall (Fairy Palace), came into being.

The New Palace was not just a new building, but a complete set of halls and courts and private residences and gardens, including a special court on the east for the Crown Prince, a library, offices for the Secretariat and the Chancellory, etc. A hundred thousand people from fifteen neighboring districts were conscripted for labor. All officials were asked to contribute one month's salary to help toward the expense. Everything was new, and bigger and grander than the Old Palace.

Unfortunately, the ghosts appeared again in the New Palace, which brought the relations of the royal couple to a crisis.

The ever-active, restless Lady Wu began to wear the king

out. Novel buildings, novel titles, novel creations delighted her. On February 4, 662, the nomenclature of all government offices was overhauled for no apparent reason. (It was changed back again eight years later.) It gave her the sense that she was doing things, and not following the routine of past sovereigns. She believed in the magic of words and symbols. She changed the name of her third son Jer, to Shien, then back to Jer again, and her fourth son's name from Shyulun, Lun, and then to Dan. She loved to change the reign-titles. Once a farmer in the provinces had seen a crocodile during a flood. The crocodile *could* be a dragon. It had *got to be* a dragon, that most auspicious symbol of the Emperor, she was quite sure. She had the reign title changed to "Dragon Inauguration" (661). Now upon completion of the new throne hall, the Hanyuan Hall, she changed it once more. Someone had spotted a deer's toe-bone thrown away from the imperial kitchen and reported that perhaps it was a unicorn. The appearance of a unicorn was associated with the advent of a saint. So a unicorn it had to be, and the new reign was entitled "Virtue of Unicorn" (664).

At this time Madame Holan, the Duchess of Han, was a constant visitor at the Palace. As Lady Wu's sister and a close member of the royal family, she enjoyed the privileges and intimacies which were forbidden the other ladies of the court. She ate at the same table and was seen in the Emperor's company constantly. Taunted by his wife with not being a man, Gaotsung sought the company of the Duchess of Han. Gaotsung liked her company and also that of her teen-age daughter. And the Duchess excited him as Lady Wu could not.

I have to go into this because I suspect that my father, Prince Shien, was probably born of the Duchess, and it had certain consequences in further disrupting the royal household. It was, after all, Lady Wu herself who started the rumor in court circles, spread by her maids at the time when she was about to degrade and exile my father.

Gaotsung's attentions to the Duchess did not escape Lady Wu's eyes. He was happy as he had not been for years. Conceivably, two sisters might join hands to monopolize between themselves the favors of the king, like the two sister queens of Han Chengti. But it would be too much to expect of Lady Wu.

The second blow came.

One day, the Duchess died of convulsions after a dinner, evidently from arsenic poisoning. One had now to get used to the idea that men disliked by the queen were usually sent to exile only to die a thousand miles from the capital, with nobody caring; but women liked by the king had the habit of eating something wrong inside the Palace and falling down dead. Such a thing should not happen in the royal kitchen, since there were officers there whose special responsibility was just to prevent such accidents. Who could have poisoned her? There should have been an investigation. But who cared, if the poisoned woman's own sister, the queen, did not? The theory was, Lady Wu could not have poisoned her own sister. She grieved, very convincingly, for the lost sister and had her buried with proper honors.

Gaotsung was stricken with deep grief and remained disconsolate. He was not a fool. He revised his estimate of the woman he had married. He now both despised and feared her. Empress Wang, Lady Shiao, and now the Duchess. Where was the ax to fall next? Curiously, the affair gave him a sense of guilt; he felt he was responsible for her death. He refrained from making open charges. In any case, it was the first case of arsenic poisoning in the royal family. Grandfather had no one to unburden his thoughts to now. He felt the walls were closing in around him, that, dependent as he was on the Empress in public life, he had no more freedom at home, that his steps were watched and circumscribed, that he must not come near any red skirt. Red skirt and arsenic had proved to be inseparable.

Outwardly, the king and queen appeared very affectionate to each other; but she sensed his revulsion for her. She wanted to make it up to him, and took good care of him and would coddle him as she would a child. Sometimes she almost convinced him that she loved him as once she did. She could simulate passion so well, and Grandfather was susceptible. All doubts and suspicions of her part in the poisoning could be submerged in a voluptuous embrace, and if Gaotsung thought of the persecutions of Wuji and others, it was of course all politics. But Grandfather was very unsure of himself in company. It always seemed that in her presence he was bound to do something wrong and have his mistake pointed out.

Slowly, the idea was formed in Gaotsung's mind that he must get rid of the Empress. He had visions of freedom, visions of a king surrounded by beauties attending to his wishes, visions of a free hand in government and of his wishes being obeyed implicitly. How was he to do it, with the court packed with men like Shyu? He wished Archduke Wuji were alive, and Suiliang and Han Yuan. General Li Tsi was now winning victories in Korea, but he was noncommittal anyway and in truth might be considered Lady Wu's man. Where would he look for a minister who would assist and support him in this plan to reassert his power as king?

Strange doings were now taking place in the New Palace. In the year 663, after its completion, an opportunity presented itself. The purpose of the new buildings was for Lady Wu to get away from the haunted Old Palace. But the ghosts now seemed to follow Lady Wu into the New Palace—understandable because the two palaces were connected. The distance was easy for humans to cover in a fifteen minutes' walk, not to speak of ghosts. Lady Wu invited a sorcerer, Guo Shingjen, to exorcise the spirits by incantations and the burning of charm papers. Such suspicious goings-on continued for nights. One could never tell what the Empress hoped to gain by these nightly sessions. She and the Taoist priest were alone night after night.

Lady Wu's nightly sittings were reported to the Emperor by a eunuch. Gaotsung became suspicious. He would go and see. Passing through a long, covered corridor, he could see a maid watching at a corner. She disappeared immediately upon his approach. He could see her shadow flitting against the dimly lighted gauze windows. The Hanyuan Tower was in the southwestern end of the New Palace, connected by a covered corridor. Gaotsung drew up sharp at the corner, where he could see lights from the second story. What should he do? Break in upon them? He was sure that the sorcerer had been warned now, as he saw the lights in the room go out. He would not risk it and silently retraced his steps to his own room.

The next day, Lady Wu sought an opportunity to explain.

"What were you doing hanging around the Hanyuan Tower last night?"

"Oh," answered Gaotsung, "I was just taking a stroll. I needed some fresh air."

"In the dark, unaccompanied? You should be more careful. As a matter of fact, I thought you were coming, and the Taoist and I were expecting you to come up. Why didn't you? Why didn't you come and watch, and listen to his incantations?"

"Oh, no, why should I? I am not interested."

Gaotsung had successfully put Lady Wu off her guard. A week passed. He was going to catch them. Luckily for him, the maid was not at the corner and when he came close to the foot of the tower, it gave her a fright. She screamed and rushed upstairs, and Gaotsung followed her up, giving no time for a warning. The sorcerer and Lady Wu were caught in an embarrassing situation. The sorcerer was adjusting his girdle. And Lady Wu—he had seen her in such attire so many times in bed. The sorcerer immediately made a gesture to get up from his cushion on the floor, where two winecups were standing beside it.

Lady Wu's voice was flustered, as she said somewhat sheepishly, "Why, so glad you have decided to come and watch the prayers. We've just been having a little rest between the intervals."

"I see," said Gaotsung and turned to go down.

"Why don't you stay and watch the prayers? We've darkened the room because absolute silence is necessary." There were three or four red candles burning on the tables.

"Why do the prayers have to be watched?" said Gaotsung. "Can't he do it alone? I thought the exorcising of spirits should take place around the grounds, not by saying prayers in a closed room at night."

Gaotsung had already started down the staircase. He had seen with his own eyes. It was enough. He left the lovers gasping for breath.

His mind was made up. In fact, he was happy. He had found just the kind of excuse necessary for deposing an Empress. All he needed was courage. Lady Wu came into his room half an hour later.

"Why didn't you stay? You left in such a huff of anger. There was nothing wrong. What do you suspect?"

"I suspect nothing."

"You should have stayed. The place is haunted. You don't know how much I suffered. I am sure the Taoist's magic will work. And it is so fascinating. I wanted to watch."

"With winecups on the floor, I suppose?"

"Oh, my husband. I assure you it was all innocent. . . ."

He studied her. "You may be an empress, but to me you are but a bitch, you paragon of virtue—nothing but a bitch!"

To her disappointment, her explanations and her advances were of no avail tonight.

"Well, then, I will leave you. Think it over and you'll realize that I am doing right."

The next day he confided his thought to Vice-Chancellor Shangguan Yi, the one he could trust. Shangguan was a poet who had created a vogue much imitated by the poets of his day. The poet agreed with him and reminded him that he was a king.

"All you need do is issue an edict. But no one should know about it. I shouldn't mention adultery. Practicing black magic within the Palace is itself a crime, for which Empress Wang was deposed. I would mention the poisoning of the Duchess, but it should be part of a general charge, couched in general terms. The persecutions of old ministers like Wuji and Suiliang would get general sympathy. But general statements, showing that she is unfit to be the Empress, should be enough."

"All right, you draft the edict," he ordered the Vice-Chancellor, "but keep it a strict secret."

It was not quite as simple as he had thought. That evening Gaotsung was sitting with the draft on his desk. He had been only deceiving himself for he should have known that his every movement was reported to Lady Wu.

Suddenly in came Lady Wu, fire in her eyes, and she fixed him with an incredulous stare. Gaotsung's face paled as if struck by an apparition.

"Is this true?" his wife demanded.

"Is what true?"

"Don't pretend. I have been accused by a eunuch of seeking sorcery— Don't interrupt me! Where's the edict?"

Her eyes traveled to the scrap of yellow paper lying on his desk. Gaotsung fidgeted in his seat.

"No, no," said the Emperor. "It's only a draft."

"Give it to me!" the wife roared.

Gaotsung quickly handed it over, as a matter of habit, and Lady Wu took time to glance at the text and get the general tenor of the charges against herself. She tore it to pieces.

"Who put you up to this?"

Gaotsung was silent.

"This is Shangguan Yi's handwriting. I know. Isn't it?"

Gaotsung nodded.

"Don't you think that I know that you and he were shut up in the Chancellor's office for two hours this afternoon? I knew even the text before I read it."

Gaotsung was silent.

Grandmother sat down. "I really must have a good talk with you," she began. "I have been wanting to say something for a long time, and I may just as well say it now. It was extremely foolish of you to listen to bad advice. I only wanted to exorcise the evil influences from the New Palace and you flew off your temper like a child. . . . Have I ever failed you as a wife?"

Gaotsung was silent.

"What I wanted to say is this, and this is a good opportunity to say it. Lately I have seen you getting more morose and irritable. I laid it all to your bad health and said nothing. I've been so busy, with all the new buildings and state affairs. What do I do lying awake at night? Thinking ahead, planning things, making decisions on the personnel and policies, all to help you. If anybody wants to take my place, let her have it. I am quite willing to lay down this burden of trying to make a great king out of you. . . ."

Grandfather was confused, shaking and dizzy. He hated to talk politics just now. "Will you leave me alone?"

But the Empress continued. "I will not talk about my deceased elder sister. It's silly of you to suspect me as having had a hand in it. But I know there's something underneath it all. I've had to do many things I did not like to do. Wuji and Suiliang, for instance. You are too soft-hearted. Why, if it had not been for my insistence, heaven knows where we might be today! I was always in the right."

"I know you always are— You can't help it."

"But it is true. Luckily, the secret ring was broken in time. Do you suppose you would be still sitting securely on the throne if I had not been firm? The whole point is, a king should feel and act like a king. I am here to help you. Why have I had the New Palace built? For you. I have never spared myself, have I? I want to help you to become a great king, a strong king. You ought to have more push and confidence. Look at our great empire! The Turkis, the Thibetans, the Khotans, the Kazaks beyond the Kunlun Mountains are suing for peace. It looks as if Korea will be subjugated soon. I know I can do it. I have all these great plans for you. We will build new palaces and monuments, establish nobles, outshine all previous reigns. Be a king! Hand in hand together we can do it. And here you are, doing an utterly foolish thing listening to bad advice like a child!"

Gaotsung almost reeled before this bombardment. His head was dizzy with the emotional excitement, his body and soul aching for a rest from the necessity for making decisions. Finally, he said gloomily, "I believe you could run the government yourself, without me."

"I believe I could. But I want only to help you. You are so ill. Now go to bed early and try to have a good sleep, and forget all that nonsense."

Gaotsung threw back his head in resignation, his thought of freedom evaporated.

Lady Wu had by her quick action averted a near-catastrophe. The fact that the Emperor could even entertain for a moment the idea of doing without her came as a terrible shock to her. Back in her room, the more she thought of it, the more enraged she became. That anyone should ever think of deposing her! It must never happen again.

She knew she held the stiletto in her hand. She would teach a lesson to all her courtiers, once and for all. To have a minister killed was so easy, a fiat would do it. She called Shyu in, and Shyu suggested that Shangguan Yi had once been in the service of Jung when he was Crown Prince. Obviously they were members of the traitorous Jungite gang! Labeled with this crime, Shangguan was beheaded in a public square in the city, and his family were turned into slaves at the disposal of the government. It was as a slave girl that Shangguan Yi's granddaughter, Wan-erl, later entered the Palace. It is one of the ironies of fate that the poet's granddaughter was to play havoc with the court during Jungtsung's reign. We shall meet her at the end of the story.

The shadowy conspiracy around Prince Jung had been overused and had become stale. Lady Wu thought his usefulness was finished. Shortly thereafter the poor young man, who had been living in constant fear of assassination, was accused of consulting sorcerers and dream-interpreters, which was strictly true. The unfortunate stepson who had prayed for peace found it at last. He was ordered to hang himself, instead of being executed in public—a prince's privilege. He was only twenty-two. Gaotsung, the father, could not save him.

❋ 9 ❋

Red skirt and arsenic are inseparable, as I hinted elsewhere. One murder, as usual, leads to another. Since the brief aborted attempt at freedom, Grandfather's condition grew steadily worse. His neuralgia became persistent and more painful. Some mornings, his pains and splitting headaches would leave him exhausted, and he became morose and listless during the day. When the Chienyuan Hall was being built in Loyang, he was seen amusing himself with the most trivial activities, like picking up the carpenter's tools and cutting up things and polishing them himself. It seemed to make him happy. Apparently he had resigned himself to letting his Empress do the governing. Or he would be examining his treasures of jade, amber, midnight pearls and other rare antiques with the Duchess's daughter, Sansan, who was now a pretty girl of eighteen. And let the Empire be damned.

In the next ten years, he had several breakdowns. He often excused himself from the audiences held in the unearthly dawn hours. If he was there, the ministers could not be sure whether he was listening or not. Henceforth it became the established routine for the Empress to sit behind a beaded curtain at all court sessions, participating in questions and replies, and the ministers learned to listen for a broad feminine voice rather than a man's. It was bad manners of course, but her excuse was that she was helping her ailing husband and, as she thought, in all conscience he needed it. It became then the general custom, in private talks and in official communications, to use the plural "Their Majesties" (*erh sheng*), rather than "His Majesty," referring to the sovereign.

The tireless Empress was wearing Gaotsung out. While he would have been content to sulk in his palace and watch the goldfish and the peonies in his garden in the company of Sansan, Lady Wu was forever doing things and dragging him about. She started building a new palace, the Chienyuan Hall, in Loyang in March, 665. In April, she was holding a military parade. And already preparations were being made for the most ambitious royal visit to the Sacred Taishan, a journey which would take six months!

Could he be excused from the journey of six hundred miles on mule carts? No, of course not. The occasion was no less than *fengshan,* worship of heaven by the Emperor on the Sacred Mountain. It was both a pilgrimage and the celebration of a great reign.

"Of course, you have to go."

"But the Sacred Mountain is way out in Shantung, six hundred miles from here. I'll be a physical wreck before the trip ends."

"Don't worry about that. The preparations will be made for our stops and our comforts all the way."

"Yes, and we will be on parade all the way for the villagers and townspeople to gawk at. What do you want to hold the *fengshan* for?"

"To thank God for the peace and the Empire. Taitsung did have one, why shouldn't you?"

"The peace and the Empire be damned! Can I bring my crickets?"

"Don't be frivolous."

"Not at all. I am serious. You have to have at least four attendants for the crickets. How many people will there be in our party?"

"Several hundreds."

"Good heaven!"

"The chief ministers and all the courtiers will regard it as a favor to be permitted to accompany us on such a grand outing. Including the servants, there may be a thousand. Won't it be glorious? A whole court on parade!"

"Will Sansan come with us?" Sansan had been made Duchess of Wei since her mother's murder.

"I don't see why she should."

"Then I am not going."

Sansan was a young girl, good-natured, brought up in royal luxury, prone to laugh, and yet completely innocent of the wicked ways of men. She was so gentle by nature that once at a cricket fight she cried when she saw a defeated cricket limp about with one leg, and Grandfather was affected too, and then they both started to smile and thought nobody else would understand them. Nobody had told her why her mother had eaten something wrong and just died, since the whole imperial household, including the kitchen help and the servants, would never suggest the thought that it was anything but an accident. Her aunt had reassured her that the royal kitchen was scrupulously supervised; she couldn't imagine what it was that killed her; it was just her fate. And the young girl had accepted that version. The first year she wore mourning for her mother while living in the Hanyuan Palace, and the following year, when they lived most of the time in Loyang, she had accompanied them.

Her complete ingenuity fascinated Gaotsung. The Emperor was her uncle. And she would sometimes put her arm around him when they strolled around the garden.

"Stop it," said Gaotsung.

"Why?" The girl withdrew her arm, puzzled.

Grandfather remained silent for a few seconds before he said, "Your aunt may be watching. You'd better watch your step."

"But why? I don't understand."

"You don't?" Grandfather drew up and fixed a solemn look on the young girl. He turned his head aside, looking at the distant hills, and made an audible sigh.

Slowly, he said, "I killed your mother— Don't misunderstand. I was responsible for her death because your mother and I were such friends. I am sorry I have to tell you this."

As Grandfather whispered to her the story, Sansan was horrified. Sororicide was unimaginable to her innocent mind.

"I am telling you this in secret. Of course it was arsenic poisoning. Your aunt is capable of anything. That's why I say: watch your step. Don't ever let your aunt think that I am very fond of you. If anything happens to you, it will be on my conscience."

"But Uncle!"

"Yes, I mean it. I never forget your mother. The least I can do is protect you."

Grandfather's intentions were entirely noble. But he should not have let such a young and simple girl into the secret of a murder. Sansan now accompanied Grandfather and Grandmother on the trip to Taishan.

The *fengshan,* or worship of Heaven on Mount Taishan, was an august ceremony not to be lightly undertaken, and was celebrated only on very special occasions. The preceding Emperor, the great Taitsung, had celebrated the *fengshan* in the eleventh year of his reign, in commemoration of the restoration of peace and unity in the country. But when another *fengshan* ceremony was proposed in 641, to celebrate the successful conclusion of the Turkish campaign, a comet appeared in June and the trip was canceled. For the august ceremony meant the conferring of a title on the Sacred Mountain God by the Emperor, and was at the same time a commemoration and a prayer, informing Heaven of the success of one's reign and thanking Him for His help and protection. Lady Wu remembered seeing it as a young girl when serving Taitsung. How she had loved it—not the religious service, but the pageantry and the social glitter.

The *fengshan* was a long, slow imperial procession across the country, upsetting the government routine for a year and the entire countryside on its path for half a year. It practically meant moving the whole court on an extended journey involving tens of thousands of men and horses and carriages and cattle and the imperial and princes' guards. Accommodation at the stopping places had to be provided for all the princes and dukes and generals and their families and retinue. It put all the local officials in a flurry. Woe to the man who should offend one of the princes passing through!

The order for the convocation had been issued. All princes and all high ministers, excepting those on duty at strategic posts, were to assemble at Loyang to participate in the royal pilgrimage. When the time came, the streets hummed with people and the suburbs swarmed with soldiers and horses, looking like a military encampment. For in addition to the members of the court there had assembled the princes, tribal chiefs and official representatives from Turkey, Persia, Khotan, India, Kashmir, Ujana (in North India), Kunlun (Chinese Turkestan), Japan, Korea, Sinlo and Baitsi (the last two in South Korea). It was a colorful cavalcade, each prince's followers forming a unit, with its colors, parasols, insignia-carriers, guards and footmen. Records of the trip describe the procession as extending thirty miles, and the highways were choked with carts and horses and camels and Mongolian felt tents. At night one could see a row of round tents around villages and on the plains. In fine, all the dust of three provinces was given a complete shake-over.

It was a long, cumbersome journey. In November the

procession stopped at Yuanwu, and in December they crossed into Shantung and stopped at Tsichow (Tsinan), where they remained for ten days' rest before proceeding to the Taishan.

The ceremony at the Sacred Mountain was planned to take place on New Year's Day. All officers connected with the program were to gather at the foot of the mountain ten days before, and take up their posts. On January the first the worship of Heaven was to take place at the mountain; on January the second a select group was to go up with the Emperor to confer a title on the Sacred Mountain; on January the third the worship of the Earth was to take place on the plains again. The Emperor himself and those participating in the ceremony had to purify themselves several days ahead by ablutions and sexual abstention.

There was, however, a novel aspect to the situation which invited a great deal of criticism and some ridicule at the time —the role of the Empress in it. In going over the program, Empress Wu had, to her immense distress, discovered that she herself was not included in the ceremony at the top, as she should not be, according to tradition. This was before they had started, and she had written a very decorous memorandum to her husband showing why this gross mistake should be rectified—a gem of modesty. Written in the rather pompous style of parallel constructions, it is worth recording here on account of its delectable sentiments.

> The ceremony of worship at the summit is in entire accord with the ancient tradition; but that of the worship below leaves something to be desired.
>
> For I notice that at the worship of the Earth the spirits to share the offerings are the previous empresses, while the service is rendered by the men ministers; this in the opinion of your humble wife may be due to a mistake of judgment.
>
> Even as the honors to Heaven and Earth are based on

a clear recognition of the sexes, so, according to the teachings of the classics, the distinction between domestic and extramural affairs must be discreetly observed.

For even as the altar of the God of Earth is square (and that of Heaven, round), so the offerings of jade should be a duty proper to the feminine.

Moreover, one does not suppose that the spirits of the empresses will condescend to show themselves in men's presence; it is as against common sense as it is inconsistent with the august conception of the sacred functions.

Your humble wife has the honor of occupying the queen's chambers; her duties have included the serving of food for her ancestors and her earnest desire has ever been to glorify the table.

This desire has been deepest in my heart, and my filial piety has need of being given expression at the formal sacrifices (at both places).

Alas, that I was unable to serve my ancestors in their lifetime! How would I dare to be idle at the offerings to the dead?

That is the reason why I lie awake at night, and my thoughts permit me no rest; I sit up in bed and look up toward the souls above.

It is my hope that on the day of the ceremony I may lead the ladies of the court to assist personally at all the wine offerings, in worship and in piety, to give expression to a heartfelt desire and fulfill a solemn function;

So that my presence may serve as an example for future empresses to follow, and the feeble light of my candle may contribute a little to the brilliance of your sunlight.

Signed: Your humble wife,
Wu Jao

The matter of protocol and the rituals and forms of worship had always been a subject of grave study and learned discussion by the pundit guardians of classical tradition, down to the minutest details. However, the Empress's innovations in this instance were accepted by her husband. She *was* going to the top. Otherwise, the strong probability was that the whole commemoration would have been called off. The unthinkable simply does not happen. The "feeble candle-light" joined the others.

All night, lights were burning brightly in the special building where the Emperor stayed and purified himself in preparation for the worship of Heaven. An altar, enclosed by three concentric terraces and planted around with the yellow flags of the Emperor, had been specially constructed. The altar was round and painted blue, the shape and color symbolic of heaven. Below the altar, on the outer terrace, an enclosure was set apart for the orchestra. The musical stones and bells were set up in place at the back, while the drums and the other instruments ranged in order as at the ancestor worship. On top of the altar was the prayer or sacrificial message engraved in jade, besides three spirit tablets, also in jade, each one foot and two inches long and one inch and two-tenths wide, on which the names of the spirits were engraved in gold. The one bearing the inscription *The God of Heaven* was to be sealed up after the ceremony and buried at the altar ground, while the other two, bearing the names of the Emperor's father and grandfather, were to be put in gold boxes and brought back to the imperial ancestral temple for safekeeping. These tablets were placed on a stone table four feet high and five feet square, covered with blue embroidery. After the libations and prayers, the "sealing-up" took place. The prayer message was placed in a jade box, sealed with the imperial seal in gold powder, and tied five times around with a gold thread. The jade box was then placed in a hole in the table, previously prepared, and the whole altar was then covered up with symbolic colored soil, forming a mound which marked the consecrated spot.

The three ceremonies taking place on three successive days

were to a large extent similar. The worship of Heaven took place early, at dawn. After a repose, the Emperor, accompanied by participating officers, went up to the top of the mountain, where they stayed overnight. It was only two or three hours' climb and the road was well paved with broad panels of stone. On the next day the ceremony at the top was performed, and the party returned to their quarters below on the same day.

On the third day the worship of the Earth took place at the foot of Sacrifice Hill (*Shershan*), over a mile away. The spirits to share the offerings were the Emperor's mother and grandmother. The difference was that the altar was square and painted yellow, color and shape symbolic of the earth. Instead of the "thunder drum" used at the worship of Heaven, the deep bass drum was used.

There were three offerings. It had already been established that the Emperor was to make the first offering, Empress Wu the second, and a queen consort of Taitsung the third, to make it consistent with Lady Wu's insistence on having women at the service.

The program followed the usual routine. There were special songs sung by the court choir at every step, accompanied by the bells and musical stones and orchestra. Twelve bells were placed in a circle, conforming with the positions of the zodiac. The orchestra had been enriched by the introduction of Turkestan (Gweitsy) musical instruments, both string and woodwind. It consisted of the five-string *pipa* (lute), bass and small zithers, *pili* (a short pipe of Turfan [Turkestan] origin whose sharp, shrill notes were said to frighten Chinese horses in battle), oboes, flutes and various clay pipes and drums.

The ceremony opened with a succession of chimes from the bells and stones. The fire was lit below the altar, its curling smoke rising on the air to welcome the spirits. The choir

It is strange that an astrologer should be the cause of the co-regent's downfall. In the winter of 679-680 the astrologer was murdered on the way between the two capitals. Changan and Loyang were separated by over a hundred miles, passing through the mountainous Tungkwan Pass coming down straight to the bank of the Yellow River. It was a natural boundary separating the regions east and west of the Pass, known as Kwanjung (Tungkwan West) and Kwanwai (Tungkwan East). The murder occurred on a mountain path. The murderer was never caught, and there was no evidence of Father's complicity in it. I do not exclude the possibility that Father might have had a hand in it. It would be good to rid the Palace of the pernicious influence of the priest and charlatan.

Again it was not clear what the astrologer Ming meant to the Empress personally. Whatever the relations between Empress and charlatan, Lady Wu flew into a rage when the news of the murder reached her. She at once suspected her son of the murder. What was he to her? The legal machine was set rolling. Father was summoned to Loyang, and in his absence a search was made of his residence. Three hundred weapons were found in his stables. On the one hand, as I have said, Father could have taken this measure for self-defense. On the other hand, the weapons could have been taken from the armory only a short distance away in the outer Forbidden City, planted there in his absence and then the search made. Father was charged with a conspiracy to revolt, though it is hard to imagine what he could do with three hundred spears and armors and shields. Revolt against whom? The charge was all the more ridiculous, considering that he was already the crown heir, with the throne in sight.

Anyway, the evidence was there, even as Empress Wang's wooden figurine had been there, discovered under her very bed. The co-regent was caught red-handed. Grandmother chanted the invocation, and the orchestra struck up, signaling the arrival of the Emperor. He came, clad in his full royal attire with a crown of twelve tassels, and slowly ascended the steps amidst further singing. At the altar he sanctified the offerings, drank the wine, poured the libation and said his prayer. At every step an appropriate song was chanted to the accompaniment of music. As the Emperor descended, the graceful *chingshan* dance, done in slow steps, was executed by one hundred and sixty-four dancers clad in silk cloaks with broad sleeves, tied-up trousers and black jackboots, their hair done up in black false coiffures.

Now the Empress's gold and blue carriage arrived. During the intermission the choir chanted the change from "civil" to "military" dance. The war dancers, clad in silver armor and armed with spears, entered the terrace in formation. These two dances, the civil and the military, were symbolic of the two sides of an emperor's rule, the one emphasizing the pursuits of peace and the other his military might.

The Empress, wearing the imperial crown with twelve strings of pearls coming down in front of her face and dressed in a pheonix-embroidered gown, went up the steps assisted by her ladies-in-waiting. On both sides of her, maids carried a richly embroidered broad band of silk on poles, to shelter her from public view. The richness of the embroidery was a subject of comment and criticism by many pundits who regarded this ostentatious display as not in accordance with the spirit of this solemn occasion. It was a religious service, not a social party.

It was the first time in history that a woman participated in this august ceremony, but of course she was Wu Tsertien, out to break precedents and set "examples for future empresses to follow." That she later decided to close down some of her husband's ancestors' temples and cut off their food is of course another story. There she knelt down before the spirit tablets of her mother-in-law and grandmother-in-law, and tended the offerings. At intervals, the bass drum and bells punctuated the different steps. Her face shining with inward satisfaction, she slowly descended, her maids carrying the spirit tablets behind her, to the accompaniment of the glittering dance of spears of the war dancers. She had lived and worked for this supreme moment, taking the part of Taitsung himself at this function as she had witnessed it when she was a girl of fifteen newly come to his service. Of course it was the pomp and glitter which excited her; of its religious meaning she had no idea and did not care.

After the third offering, the service was concluded. The following days were given over to social parties and entertainments. On January the fourth the Emperor and Empress sat in court to receive the congratulations of officials and foreign representatives. On the fifth, a series of edicts was issued. The name of the reign was again changed, to "Sanctification by Heaven" (*Chienfeng,* 666-667); a general amnesty was declared, peers were created, titles were conferred and officials of lower ranks received an increase in salaries. Taxes were forgiven the people of the Taishan district and along the route of the imperial pilgrimage. Beef and wine were given the people for the seven-day celebration. The following day was given exclusively to dinner and entertainments. A dinner was given by the Emperor in the open on the terraces, with music and colorful folk dances, some volunteered by the foreign representatives. There was, among other things, a short popular comic act, the "Shimmy Sister" (*Dayaoniang*), showing a wife who shimmied every time at the approach of her frightfully ugly husband. The spectators joined in the cry "Oh, shimmy, sister!" at these moments. It never failed to arouse a great deal of merriment.

The "Dance of Slashing the Enemy," created by Taitsung and steadily revised and improved, was given by one hundred and twenty-eight persons. The war dancers were clad in silver armor, holding spears and battle-axes in hand, preceded by a color-sergeant in golden armor. In eight units, they formed and re-formed in changing movements, with clashes of weapons, re-enacting the different outstanding episodes in Taitsung's defeat of the enemy. It was very realistic —actually an enacting of battle scenes—which always impressed the spectators and moved Gaotsung to tears.

The royal party returned to Loyang in April. They had been away exactly six months.

While on the journey, something unpleasant had happened. At this time, two of Gaotsung's sons and Lady Wu's stepsons, Shangjin and Sujiay, had been exiled for ten years, and the father longed to see them. He had suggested having them come back to the capital for the *fengshan* occasion so that father and sons could be reunited again. They were boys of eighteen and twenty respectively, and Sujiay, born of the ill-fated Shiaofei, had been exiled to Kiangsi, 700 miles away. But the father had been overruled by the stepmother. Sujiay had written a sentimental letter begging for permission to come home. The letter was secretly forwarded by Jang Jienje. Grandmother characterized this letter as "grumbling," had him charged with bribery and further degraded and banished.

But something more unexpected was to happen. Lady Wu had three uncles and a number of cousins. It will be recalled that Yuanching and Yuanshuang had been demoted and exiled on account of their insolence. Yuanching had died immediately upon arrival at his destination, and Yuanshuang, later implicated in some charge, had been condemned to death. On their visit to the Taishan, two of the cousins of Lady Wu had come to join them, one of them being a magistrate in Shantung. It was natural for Sansan to meet her uncles and talk of family affairs.

The cousins, Weiliang and Huaiyun, had heard of what happened to Yuanching and Yuanshuang and to Sansan's mother, who was their cousin. Sansan had been indiscreet and had told them how her mother died of arsenic poisoning. Somebody must have eavesdropped and reported this to Lady Wu.

Lady Wu pretended not to know and cordially invited the two cousins to accompany her back to the capital.

It was another one of her clever moves. Sansan had talked, but Grandmother would not do something obvious by repeating what she had done to her mother. So, shortly after their return to the capital, Sansan died of arsenic poisoning; the culprits were ostensibly the two cousins. It was an unsolved mystery.

The circumstances were as follows.

One day the brothers Weiliang and Huaiyun came to dinner. Upon Grandmother's suggestion, they had brought along some special delicacy. The Emperor was expected to come to dinner, and while they were waiting, the special appetizer was served. Sansan was given some and was seized with a terrible pain. Her face turned deadly pale and all her insides were burning. Blood spilled from her nostrils. She was forced to leave the room and was taken to bed. Dinner was interrupted. No one else suffered from the poisoning.

The Emperor arrived and was horrified to see the young woman writhing in pain, life visibly ebbing out of her. He remembered that her mother, the Duchess of Han, had died in the same manner, in spite of the most rigid control of the kitchen.

That very night, the girl passed away. That a fair young woman should be snatched away in the prime of her life! The Emperor's heart was broken, and he was filled with bitterness. Such vileness, such underhanded meanness and contempt for a young life.

The brothers were horrified, too. Grandmother was in tears, calling, "My poor niece! Her mother was my only blood kin, and now even this, her only seed, must be taken away from me. . . . Why, these murderers!" she exclaimed in anger. "They intended to poison Your Majesty, I know. She happened to take it. My poor niece!"

It was then *prima facie* a clear case, and Lady Wu was the witness, though a more careful inquiry regarding the time between the arrival of the appetizers and their being served, and about the person handling them in the interval, might have elicited certain clues. What was less easy to explain was why the others who ate it—Lady Wu and the brothers—escaped. It was certain, then, that only one of the appetizers contained the deadly poison. How would the accused make sure that the right one was served to the murdered woman? But we are only trying to establish responsibility for a guilt committed decades ago—a futile occupation. The brothers were summarily executed.

Three persons who could have talked were thus safely put out of the way.

❋ 10 ❋

Grandfather felt now like a lonely, imprisoned bird in a golden cage, with not even another bird for his playmate. He had shifting pains and his symptoms grew daily worse. His hair began to turn white at thirty. His comfort was his son Hung, the Crown Prince, who promised to be a good successor to the throne. Prince Hung was a spirited, handsome young man who carried himself with dignity. Hung was Lady Wu's own firstborn son, and nobody was going to kill him, of course.

In 673, His Majesty was so ill that the Crown Prince was ordered to attend to the affairs of the ministries, while the Emperor and the Empress often stayed away for months on end at the eastern capital. More important matters were referred to "Their Majesties" in Loyang—in reality to Her Majesty, since the other Majesty was bedridden.

Externally, the Empire was carrying on wars successfully with its neighbors, for Taitsung had left behind a well-disciplined army and experienced generals. The frontiers were extended to Korea, Inner Mongolia and beyond Turkestan.* As was to be expected in relations with remote foreign tribes, the so-called subjugations were temporary; revolts flared up again and again. The Eastern Turkish Confederacy had been broken up; the Western Turkish Confederacy had risen to take its place, which now extended to Kokonor and Western

* Including present-day Kazakhstan in the USSR, where the poet Li Po was born in 701.

Mongolia. In 667 the old general, Li Tsi, had won a decisive victory over Korea and some thirty thousand Koreans were resettled in the interior of China. In December, 673, the Turkish kings of Suler and Gungyuay in the region of Tashkent and Samarkand came to Changan to pay their tribute and ask for peace, and in December of the following year Firuz, son of Yesdegerd, the last Sassanian king of Persia, driven by the rising Moslem power, came to live in Changan as a refugee.

The capital Changan (modern Si-an) was colorful and vibrant with the costumes of men and women of different tribes—Indian monks, Japanese students, Zoroastrian Persians, Manichaens, Nestorian Christians,* and Syrian Jews. Taitsung had been liberal with foreign merchants and missionaries, and many had come to settle in Changan, where they were allowed to worship in their own churches. It was in this period that Shyuanjuang, who had lived for seventeen years in Afghanistan and India, brought back 657 Buddhist Sutras and was occupied with the tremendous task of translating them. This was at the Yuhua Temple in the suburb of Changan, assigned him by Gaotsung.

Briefly then, during the first ten years of Lady Wu's tenure as Empress, the Emperor regularly, and the Empress occasionally, saw the courtiers at audience; during the second ten years, the period of the "Two Holies" or "Their Majesties" from the death of Shangguan Yi the poet in 664 to 673, the Emperor and Empress regularly did so together; during the last ten years, the period of "Celestial Empress" from 674 on, she regularly, and he occasionally attended the audience.

Lady Wu started the Shangyuan regime (674-5) with a great deal of *éclat* and fanfare. The new era was ushered in with a high-sounding political program. Her ability as ruler

* The Nestorians came to China in 635 in Taitsung's time, and the Nestorian Tablet, discovered in the early seventeenth century in a temple outside Si-an, is now in the British Museum.

and her remarkable political skill are shown in a letter she wrote as a "humble wife" to her husband and caused to be published. It contained a list of twelve grandiose governmental reforms, calculated to increase her popularity. The Twelve Points were: 1) Promotion of agriculture and sericulture and lightening of labor service; 2) remission of taxes for the northwest provinces; 3) *disarmament and peace through moral regeneration;* 4) ban on extravagance; 5) relief as far as possible of army conscription; 6) freedom of expression; 7) discouragement of dishonest officials and yes-men.

Then followed more specific, more original proposals: 8) All officials, from the Princes and Dukes down, should study Laotse (of the same clan name Li as the royal Tang House); 9) the period of mourning for one's mother should be three years, even though one's father was still living (embodying the principle of sexual equality); 10) retired officials were to keep their titles and ranks and honors of office; 11) the salaries of metropolitan officials from the eighth rank up should be increased; and 12) a review should be made of officials obscured in long years of service, and recommendations made for their promotion according to merits. The immediate effect of the last three points was to make her popular with the rank-and-file of officialdom. On the whole, these were reforms that almost any politician with an eye to popularity could think up. It would be very hard to have objections to them, especially "peace through moral regeneration."

Trouble seemed to dog Grandfather's footsteps. In 675, there came a crisis in the imperial household which could not have happened normally and which embittered Grandfather greatly.

Hung, the Crown Prince, was the scholarly type, idealistic, not too practical, and sensitive like my grandfather. Ever since his childhood, he had been carefully trained as a crown prince, with the best scholars of the land as his tutors, a training which included attending government offices and familiarizing himself with office routines. He was now twenty-three and given ever-increasing responsibilities. He was left in charge of the government at Changan in 671-672 while his father was ill in Loyang, naturally with selected ministers to assist him. He had married the daughter of a scholar. Besides his father-in-law Bei Jyudow, he had surrounded himself with a number of scholars.

Everything looked promising for the Crown Prince and his young wife. A lover of literature and history, he had, with the help of his scholar friends, compiled an anthology of beautiful passages from literature and the classics, upon the completion of which the Emperor awarded him 30,000 pieces of silk as appreciation. The Emperor loved him. Once he said to his courtiers, "Hung is the right sort, a gentleman. I am very proud of him. He has never been rude or discourteous to the ministers."

While learning the art of government, some of the best qualities of his grandfather, the great Taitsung—his humanity and concern for the people—were early revealed in him. The conditions of the soldiers' life touched him profoundly. The best thing he did as a prince was the abolition of the confiscation of the wife and children of a deserter as slaves. To be sure, this stringent measure partly accounted for the good discipline of Taitsung's army. However, he had learned, as he wrote in a letter to the throne, that many soldiers were not deserters but were treated as such. Many failed to show up after battle for a number of unavoidable reasons. Some, for instance, were trying to swim across a river and got drowned; some fell ill and turned up late for duty; in fact, any kind of accident could have happened after a battle, and some were captured by the enemy. The regulations of the army took account of the dead in battle and punished the families of the missing. Thus many of those unaccounted for were treated as deserters and their families sold as slaves. He quoted the classic *Tsojuan*: "Rather break the regulations than kill an innocent man." He requested a clearer definition and distinction of the different classes of missing soldiers. Thus, through this action, many of the soldiers' families were spared the ignominy and hardships of slavery, even though such slavery service was limited in period and could be redeemed.

During the great famine in the winter of 672-673, following a widespread drought that summer, the northwest was badly hit. People were dying of starvation. Prince Hung discovered that the soldiers were being fed on a ration of cooked elm bark and berries, and he ordered that rice from his own house be given to them. He also petitioned that the government land at Tungchow be given to the poor to farm.

Such a temperament was bound to bring him into direct conflict with his mother, Lady Wu. Maintaining discipline and carrying out justice he could understand, but sheer meanness, pettiness and unnecessary cruelty enraged him. When he visited Loyang, he discovered that his stepsisters, the Princesses Yiyang and Gao-an, daughters of the murdered Shiaofei, had been living in the back courts, completely forgotten and neglected by everybody. They were now about thirty and no marriage match had been arranged for them. They just had no way of marrying. It was scandalous.

He spoke to his mother. "By the teachings of the sages, girls should be married when they are of age. Why aren't my sisters married? They can't do any harm. You could make arrangements for them."

Grandmother could not deny the justice of this observation. She had thought she had already been too liberal to these stepdaughters. Shiaofei's clan relatives were branded as "vultures" and exiled, yet she permitted these children of hers to live right in the Palace. She hated to have her mistake pointed out. She said that she had just forgotten, and she would marry them off. She gave away the Princesses to two palace guards. This was less than fair; after all, they were the king's own daughters. But Grandmother felt like a cat who has his fur rubbed the wrong way. She never wanted her son to be a judge of her conduct.

However, one month later, in April, 672, a more serious murder of a helpless woman occurred in the Palace, which made Prince Hung boil over. His wife was unhappy. Born of a scholar's family, she was what we call a dutiful daughter-in-law, quiet and correct. Being the daughter-in-law of Lady Wu was not easy. Grandmother disliked her and she knew it. Another daughter-in-law, Prince Jer's wife, Jaofei, was now the target of grandmother's hatred. Her mother was no other than Princess Changlo. Since the marriage, Princess Changlo had lately been coming to the Palace, and unfortunately she was seen too often in the Emperor's company and seemed to get along very well with him. Lady Wu took no risks. She had Changlo and her husband sent away to a post in the provinces, and forbidden ever to appear at court. This had nothing to do with her daughter, of course. But Prince Jer's wife was shut up inside a house. Food was supposed to be brought to her; whether it was or not, it was not known. In a few days, the door was broken upon and she was found dead of starvation!

Prince Hung was bursting with anger. He could not stand such meanness, such uncalled-for cruelty. Why had they broken in the door? Because the door was locked. Why did they suspect that she was dead? Because they saw no smoke coming from the chimney, and they were supposed to bring in raw meat and vegetables. Why couldn't they bring her cooked food, and why did a prince's wife have to be treated like a prisoner and do her own cooking? She had done nothing to be accused of. There was no need to persecute the daughter on account of her mother. Prince Hung knew that she had been starved to death by his mother's orders. Her husband, Prince Jer, had not even dared to go near her or see her when she was confined. There was a difference between Prince Hung and my father, on the one hand, and the younger two, Jer and Dan, on the other, who were made of a softer caliber and were more to Grandmother's liking.

If Prince Jer would not protest, Prince Hung would. He sought an opportunity to speak to his mother. Grandmother knew this son of hers. When he came in, her face was grim. Even in the imperial family, formalities were not relaxed. Prince Hung felt and spoke like a crown prince, young and dignified and sure of himself. He addressed her as "Your Majesty." His sister-in-law, he thought, had been a dutiful daughter-in-law. Grandmother frowned. She was dead. What was the point of bringing it up?

"I recollect that Your Majesty wrote a book about the lives of virtuous women. It is a poor comment that a virtuous woman should be allowed to starve to death in your own house!"

It was a bombshell. Grandmother's fury was terrible to behold. What did he mean? What was he trying to imply? Prince Jer's wife had been rude after her mother was sent away. She was sullen and silent for days. Was she not being disrespectful? Was that what he called being a dutiful daughter-in-law? Was it wrong for her to punish her for her insolence? And if the poor young fool chose to starve herself to death, why blame her for it? "And don't forget your manners. Don't presume to tell me what to do!"

"I am not presuming," retorted the son. "On the other hand, I thought you would like your subjects to speak frankly and freely. I remember freedom of expression was one of your Twelve Points, so that wrongs may be righted, injustices redressed. I am just trying to be helpful. Sometimes it helps. If I had not taken the liberty to speak to you about the Princesses Yiyang and Gao-an the other day, they would have grown up into spinsters. Is that necessary? And really, you might have had them married into scholars' families, not to guards! They are the king's own daughters."

"You can withdraw!" said Lady Wu grimly, her voice settling back into a frightening coolness, her face tightened hard and flat, her eyes narrowed into slits.

Exactly eighteen days later, Prince Hung died of poison while visiting Hobigung in the company of his parents. Again, he "ate something wrong." And Hung was her own firstborn son!

It would be wrong to measure Grandmother by ordinary standards applicable to us common men. My father received even worse treatment at her hand. I believe at this period the Princes were just so much political capital for her to gamble with, and she had so many and could spare one or two. The best explanation is to accept the fact that individuals are born differently, and in Grandmother we are dealing with a very rare, indeed a unique, individual.

The final score was as follows: of Grandfather's eight sons, one died young, Grandmother killed five including two of her own, and the remaining two were imprisoned by her for over a dozen years, not counting the infant girl whom she strangled.

Prince Hung's death precipitated an immediate crisis. That very night, the royal couple returned to the Palace. Gaotsung loved his son above everyone else. He had stood for enough. He had seen six or seven murders in his family—wife, concubine, sister-in-law, niece, daughter-in-law, Prince Jung his eldest, and now this! He was unable to see his sons Sujiay and Shangjin—now banished and forbidden to return to the capital. He had been angry enough a month ago when

Princess Changlo, his half sister, was dismissed from the court and forbidden to appear again just when he was beginning to enjoy her company. He was sick of it all.

That evening Grandfather, His Imperial Majesty Gaotsung, was shaking with rage. My father Shien saw the whole thing. His Majesty actually broke out in tears over the death of his son. He refused to come to dinner, and when he did, he refused to eat. As reported in the Palace, he looked a broken man. He sat looking glumly at his Empress.

"Don't be so upset. You must try to eat."

All of a sudden, Gaotsung sprang out of his chair, and brushed the plates and sent them crashing to the floor. His hands shaking, his hair disheveled, his voice hollow and yet filled with trembling emotion, he pointed at her.

"You, you, you!" he shouted, eyes blazing. "You murderer of my son!" Lady Wu blanched at this unexpected fury, but kept her eyes on him. The king continued, "I know you, and I have had enough of this. You cannot tolerate one person in the world except yourself. Why did you exile Princess Changlo and send her away from me? Why did you starve her daughter to death?" He went closer to her. "How did Sansan die? Tell me how did Sansan die? Because she knew too much?"

Lady Wu's face was deathly pale. The king raised his hand and made as if he was going to strike her down. Suddenly, his strength gave out. His arm flailed and dropped and Father caught him just in time as he started to collapse to the floor. He was carried to his room, his eyes still blazing and his breathing hard. The Empress had abruptly left and did not go to see him. Never had such a thing happened before in the Palace.

My father, Shien, stayed with him.

"You take over," he said in a tired voice. "I want to abdicate. Leave me alone. The Empire be damned! . . . Leave me alone," he groaned.

That night, a physician attended upon His Majesty. Father heard him repeating in his sleep, *"Leave me alone."*

The next day Gaotsung sent for some of his ministers and indicated his desire to abdicate in favor of Father, Prince Shien. "I have had enough of this. Let my son Shien take over. The Empress is for 'peace through moral regeneration'; I just want peace, with or without moral regeneration."

Ho Chujyun and the other ministers demurred and strongly counseled against it. His Majesty was probably too much upset by the death of the Crown Prince.

The Emperor thought it over the next day and changed his mind. In his deep sorrow for the Crown Prince, he did an unprecedented thing. He conferred on the dead Prince the title of Emperor and ordered that he be buried with imperial honors, although the period of national mourning was shortened to thirty-six days. His spirit tablet was sacrificed to according to the rank of an emperor, a practice which was kept up until a few years later. A fabulous mausoleum was ordered to be constructed. It was so extravagant and involved so much hard labor that a group of workmen revolted, threw stones at the foreman, and disappeared.

Prince Hung's wife, Princess Bei, fell ill. She didn't want to live. A year later she died of sorrow and mortification.

❋ II ❋

I remember I was five when Father returned to Changan the capital in July, 675, and told the family about the horrible tragedy which overtook his elder brother and some of the scenes which I have just described; and then, rather casually informed us children that he had been made the Crown Prince. Of course, Mother and the children had heard about it (Father had been declared crown heir at the eastern capital), but curiously there was no joy in Father's face. One of the things I can never forget was when he said, "I shall never eat at a dinner with Grandmother if I can help it."

Nevertheless, to be the crown heir was something great, something exciting in the eyes of us children and it made changes in our way of life. Father had been governor of Kansuh up to now, but we had always lived in Changan. A month later, we moved into the New Palace. I remember that Father's books alone filled three carts. Father was twenty-two then, and there were three of us brothers, Shoushun, Shouyi and myself, the youngest. I had seen Grandfather and Grandmother a few times and we heard vague stories about the *fengshan* trip and of somebody poisoning our Cousin Sansan. But I couldn't remember Grandfather at all at the time, for he was bedridden and stayed away at the eastern capital with Grandmother. His condition seemed considerably worse after the *fengshan* trip and all the domestic troubles. That spring, I was told, he had stopped giving audiences.

We were living in the old capital, as I have said, and in a way Father was quite happy. He was very jolly and played a lot with us children. There is a football field in Dungwan, or Eastern Park, next to the Palace, and plenty of opportunity for hunting and sports. He loved horses and falcons, and I learned even as a child to have a falcon rest on my wrist, except that I was always scared because of the bird's fearful-looking eyes. Like the present sovereign and like his grandfather, he had a passion for tall horses, excellent breeds from Tienshan (in Turkestan). I used to admire him and watch him riding around the park.

"One day you will be Emperor, Father," I said to him. He hardly gave a nod, but his lips curled in a smile. Grandfather was not expected to live very long and we brothers discussed this among ourselves.

Father was gay and robust, a good swordsman and an archer of sorts. But he was also brilliant in his studies. He was reputed to be able to recite five hundred words of poetry and read, at the age of six or seven, the *Shujing* (Book of History, the most difficult of the Confucian classics in the archaic language). At this time he was occupied with a group of scholars in compiling the *Commentary to Later Han History,* for which he will always be remembered.* This was a most ambitious undertaking, involving exegesis and research on archaic dialect words and pronunciation of geographical names. The difficulty of the undertaking and the enormous learning and painstaking work required will be appreciated by scholars.

Upon completion of the great editorial work, under his name as the chief editor, he received a special commendation from the Emperor, as follows:

* This has remained to this day the standard commentary on *Houhanshu.*

> Crown Prince Shien has attended to the affairs of the government and executed his duties ably and conscientiously. While he shows patience and thoroughness in his work, he also has on many occasions shown generosity and forgiveness, as a king should. In his spare hours he has devoted himself to scholarly research and drunk deep of the wisdom of the Sages. He has delved into the archives, brought to light the beauty and wisdom of the past, and always approved of what was good and righteous. It gives us great pleasure to note that here is evidence of a good ruler and that he will be worthy of the sacred trust of the Empire. Let him be granted five hundred pieces of silk.

He was, however, a more practical and all-around character than his elder brother, Prince Hung. Wary of Prince Hung's untimely death, he preferred to stay away from Grandmother, particularly from her dinners, and live in Changan. Grandmother sensed this and resented it. The future sovereign was drifting away from her motherly wings. In 679, Grandfather had another stroke and Father was named co-regent. He seldom visited his parents if he could help it. Besides, the mother-and-son relation had grown strained, and he didn't want what had happened to his elder brother to happen to him.

This arrangement of living apart from Grandmother's presence seemed to suit us very well, but it did not seem to suit Grandmother. Father made a few trips to the eastern capital to see his father, now progressively worse. Grandfather's eyes were failing and his splitting headaches grew more persistent. Once he was given acupuncture and was able to see better for a time. Since being made co-regent, Father gave more of his time to affairs of the government, for at any moment, Grandfather might pass away.

Father's reputation was well established and he was highly spoken of by everybody. He was twenty-seven, not a young weakling, and not an idiot likely to accept anyone ruling in his name.

About this time, the old rumor was revived from the Palace about his being born of the Duchess of Han. I am sure Grandmother had this rumor spread on purpose. He had also received several angry letters from her, reminding him of the duties of a good son. This made Father very uncomfortable. He didn't know what was happening, or was going to happen. It is even possible that he took measures to defend himself by storing weapons in his stables.

Grandmother now had a Taoist priest and fortuneteller, Ming (Tsungyen), whom she often saw. Grandmother's love of priests was notorious. Priests and doctors had entrée to the queen's chambers. In the light of what had happened before and what was going to happen soon, the priest's visits reflected ill on Grandmother's character, since there was no good reason to suppose why she should require such visits, which had been going on for a year or two. Grandfather was bedridden, and it was not likely that she could be caught again.

The priest, having become intimate and close to the Empress, and perhaps conveniently falling in with what he knew she liked to hear, said that my father's sharp, well-chiseled facial features did not presage a long life or good luck (true enough, according to prevalent fortunetelling), that the fires of his intelligence were not subdued, his nose too pointed, etc.; that Uncle Jer, on the other hand, resembled the great Taitsung; that Uncle Dan had the best physiognomy of all.

All this sounded very suspicious, coming at this time, and caused a further estrangement between mother and son. Father hated all this mummery and superstition and despised women who believed in it. Grandmother did not try to conceal the fortuneteller's predictions, and Father did not try to conceal his contempt for the priest-astrologer.

had no difficulty in persuading a certain Jao, an employee on father's staff, to testify that the murder of the astrologer was his work. The confiscated arms were shipped to Loyang and publicly burned at the Tientsin Bridge in front of the Palace. The highest ministers were appointed to a committee to examine the case, and returned the verdict they knew Lady Wu wanted and demanded. The price of treason was death. Lady Wu declared that, for the sake of law and order, she was willing to sacrifice her personal feelings toward her beloved son. The interests of the state came first.

The motive for this strange move against Father was not clear until events happened subsequently.

Gaotsung thought of the fate of his other sons, Jung and Hung, and shuddered. He pleaded leniency. Any number of reasons could have been advanced to mitigate the punishment. As co-regent, Father had made a good record; there was no clear motive for revolt, in fact no need for him to do so; the presence of weapons in a co-regent's residence was not sufficient proof of intention to revolt; and as for the murder of the astrologer, *who really cared?* Above all, the king had the power to pardon. He could always overrule his ministers. Looked at sanely now across the decades, the case seems preposterous that a co-regent should pay with his life for the murder of a fortuneteller. Had it not been Grandmother's predetermined purpose to get rid of her able and independent-minded son, there would have been no search of his house and no prosecution at all.

Our family was so broiled over the catastrophe that we did not try to think. As I see it now, Father must have said something very offensive to Grandmother about her affair with the astrologer, who was personally hostile to him. That would have justified Grandmother's anger. But Father never told us about it.

The result was a temporary compromise which satisfied

Grandmother. Father was deposed and imprisoned; the heir was changed. Prince Jer was next.

I was ten when the tragedy struck home. We had always lived in luxury. I was seized with such fear as only children know. The next year, Father was banished to Chengtu (Szechuan), but we three children, being young, remained in the Palace. There Father languished, without communications, accepting his fate in silence. He was to be killed in good time but not just yet, while Grandfather was living. We children never saw him again until the death of Grandmother, when his remains were brought back to be buried with his ancestors.

We went over to live in Loyang. But we were confined in the back courts. Only on occasion were we permitted glimpses of Grandfather and Grandmother. We did see Princess Taiping, who for some reason took an interest in us. She was about fifteen or sixteen, just before her marriage to Shuay Shao. After her marriage a year later, she lost interest in us and we saw very little of her. But what a lot we began to hear about her doings around the Palace!

In December, 683, Grandfather passed away, and to our great surprise, two months later, in February, 684, Uncle Dan, declared "Emperor," came to join us at the back courts with his entire family held *incommunicado*.

In this connection, let me interpolate here something which happened very recently as I write these memoirs. A strange result of my eighteen-year confinement in the Palace is that I have become a weather prophet.

Recently I have been credited with clairvoyant powers. It was April and the weather had been sunny and dry, and the Prince of Chi, His Majesty's brother, had come to see me. I felt vaguely unwell and out of sorts. "I bet it is going to rain," I said. Surely enough, in half a day's time, the weather changed and there came a pouring rain which continued unabated for over ten days. Then again at dinner I said to the Prince of Chi, "It will clear up soon." There was no sign of a break in the sky. My cousin was incredulous. "Take my word for it," I said. Indeed the next day, the rain stopped and the sky cleared again. My cousin told His Majesty about it, crediting me with being a weather prophet, and His Majesty asked me if it was true.

"I have no magic," I replied. "During my youth, when I was shut up inside the Eastern Palace, I used to receive floggings about three or four times a year at the hand of the Wus. You were too young to remember. The scars healed, but the effect remains. When the weather changes, I ache all over inside my bones, and when it is about to clear up, I feel well again. That's how." And I added: "Thanks to Grandmother."

The atmosphere tensed at once. It was as if I had committed a social *faux pas.*

Here ends the first part of my memoirs, preoccupied chiefly with the tragedies inside the royal family.

Book Two

❋ 12 ❋

It was wonderful—her husband the Emperor was dead. It was wonderful—she was now a widow. Her day had come. She was now sixty, but she enjoyed remarkable health. Her teeth were intact and her appetite, in more senses than one, was wonderful. She was bursting with energy. The world lay spread at her feet, for her to enjoy and to rule.

Of course there was the slight matter of having a son on the throne. Jer, her third son, should now be crowned Emperor, or should he? Jer, as everybody knew, resembled his grandfather, Taitsung, most among the brothers. He was then twenty-eight. Lady Wu was debating in her mind whether this was what she really wanted, whether after all something more drastic might not be attempted, either by a forged edict, or by a *coup d'état,* to put herself on the throne at once. She was, as a matter of fact, tired of appearing to play the second fiddle, either as the spouse or as the mother of a ruler, and never wielding the royal scepter herself.

Chancellor Bei Yen was greatly puzzled. Usually the new king is proclaimed a day or two after his predecessor's death. For six days and six nights she debated this question in her mind. Her great tact led her finally to refrain for the present from drastic moves but to decide in favor of *legitimacy.* This reasoning enabled her to yield to Bei Yen's insistence and have Prince Jer proclaimed Emperor on the seventh day.

A whirlwind now began to be felt in court, which, anticipated by some, shocked everybody by its speed and violence.

The storm broke sooner than anybody had expected. Grandmother dethroned her son hardly two months after her husband's demise and imprisoned him, and then had him banished. This was the fourth time she had deposed a son. On February 5, 684, she arrested the Emperor and literally had him dragged off the throne on a flimsy pretext.

It seemed that Prince Jer had had a quarrel with Chancellor Bei Yen. He had wanted to make his father-in-law Lord Secretary, one of the top royal assistants, and Bei Yen had objected. The father-in-law had no official standing and therefore no qualifications for such a high post. An exchange of hot words followed.

"I am Emperor, don't forget," said the young sovereign. "I could even turn over the Empire to him if I wanted to."

These words, tossed out in the heat of argument, were all that Lady Wu needed as an excuse to dethrone him. The young Emperor was unaware of his danger, like a young deer grazing happily in a pasture. Lady Wu pounced upon her son with lightning rapidity.

Secret arrangements had been made with a general of the imperial guards. On the morning of February the fifth, soldiers were posted all over the Palace. The officials gathered as usual for the audience at the throne hall. To their surprise, Lady Wu appeared, leading the young Emperor behind her. Just as the latter was about to go up the steps of the throne dais, he was abruptly stopped by Chancellor Bei Yen, who, pulling out a scroll from his sleeve, solemnly read the Empress's edict deposing him and sentencing him to confinement in the Palace. He was hereby demoted as Prince of Luling. The captain of the imperial guards came up and laid his hands upon him.

"Take your hands off me!" said Jer in utter bewilderment. "What is my crime?"

"Your crime?" shouted his mother. "Crime enough when you wanted to turn over the Empire to your father-in-law."

Of course, Uncle Jer had said this in a moment of anger. Certainly a hypothetical statement exchanged in a quarrel could not, and should not, be taken seriously, and certainly was not sufficient cause for the removal of a king from his throne. But protest was of course useless.

Emperor for exactly fifty-four days, Uncle Jer suffered himself to be dragged from the hall in the presence of all the courtiers. The latter were stunned. Anything so high-handed had never been seen. He was temporarily confined to the Palace, the next month was taken to Fangchow, and before the month was out removed again to Jyunchow (both in modern Hopei). His father-in-law was banished with his family to the south.

Incidentally I may mention here that Uncle Dan, who had come to join us at the back court as the Emperor of All China, had his personal name changed again. He was Dan part of the time I was with him and Lun the other part. When he was born, he was called Shyulun; he lost the "Shyu" and became just Lun in 669, became Dan in 678, Lun again in 690, and Dan once more in 698. The same oscillations took place with regard to Prince Jer's name. What this did to a man was perhaps to beget in him a hesitant sense of his own identity.

Now began my period of confinement within the Palace with my brothers. As orphans of a convicted and disgraced prince, already deprived of his ranks, we were shut up with Uncle Dan and his family. We were forbidden to put our foot outside the palace gate and ventured outside our quarters in the Eastern Palace only by express permission, as when attending dinners in the main part of the Palace. We learned to talk in whispers and felt like helpless children of convicts, tolerated and living by the grace of Grandmother's permission, as if under a huge black shadow, fierce and mighty and without appeal. At any time any one of us, Uncle Dan included, might be killed or permitted to hang himself. Uncle Dan, having seen all that had happened to his brothers, was rendered innocuous, playing the part of the docile obedient son. For eighteen long years I never saw the streets of Loyang. What we knew of court politics was learned indirectly by hearsay, though we heard enough of the "revolution" to set one's hair on end. For our own protection, we kept to ourselves and consoled ourselves with the thought that our lot was no worse than occasional insults and floggings, at the hand of the Wu nephews.

A hard sense of personal survival compelled Uncle Dan to pretend to hear nothing, see nothing and say nothing. He was held *incommunicado.* It was actually safer for him inside the Palace than at some remote place of exile—as witness my father's fate. There was no coronation ceremony for Uncle Dan. Grandmother merely sent a scroll, through her nephew Wu Chengtse, appointing him "Emperor."

Those were hectic days in February, March, April of that year (684). Too many things were happening. The public had hardly time to regain breath before another blow from Lady Wu's iron hammer fell. It justifies the charge in Lo Binwang's Declaration of War (p. 141) that "the orphans were abandoned when their father's grave was hardly dry." In fact, Gaotsung's mausoleum had not yet been started.

My father was still living under detention at Chengtu. I was fourteen then, having been away from my father for over three years. Grandmother had too much respect for Father's ability and feared him more than the other remaining sons. He might be able to start a revolt, serve as a rallying point of support for rebels to her regime, or get in touch with his brother, Jer. Lady Wu exercised forethought and took precautions.

Three days after the arrest and forcible ejection of Prince Jer from the throne, and two months after Grandfather's death, she sent a captain of palace guards to Chengtu. The mission was "to search his house and protect him from accidents." The court emissary first shut him up in a back room, then compelled Father to hang himself. A poem, written before his end, has been preserved. It is called the "Song of the Cucumber Plant."

> A cucumber plant below the Yellow Terrace;
> Its fruit is ripe for plucking.
> One plucking will do it no harm;
> Two pluckings make the plant look thin.
> It will survive three pluckings still,
> But with the fourth plucking,
> Carry the bare vine home.

This refers evidently to the deaths of Jung, Hung, and the imprisonment of Jer and Dan.

When the news of Father's suicide reached the capital, Grandmother ordered a public mourning ceremony with sacrifices to his spirit at the Shienfo Gate, at which she took part as the bereaved mother.

It was "all a mistake" on the part of the emissary Chiu (Shenji), it was said, and Chiu was dismissed to a lower post in the provinces. However, hardly half a year had passed before Chiu was recalled and restored to his original post. The public then understood that he had carried out the Empress Dowager's orders and it had been no mistake after all.

Grandmother was now on the rampage. She did extraordinary things, amusing things, spectacular things and not-so-rational things. It was all very feminine in character. Grandma, it must never be forgotten, was a woman. If one does not take sides or is not burdened with a sense of loyalty to the Tang House, as we Princes are, it is possible to enjoy the spectacle of a grandma going on a spree. She felt and acted like a poor man who has unexpectedly come into a fortune.

Grandma, I believe, really believed in the power of words, blessed words, felicitous words. Words, properly handled, were bound to create an atmosphere. By everybody saying "Happy Birthday," a birthday can become quite happy. Loyang was proclaimed *Shendu,* or "God's Dwelling Place." Apparently she had no use for false modesty. A new flag was adopted, gold with purple, ostentatious and bold. By an imperial edict, the nomenclature of the entire administrative system was overhauled once more and new names of a festive, floral character were given. To mention only the top posts: the Imperial Secretariat on the left of the throne hall was renamed "Terrace of Male Phoenix," and the Chancellory on the right became "Tower of Female Phoenix." The imperial library was called the "Unicorn Terrace" and the Office of the Cabinet was "Terrace of the North Pole" (Wenchang). All suggested the Fairyland of the Fairy Queen-Mother of Heaven. That her earthly role might be in harmony with the cosmological scheme of the universe, the names of the six ministries were correspondingly changed. The Ministry of Civil Service became the "Ministry of Heaven," and the Ministry of the Interior, the "Ministry of Earth." The Ministries of Ceremonies, War, Justice and Public Works were changed respectively to "Ministries of Spring, Summer, Autumn and Winter." In the center of this splendid Bright Mansion, in the center of God's Dwelling Place, sat the goddess, for the time called inappropriately "Empress Dowager." The time was not yet for her to call herself "Holy

Mother Divine Sovereign" (*Shengmu Shenhuang*) but it was bound to come.

It would seem that Grandma was very happy—in fact, excessively gay—at this period of her triumph. She was now the sovereign. A sovereign always has several mistresses or concubines. The problem came up: How was she to have a concubine? Obviously, the concubine would have to be a man.

And now the mad monk rose to dominate the court life. In the end, Grandmother achieved a great notoriety—in teahouse gossip and among minstrel singers—and became a more popularly known figure through these affairs with the monk and her subsequent lovers than she could have hoped to achieve by her wildest political dreams or actions.

The mad monk, Shuay Huaiyi ("Embracing Righteousness"), was originally neither a monk, nor so named. As I have mentioned, he was a wrestler in a medicine show in the streets and squares of Loyang, the wrestling and boxing being the lure to attract customers for his pills and ointments. Tall and husky, he was known to be an exhibitionist in the technical sense of the word, and a braggart of his sexual prowess. We children saw this boxer-monk passing in and out of the Palace, a big chunk of muscle walking with his characteristic swagger, the kind you see in young men about town. He breathed masculinity from every pore of his being. His original name was Feng "Little Precious," as I have said in the beginning. Through a palace maid, he had come to know Princess Chienjin, then Princess Taiping intimately and the Princess, having confirmed the real basis to his sexual boasts, warmly recommended him to her mother, Lady Wu. Lady Wu was delighted with him and sent for him constantly, though secretly at first. Little Precious Feng had never thought particularly about his name, but the name in a husky, grown-up man was not only vulgar, but obscene. The name Huaiyi, or "Embracing Righteousness," was a great improvement upon "Little Precious." Princess Taiping and Lady Wu—mother and daughter—shared all their secrets as they had always shared their palace intrigues and cabals.

Lady Wu now found herself in Shuay's toils, unable to live without him, forced to let him do all he wanted. Deficient in the maternal instinct, Grandmother discovered she was just a woman, powerless before a common boxer. Her hardness, her emotional suppressions, her stern sense of politics, melted before the ardor of "Little Precious."

Or perhaps the opposite was the case. Perhaps, in her mind, these carousals and revels were part of her conception of regal splendor. Perhaps, in her florid imagination, all this wining and carousing and debauchery was also condoned and enjoyed by the gods and goddesses—which constituted Heaven. As will be seen in a later chapter, the mad monk guided her steadily and systematically toward the belief that in the public's mind she was Buddha reborn; and it was under his influence that she had Tientang (or Hall Celestial, current name for Paradise) built, towering three hundred feet high behind the throne hall. A strange halo of fantasy, sensuality, and terrestrial and divine glory surrounded this godhead as long as the monk was her lover, and the spell was broken only when he became unfaithful to her. While it existed, it gave her faith and inspiration for going ahead with her political program; a Buddha reborn and come to earth to judge the righteous and the wicked—those who believed in her and those who did not. Lady Wu herself acknowledged that the adoption of Buddhism contributed to the success of her new dynasty.

Confident of his hold upon the Empress, the abbot did not change his ragamuffin's ways. A braggart and a coxcomb, he became a terror in the streets of the capital. Mounted on horseback and preceded by servants wearing Palace uniform, he cantered or galloped through the city. Anyone who failed to get out of his way quickly enough was liable to receive a few whacks from an iron chain. Once he beat up a public prosecutor in the streets because the latter had impeached him. Inside the Palace, he was received and treated like a prince consort, which in fact, if not in name, he was. He was given horses from the imperial stables and court officials abjectly bowed when he passed. The Empress's favorite nephews, Chengtse and Sanse, courted his favor by acting as his lackeys, holding his horse for him to mount and dismount.

Once the abbot came into the Palace through the front gate and stalked through the office of the Imperial Secretariat on his way to the Empress's court at the back. The Lord Secretary, Su Liangtsy, was an elderly, dignified old man. Su accosted him as a matter of ordinary courtesy, but was ignored. Su was enraged.

"How dare you, baldhead! What is your business coming in here?"

The mad monk's eyes rolled and he facetiously gave a few swift, beautiful parries with his crooked arms. "Wanna fight?" he said in his street slang, his legs spread in a fighting position. He looked especially comical that afternoon because he was unshaved and was wearing purple, which was incongruous with his uncouth face or with the office of the Secretariat.

Duke Su ordered the guards to eject him by force, and a scuffle ensued. After subduing him, the guards gave him a dozen slaps on the face.

Abbot Shuay hurried off to the Empress's court at the Yingshien Hall and complained. When Lady Wu heard what had happened, she broke out into great laughter.

"Who told you to come through the front gate? You should have come in from the north."

Duke Su was untouched. Wisely, very wisely, Lady Wu did not care to make an issue of it.

As Lady Wu did not wish the abbot out of sight and would rather not have him spreading stories in the city, she now put him in charge of the buildings and garden of the Palace. The abbot had told her that he understood architecture, or at least could build buildings. Thus a somewhat barefaced pretext was found for his constant presence inside the back courts of the Palace.

Even so, the women's quarters in the Palace were, by a long-established tradition, accessible only to women and eunuchs. The presence of an uncastrated man inside the ladies' courts caused many tongues to wag. A certain Wang (Chiuli), court censor, took his duty seriously. He submitted a petition to the throne that the abbot should be castrated if his continued presence in the ladies' quarters was desired, so as to "preserve the virtue of the maids and the chastity of the ladies."

Lady Wu roared with laughter when she read the petition. It was very funny, she thought. Again, wisely, she ignored both the letter and its writer.

Of this abbot and his religio-political extravaganzas, more in a later chapter.

❋ 13 ❋

All thoughtful persons had been shocked and disturbed by the happenings of the recent months, the dethronement of one young emperor and the imprisonment of another in quick succession. Questions were asked, if only in whispers. What was the Empress Dowager trying to do? The people sympathized with the imprisoned young Princes, for their hearts belonged to the great Taitsung, and these were his grandsons. She had better not touch the Imperial Ancestral Temple of Tang.

To observant eyes, the most significant danger signals were the promotion of Wu nephews and the setting up of the Wu ancestral temples in Loyang. At this time, the Wu relatives were rapidly promoted to positions of power, while the Tang Princes were gradually eased out. As Lady Wu had three uncles, there were still fourteen of her nephews left, among them Chengtse, Sanse, Yuning and Yitsung. Chengtse was the most ambitious and active of them all. Without proper education, a snob and a bully, but a petty politician, he was made Lord Secretary in May. But with all his gaucheries, even Lady Wu could not stand him. His acting lord secretaryship did not last over a month. The people's private comment at this time was that the abbot "patted the behind" of the Empress, Chengtse and Sanse "patted the behind" of the abbot, and the general run of ministers and officials "patted the behinds" of the Wu nephews. Other nephews were given the rank of general or received posts as chiefs of various independent bureaus.

Here was an anomalous situation. Lady Wu was taking too much licence. After all, the Tang House was prolific. Both Emperor Gaotsung and his father Taitsung had a dozen brothers, men between fifty and seventy now, and they all had many children.* There were at least three dozen members of the royal household of princely rank. Among these were Yuangwei, Yuanjia and Lingkwei, Taitsung's brothers, men of great culture and refinement. The Wus were haughty, but crude. Yet the critical posts, like the commanders of the two capitals and of the Forbidden City, were in the hands of the litter of Wu nephews. It was subversion from within.

What attracted the most public attention, however, was Chengtse's proposal to erect ancestral temples of the Wus in royal style at the capital. It was a clear sign of the intention to found a royal house of the Wus. The Wu family temples already existed in Changan; now new ones were set up in the eastern capital in the style of royal ancestral temples. Lady Wu's ancestors had previously received posthumous honors of various ranks. But now, for five generations back, these ancestors, both men and women, were raised to the rank of princedom.

Ugly rumors were current and the people's hearts were troubled. The Empress was clearly planning subversion. Something must be done by someone, for the people never forgot Taitsung. The two "emperors" (Jer and Dan) were in prison and powerless. Other Tang princes, brothers of Taitsung and Gaotsung, and their children, now scattered in

* Taitsung's father had 22 sons and 19 daughters; Taitsung had 14 sons and 21 daughters; Minghuang had 30 sons and 29 daughters. Poor Gaotsung had only 8 sons and 3 daughters. Shouli, Prince of Bia, had about 60 children, all mediocre.

the provinces, watched the signs of the times with grave misgivings.

It was left to a group of scholars to raise the banner of rebellion.

Li Jingyay,* who led the revolt, was a grandson of General Li Tsi, who had years ago officially presided at the coronation ceremony of Empress Wu. A group of five or six scholars and cashiered officials met at Yangchow. Stirred by the obvious trend of events, and sensing that the whole nation felt as they did, they started the revolt, took over the local Yangchow troops and arms by a ruse, chose a double of my father Prince Shien, saying he was not really dead but was with them, and declared war on the usurper. Their cause was popular and their hopes were high. In a fortnight they claimed to have raised 100,000 troops.

It began with the famous Declaration of War written by Lo Binwang, which has become a classic. When this manifesto reached the capital, it produced a greater sensation than the news of the rebellion itself. It quickly passed from mouth to mouth, and some of the scathing lines stuck. For, apart from its style and sonorous rhythm, it gave expression to the people's real feelings, an outlet on paper for what the scholars and officials dared only whisper in the privacy of their homes. And it was so bravely and beautifully said. Read by everybody, this masterpiece of invective damaged the Empress's reputation more than any force of arms could.** It read:

* Li Jingyay is quite commonly referred to as Shyu Jingyay, Shyu being his real surname. His grandfather General Li Tsi (originally Shyu Tsi) had been given the honor of bearing the clan name of the emperor, Li, as reward for one of his great victories.

** Down through the centuries and up to the present generation, this *Manifesto of Lo Binwang Against Wu Jao* has always been included in the hundred best essays because of its style and sonorous rhythm. Every schoolchild was acquainted with it.

The Usurper of the Throne, the woman Wu, is a vile character, born of low origins. She entered the royal service under Taitsung as a wardrobe attendant, and ended up by filling the court with her scandals. She concealed her relations with the deceased Emperor and courted the favors of his son. She befouled the court with her jealousies and ensnared the sovereign with her vixen's wiles. She besmirched the phoenix symbol of the queen and led our sovereign into the path of the incestuous deer. With the heart of a serpent and the savagery of a jungle beast, she drove away the good ministers and surrounded herself with dissolute men. She killed her sister and butchered her step-brothers; she assassinated the king and poisoned her mother. Such conduct is an abomination in the eyes of the gods and a blotch upon the whole scheme of the universe.*

Now, with a yet more sinister purpose, she is casting her eyes upon the divine throne. She imprisoned the beloved sons of our sovereign and raised her thieves' brood to power. Alas! Where is Ho Tsemeng's voice of protest? Where are men like Ju Shihou gone? Signs are all too evident that she is plotting the downfall of the Imperial House.

I, Jingyay, a servant of the Royal Tang House and descendant of a duke, cannot forget the debt to the Imperial Dynasty, nor the loyal tradition of my ancestors. Is there any wonder that I feel the indignation of the Prince of Sung and shed the tears of Yuan Junshan? Stirred, therefore, by the purpose of restoring the Tang House, and believing that this is the wish and desire of the people, I hereby raise the banner of revolt, to clear the country of this monster. The chariots shall roll and the horses' hoofs shall be heard from the Hundred Yuehs in the south to the great valleys of the north. Unlimited supplies of food are available from Haining and the fleet's flags announce that the victory is near. The north wind echoes to the tramp of soldiers, and gleaming

* The last two charges are not found in historical records and were war propaganda, probably based on rumors of the time. Lady Yang had apparently died a natural death.

steel matches the cold splendor of the southern stars. The roar of soldiers shakes the mountains and battle cries rend the silence of the skies. The army's cause is just, its might irresistible.

Rise ye, rise ye, all men! Some of you are born in the land of Han, or are related to the Royal House. Some have received the sacred trust by word of mouth, or heard the royal will publicly proclaimed. Are your hearts dead? Does not the royal behest still ring in your ears? For consider, the orphans of our king are rendered helpless and defenseless while their father's grave is hardly dry. There are men who will rise to the occasion and change the course of events, serving the living as they served the dead. If they will join forces with us to restore the monarchy, I pledge by the land and rivers that the rewards are awaiting you all. On the other hand, those who vacillate and lag behind will be duly punished and regret it too late. Look around you once more, and ask yourselves, to whom does this land belong?

"Great!" remarked Lady Wu when she came to the sentence, *while their father's grave is hardly dry*. "Who wrote it?"

"Lo Binwang," a courtier replied.

"It is my ministers' fault. It is a shame that such literary talent should have been overlooked. The government could well use such a man."

Unfortunately, the leaders of the rebellion were all scholars. None of them had any experience in commanding troops. With the right strategy, the forces of the rebellion could have, as the manifesto suggested, swept over the country like a prairie fire and engulfed Lady Wu in her "God's Dwelling Place" in its flames. But there was divided counsel. The war could be won, as one of the better men suggested, only by a daring march on the capital; they would have won simply by movement. Before the government troops had time to attack, the rebel ranks would have been swelled by local armies, many of whom were loyal to Tang, particularly by the warlike boys of Shantung. Jingyay, however, chose to play it safe. He made Nanking his stronghold and chose a defensive rather than an aggressive strategy, so that in case of an initial defeat he would be able to fall back and hold out from the southeast. The psychological moment was lost; no one was interested in a separate local regime in Nanking, with a possibly protracted war under heavy odds.

The government countered now with 300,000 troops under General Li Shiaoyi. The two armies met on the plains in Kiangpei (north of the Yangtse near Yangchow), a region crossed by many winding rivers and lakes.

For a moment, the outcome was uncertain. The rebel forces were deployed in an arc north of the Yangtse, around the hills and lakes northwest of Nanking, with Nanking as the center of operations. The government commander Li was hesitant. Meanwhile, the Empress Dowager was taking no chances. There could be trouble if the commander went over with his troops to the rebels' side. She sent a veteran general with a long record fighting the Turks in the north, Black Teeth Changjy, to take command and supervise him. Commander Li's staff advised him to take quick action before the new commander-in-chief arrived and hit the enemy at his weak spots. Battles seesawed across the banks of the river, covered at this time of the year with tall, brittle, inflammable reeds. The government troops set fire to the reeds; fanned by the high autumn winds, the fire spread rapidly and threw the enemy into utter confusion. Jingyay saw his forces split, his army disintegrating into a routed rabble. He tried to rally his forces south of the Yangtse, but failed. The government troops followed in hot pursuit.

Finally, he saw all chances gone and tried to flee by boat to Korea. While waiting for the boats, held up by a storm, he was assassinated by one of the officers and the other leaders were captured. Lo Binwang, the writer of the famed manifesto, had completely disappeared and was not heard of again. The leaders' heads were chopped off and brought back to the capital as trophies. In two months' time, by November, the rebellion was over.

Twenty-five heads of the rebel leaders now hung prominently over the gates of Loyang. Lady Wu disliked rebels. Not only was Jingyay's family exterminated, but her vengeance extended to his grandfather, General Li Tsi. No matter that the Archduke had been the one to crown her Empress and made her rise to power possible, had as commander-in-chief fought right up to Pyongyang and forced the surrender of Korea, no matter that he was one of the legendary heroes in the war campaigns of Taitsung. His soul was not to be left in peace. His grave was broken open and his remains mutilated. (The commanders of the present campaign were also killed a few years later.)

While the war was still in progress, the Empress Dowager gave her courtiers a foretaste of her temper.

A rebellion like this was an excellent chance to get rid of someone, in this case Chancellor Bei Yen, who had been consistently opposing Wu Chengtse. One of Bei's nephews was involved in the rebellion, so Bei must be an accomplice, Chengtse's reasoning ran. The real reason was that Bei Yen had said that if the Empress Dowager would return the throne to the Emperor, she would take the wind out of the sails of the rebels. The Chancellor was living in a house with bare walls and scanty furniture when his house was searched.

The interesting thing about the condemnation of Bei Yen was that while the full court was assembled to determine his guilt, the argument was not whether he had or had not as a matter of fact joined the rebels, but whether he *might* or *might not* join the sedition. The conversation ran as follows:

LI JINGSHEN: I am quite sure that Bei Yen might join the rebels.

HU YUANFAN: No, Bei Yen is always loyal and honest. I am sure he would not.

LIU TSISHIEN: I am of the same opinion as Hu.

THE EMPRESS DOWAGER: I know Bei Yen would join the rebels. You people do not know the reason.

HU YUANFAN: If he is a rebel, then we are all rebels.

THE EMPRESS DOWAGER: No, I know that he would join the rebels, but you won't.

Lady Wu meant by her cryptic remarks that when it came to a question of the Wus replacing the Lis, Bei Yen would join a rebellion. She had Bei Yen killed. She was in a black mood. She killed two other generals accused of knowing some of the leaders, but without trial, by simply sending a palace officer to their posts to read the edict and have them decapitated. One was General Cheng Wuting,* who was known as "the Terror of the Turks" and upon the news of whose death the Turks held a wild celebration. The other was General Wang Fangyi, a relation of Empress Wang.

Now, upon the termination of the revolt, Lady Wu sat triumphant in the Wucheng throne room, with all the high ministers assembled before her. She said with evident anger to the gathered officials, "Do you realize that I have done everything possible for the good of the country?"

"Of course, Your Majesty," echoed the courtiers.

"For twenty years," she continued, "I have labored and helped your Emperor to rule the country and have never spared myself. I have given you your positions and power. I have given the Empire order and peace. Since the late Emperor passed away, I have never for a moment thought of

* General Cheng had sent a letter to Lady Wu pleading for Chancellor Bei Yen.

myself but only of other people. Yet the sedition was led by prominent ministers and generals. Who was more powerful than Bei Yen? Who came from a better family than Jingyay? Who was a better general than Cheng Wuting? I could, and did, put them to death when they were disloyal to me. Now any of you who thinks he is an abler man than Bei Yen, or Wuting, or Jingyay, and wants to start trouble, go ahead! If not, you had better render me the homage that is my due and not make fools of yourselves."

"We dare not, Your Majesty," repeated the officials in chorus, not even daring to raise their heads.

✻ 14 ✻

A war of insurrection, brief and quickly put down, was exactly what Lady Wu wanted. It not only stirred up all the humors in her blood and keyed up all her nerves for action. It alerted her to the danger of similar revolts, the unpopularity of her rule, and the necessity for tightening her controls and silencing all opposition. She was quite sure, and yet not quite sure. She had something on her mind, something overwhelming and audacious, and for that she needed a different political climate, a better and tighter organization, and more cohesive, obedient tools to do her bidding. Perhaps power fed by power, perhaps the very act of chopping heads gave one a tingling sense of power. But Grandmother always acted with a purpose; her actions, as future events will show, followed a well preconceived pattern. She had to have two things: a hard core of ruthless men, whether educated or not, to carry out her biddings implicitly; and she must have an efficient network of spies and secret agents to pounce upon any rebellious persons who dared to object. To justify the spies and the terror, she needed a third element: there must be a constant scare of conspiracies and threats to the state, and the tension must be kept up to justify the terror and the slaughter. Provided such a hard core of ruthless secret agents and executioners existed, and provided the spy system was properly nurtured into full blossoming, there was no reason to doubt that Lady Wu could succeed.

The spy system began innocently enough with the installation in March, 686, of a copper letter-box to be placed in all government buildings. It was a square-shaped thing, consisting of four separate compartments fitted into one another with a slit on top on each side through which informers' letters could be dropped. Any man, be he farm laborer or shop apprentice or ex-convict, who wished to give secret information on counter-government intentions, words or activities by a friend or neighbor, could drop a letter into the letter-box without let or hindrance.

The edict announcing the installation of the letter-box system was harmless enough. In the words of the edict, "These boxes are established in the hope that the people's voice may directly reach the government without obstructions, and that justice shall truly prevail upon the land." The four sides facing the four directions were supposed to promote four cardinal virtues. The East, colored green, was symbolic of Kindness; the West, colored white, was symbolic of Justice; the South, colored red, of Honesty; and the North, colored black, of Wisdom—so the edict says. Grandmother would never let Virtue alone.

However, it was not the innocent letter-box representing the four virtues which could do much harm; it was rather the use to which it was put and the real purpose of installing it which was important. Used as a means of placing false accusations put in by underlings of the hired judges to torture the innocent, it brought hell upon the officials and common people and their families. It turned every man into a potential spy for the government, neighbor against neighbor, convict against judge, servant against master, and friend against friend. No such universal spy system has existed before. Every man's single concern in life became just to survive, while the cunning and the wicked had the chance of a quick rise to power by turning informer and selling their friends and acquaintances. This was Mutual Accusation Universal, systematically indoctrinated and spread nation-wide; any citizen if he was good and loyal, should be a spy for the established regime. Never was a nation so demoralized; never did human dignity sink so low. The hot contest for survival was on.

For now, along with the installation of the letter-box system, orders were issued to all districts that anyone of whatever station in life who wished to give information on a secret conspiracy, or on a person or persons critical of the government, should be properly received by the magistrate, even if he was a convict in jail. Anyone rejecting such information or dismissing such an informer would be guilty of protecting traitors. The informer, if so he wished, could ask to go to the capital to see the Empress Dowager, provided with food and quarters on the way like a fifth-rank official. And the Empress did see him. If he was a good talker and looked like a hard-faced, square-jawed ex-convict, or a crafty-eyed instrument for her use, he would be at once promoted, made a judge or a roving secret agent at large, and be given silks and silver. On the other hand, if his information was false, or if he looked dull and useless, he would go unpunished, on the ground that he had made an effort to please the throne and his heart was in the right place. Lady Wu never wanted to discourage informers.

"Informing," or *gaomi* (also called *shangbien,* "report on conspiracy"), became the rage, and soon attracted a great number of loafers, gamblers, convicts and unemployed, as the quickest way to get rich and powerful. People at the time compared the profession of *gaomi* favorably with that of burglary. For a burglar ran the risk of sitting in jail if he failed, and had a chance of obtaining silver and jewelry if he got away. An informer had the prospect of becoming an official, with an attractive prospect limited only by his ability and energy, while if he failed, nothing happened to him at all.

It was in this manner that a number of powerful hangmen rose to power and, joined by others who came to sell their services, became a gang whose agents were distributed throughout the country, vying with one another in showing loyalty and affection for the crown by competitive cruelty. The more arrests that were made and convictions obtained, the more they proved their loyalty.

Of these hangmen of the government, there were three outstanding in their cruelty and therefore in their power and influence; Soh (Yuanli), Lai (Jyunchen) and Jou Shing. Soh was a Hu, from a barbarian tribe from the north, practically unknown till he took up informing. Lai, the most outstanding, or most infamous, was a convict, in jail for robbery when he asked to be freed to give information. Jou Shing had a more professional background, being a student of law and already a third-class secretary in the Cabinet office. There were others. Hou (Sejy) was an illiterate pastry peddler. As a judge, he made an irresistibly comic figure because he talked a terrible dialect accent in an uncouth low slang. Wang Hungyi was a village rowdy and black sheep of the family who rose to be a judge by informing on his village neighbors, who, gathered at a village festivity, were accused of hatching up a conspiracy.

The three investigation judges, Soh, Lai and Jou Shing, representing the S.J.T. (*shujengtai,* new name for the prosecutor's office), are important because they became the leading figures in the years preceding the *coup d'état.* Soh rose to be a "roving general" and secret agent chief at large with power to kill on the spot. Lai became assistant attorney-general, and Jou Shing became a vice-minister of justice, later Vice-Premier for a few months shortly before his death. The names of Lai and Soh were linked together, and the two words, which together spelled "come and raid" (Lai-Soh), became a phrase, a synonym for cruelty. The maids in official mansions would cry, "Lai-Soh!"—like saying "The Devil has come!"—when an officer from the S.J.T. knocked at the door. In nearly every case ("ninety-nine cases out of a hundred," the records say) in about a month their master was killed, the family exiled as slaves and the home broken and in ruins.

In general, each of these men accounted for the murder of hundreds of persons and the ruin of over a thousand families. Soh furnished the first example of the glittering career of an informer; Jou Shing was the main judge-executioner of the Tang Princes; and Lai, the most ambitious and the most hated and feared of all, carried on his work long after the *coup d'état*. Lai held the power of life and death over every official. When Lai was finally killed, many officials came to confess that they had in many instances cooperated with the hated man.

"Why did you do that?" asked the Empress.

"It was obvious. When we violate Your Majesty's laws, we have to pay with our lives only. But if we should offend Lai, our whole family and children would be wiped out."

Lady Wu knew perfectly well the tools she was using, and had no mercy when her secret agent chiefs' usefulness was ended. She merely told the new S.J.T. chief Lai to frame the old S.J.T. chief, Jou Shing. She secretly admired the strong, the upright and the honest men who stood up against their terror, men who went into exile for the time being. How these judges ended, and how some of the honest and fearless ministers were later recalled when her throne was secure, will be told in a later chapter.

I must dwell on these tortures and refined methods for forcing confessions in some detail, because the trials and purges cannot be understood without these details.

Soon after Jingyay's rebellion, Soh rose into sudden prominence, being the first to profit from informing as a career.

The rebellion provided a tense atmosphere for hunting down suspects for sedition. The impression was purposely created that there was a large-scale conspiracy, or many hidden centers of revolt. He was able to obtain more arrests and convictions than others. For he started and possessed unique methods of extracting confessions. One was an iron clamp, fitted on the head of the accused, with wedges for gradually increasing the pressure until the "confession" was "extracted"; not infrequently the skull was cracked if the accused was stubborn. If the prisoner died, so the prisoner died. A second method was to make the prisoner lie in a prostrate position with a stone suspended over his head for hammering him delicately or roughly, according to the prisoner's state of mind. A third was to tie up a man's arms behind him and turn him on the rack. Since Soh's object was to show as many arrests as possible, to show his efficiency and "results," it was his habit to make the prisoner accuse a number of others, friends and acquaintances, so that when a person was arrested, dozens of others were involved. The result was that Soh found himself in great favor with Lady Wu, who often gave him interviews and commended his good work. Lai and Jou Shing then followed suit.

The judicial system, of course, had completely broken down. A new concept of legality took place. Under Taitsung, no man could be subjected to capital punishment except at autumn once a year at the capital itself after review by the Supreme Court. He must have been tried at three levels of local government before he was sent up to the capital. Now a prisoner could be killed on the spot and a report made subsequently. The function of the attorney-general's office used to be investigation of cases, impeachment and prosecution. Now this office, or S.J.T., had its own two prisons, called the S.J.T. prisons. The prosecutor was investigator, judge and executioner combined. Its fifteen circuit prosecutors, officials only of the eighth rank, could, as stated in Li Tsejen's memorandum of November, 690, execute a man on the spot, and without the right of appeal.

Lai then with the help of another hangman, Wan Guojyun, prepared a handbook called *The Science of Processes* (*Lojyjing*) and elevated the methods of forcing confessions into a science. This was a very well-arranged, handy volume prepared for the use of their agents in the country, initiating them into the technical legalities of frame-ups and putting on pressures, with clear, succinct and helpful suggestions. With the *Science of Processes* and its technique of refined tortures, the judges could obtain any confessions they wanted. The four-colored letter-box was also a great convenience. When the gang wanted to involve a prince or a high minister, they would have letters of secret information sent in from widely separated districts, but identical in charges and details, and the case would be handed over to Jou Shing the lawyer for proper handling. The judges themselves would prepare the frame-up documents.

Special mention must be made of Lai's refinement of technique. One of his own colleagues made a pun about Lai's office. It was situated at Lijingmen (Bellevue Gate), just a short distance west of the Palace. His friend called it "Normally Finished Gate," pronounced with the same sounds, because once an accused entered that gate, only a miracle could have got him out again. Lai always started by pouring vinegar down the nostrils of the accused. He would be thrown into a cellar with unspeakable smells, and he would starve; prisoners were said to bite their quilts in hunger. Then the torture by nervous exhaustion began. The prisoner was submitted to interminable questionings and prevented from sleep. A prisoner would be jerked awake whenever he fell asleep, so that after a few nights without sleep his mind became groggy, and he was disposed to confess anything and be done with it.* This was extremely effective, and yet the accused would show no signs of brutal treatment; at the time it appeared so new, so modern, so progressive and so invariably successful that it was a wonder that other people had never thought of it before. I put this down because I want Lai to have the credit for this invention. If some other executioner of the people in the future should claim first honors for inventing torture by nervous exhaustion, he should be sharply reminded that Lai was the true inventor. Also playing upon a man's affection for his family was a basic principle in forcing a person to admit his guilt. Every principle in the weird purges and trials for establishing a beastly reign of terror was discovered under Lady Wu's regime.

The graphic names of the ten big cangues and racks suggest their gruesome character. According to Jou Jyu's memorandum of July, 692, these were: 1) Stop-all-Pulses, 2) Pant-no-more, 3) Howling-on-the-ground, 4) Instant Confession, 5) Horror Supreme, 6) I-am-Rebel, 7) It-is-true, 8) Dying Pigs' Rattle, 9) Beg-for-Instant-Death, and 10) Beg-for-Family-Ruin. One was an instrument for racking and twisting a man's arms and legs; another for trailing a prisoner on the ground, head in rack, with loads across his chest; another was putting heavy bricks on a pillory and jerking the prisoner from behind. These racks were displayed before the accused before trial, and usually he chose to confess what the judge wanted and would have anyway, and spare himself the pains and agonies.

According to Jou Jyu's impeachment of the cruelties, the punishments included pouring mud into a prisoner's ears, clamping on the skull, the wedge-cangue, the revolving rack,

* See *Life* of Soh, and of Lai, *Old Tangshu,* vol. 186A, and the Introduction, *New Tangshu,* vol. 209.

squeezing the chest, sticking sharp bamboo points into fingernails, suspending a prisoner by his hair, and singeing his eyes.

The frightful aspects about these juridicial persecutions are, firstly, that the informers, prosecutors, and judges were the same men, or worked as a unit to destroy anyone they or Lady Wu wished. Secondly, since the most usual charge was sedition, the family, children and grandchildren were punished by exile. Despots always know how to play upon family affections, and by threats of danger to their children or parents or sisters or wives compelled men to sign their own death warrants, which they otherwise would have refused to do under torture. Sometimes the promise of mitigation of sentence for the family was kept, sometimes not. Thirdly, by this same process people were induced to accuse their own friends and acquaintances in the hope of getting away more cheaply—an exile instead of a death sentence for themselves.

When these three methods were systematically applied, an autocrat was born, to be worshiped and adored by the millions; envied and admired by soft-headed scholars.

The ingenuities of man torturing man have no end. I thank heaven that we are back in civilization once more during the last decades. I question that man can ever sink so low as to have that happen again. By any standard, this civilization of ours must go forward, not backward.

The ray of hope that restores our faith in human decency was a number of upright men who, in the midst of these persecutions, either gladly died for their opinions or, as far as lay within their power, tried to fight the lawless barbarism of the executioner-judges. This was the case, for example, of Vice-Chancellor Liu Weijy (*Murder List-III,* No. 8). He had been heard to make the remark in private that the Empress should return her son to the helm of the government; and he was prosecuted. He refused the summons because he said that it was irregular, without the stamp of the Imperial Secretariat (an insistence upon a legal procedure which everybody had forgotten about). Under trial, he refused to retract, in spite of sharp warnings by his friends. He had indeed said that the Empress should return the throne to the Emperor; it was not a crime of disloyalty to say so and he stood by it. Nor would he implicate others, as Lai tried to make him do. "God forbid that I should turn informer!" he replied. The Empress granted him the privilege to hang himself. He wrote his letter of farewell to the throne, reiterating his position clearly and firmly, ate his last dinner with his family, said farewell to them, dressed properly in his official cap and gown, then hanged himself. This was also essentially the spirit of Wei Fangjy, Wei Shyuantung and Ouyang Tung (Nos. 17, 12 and 30 on *Murder List-III,* pp. 182-183).

There were also a number of judges who tried to uphold the dignity of the law and who refused to cooperate. Li Rejy refused to condemn a certain accused, and the case caused considerable argument back and forth among the censors. One censor-judge said, "So long as I am judge-prosecutor, this man shall never live." And Li Rejy said, "So long as I am at my post, this innocent man shall never die."

There were in particular two famous judges who, within their power, fought to defend and save the innocent. These were Shyu (Yugung) and Du (Jingjien), who were to rise to important positions at the end of the story. Shyu refused to use torture, and his staff under him were so inspired they pledged each other never even to flog a prisoner. The accused used to say, "We wonder who will be the judge. If Lai or Soh, we are doomed. If Shyu or Du, we are saved." Once in handling the case of a mother-in-law of Prince Dan, Shyu found there was not sufficient evidence. He refused to condemn the woman. The case was brought before the Empress, and Shyu argued hotly with Lady Wu, maintaining that the woman had merely prayed for her daughter's soul after the latter had mysteriously died in the Palace, that praying was not a crime, and that, as a judge, he was bound to maintain the law.

"Why do you acquit so many people, according to what I hear?" asked Lady Wu.

Shyu replied sententiously, "It is possible that I may have failed to bring conviction and let a few guilty ones escape. But acquitting a guilty one is a small mistake on the part of your servant, while protecting the innocent should be the chief concern of a great ruler."

Shyu was banished. But the Empress remembered this man, and years later recalled him to power. This was an illustrative case showing that Lady Wu knew all the time what she was doing, but permitted him to be banished in accordance with a policy she had set for the time being. Many such good men were later raised to power when her throne was secure and terror was no longer necessary. She was a remarkable judge of men and used a cutthroat or a great honest man for her own purposes.

There was Chen Tse-ang, a poet, who felt it his duty as a man to write a letter to the Empress in March, 686, when these arrests and trials were getting under way. He had only a small post in the Cabinet office, responsible for the orthography in outgoing official communications. The letter gives us a good picture of the situation in those days.

> Since the rebellion of Jingyay, it is the desire of the government to track down the seeds of conspiracy. Your Majesty has thus been led to institute purges by means of terror and tortures. The slightest suspicion leads to mutual accusations and mass arrests. Many undesirable characters have taken the opportunity to inform and accuse others in the hope of obtaining a promotion for themselves. I am quite sure this cannot be the true intention of Your Majesty.

> I know that the common people at heart want only peace and to be let alone. I am amazed that, instead of letting the rebellion die out by itself and be forgotten, Your Majesty has chosen to alienate the people's hearts by such further persecutions.
>
> I have seen hundreds and thousands of cases. In not one case out of a hundred was the accused guilty. But Your Majesty has encouraged these rapacious judges, with the result that a gang of self-seeking officials are having a free hand to destroy innocent people for their private ends. On the flimsiest pretext, a charge of conspiracy or of being anti-government is made, and frequently the arrest of one man causes a hundred to be thrown in jail. It is a common sight to see a procession of scholars being led down the streets, and every day we hear of more trials and more executions. People are saying that, for one person Your Majesty loves and protects, you have killed a hundred. The people's hearts are troubled, and they do not know where to turn. . . .

Chen's letter was of course ignored. But he was not punished, either, for his outspoken criticism. There was a point at the end of his letter. He quoted historical examples and offered his opinion, in all sincerity and goodness of heart, that such persecutions would lead to rebellions on a bigger scale when the people's hearts were truly alienated. But Chen's reasoning was only partly correct. For if terror was stepped up to the proper pitch and intensity, if mass arrests became the order of the day, if the executions turned into public parades, and if there was a country-wide mutual accusation system, opposition became impossible. Lady Wu was right and was sure she was right. Chen kept up the fight and wrote more letters, in March and October, 689, again, during the height of the massacre. Thus the poet may be said to be the first of those who fought for human conscience. Chen's record was in contrast to that of the other post-revolutionary poets of his day, Shen Chyuanchi and Sung Jywen,* who were content to write eulogies of glorious Empress Dowager and her favorites, and who were therefore literary prostitutes rather than poets.

* Chen Tse-ang, Shen Chyuanchi and Sung Jywen are the three poets of the "Early Tang" period, just preceding Tu Fu and Li Po.

❋ 15 ❋

We must now turn to the shattering exploits of the mad monk. While these things were going on, the activities of the mad monk were of a spectacular, overwhelming character.

The monk was mad, undeniably. Towering in his abbot's garb, flaunting purple silk, he had now, in his own mind, reached the ultimate of earthly glory. He had now been made a duke, and had the high ministers at his knees, and the national exchequer given him *carte blanche*. At the Divine Temple of All Creatures, on such occasions as the Shangyuan, the lantern festival on the fifteenth of January, he would load ten carts with coins and throw them to the men and women in the square in front of the Palace. He held "no-obstruction assemblies," so-called in Buddhist phraseology because all social barriers between the sexes and between the rich and poor, prince and pauper, were let down.

The fantasy struck him that he could make Buddhas rise bodily from the ground. It would be a good show. He had the floor of the Hall Celestial dug fifty feet deep. Different Buddhas, splendidly dressed in gold and silk, were hidden below. At a signal, the Buddhas rose steadily to the surface, brilliantly illuminated by a thousand candles, to the admiration of all.

It will be recalled that Lady Wu had a penchant for buildings, and to a very large extent this love affair took on the character of a mixture of architectural grandeur, political showmanship and religious mummery. The monk Embracing Righteousness was now abbot of the White Horse Temple outside the capital, where he had gathered a thousand husky young men of the boxer-wrestler type; but he himself was in the Palace most of the time and had made himself the country's first architect, occupied with two buildings: the *Mingtang,* later called the Divine Temple of All Creatures and used by Lady Wu for her court audience, and the *Tientang,* or Hall Celestial, which means literally "Paradise." Behind the building of these two temples was a political program spawned by the mad monk. The building of the Mingtang was eventually to lead to a great political crisis.

All this had a religious character. The capital had already been called *Shendu,* or nearly "God's Dwelling Place." A whole program was designed to encourage the make-believe that Lady Wu was another Buddha Incarnate.

There was no limit to the expenditures for the Mingtang and the Tientang. Tens of thousands of workmen were commandeered by the abbot. Huge timbers from the mountains were transported to the Palace, requiring a thousand persons to move one piece slowly along. The old Chienyuan Hall, the front hall of the Palace, was demolished and the Mingtang erected in its place. It stood 300 feet across and 294 feet high, in three stories. The ground floor was square, the four sides painted white, black, red and green respectively, symbolic of the four elements. The middle floor had twelve sides, symbolic of the twelve months and the zodiac, standing under a circular projecting roof supported by nine dragons. The top floor had twenty-four sides corresponding to the twenty-four constellations. The roof was round, capped by an iron phoenix ten feet high, studded and plated with gold. A huge central pillar rose from the ground to the top, and all girders, buttresses and cornices were made of the finest timber. Around the base of the edifice ran an iron drain whose running water symbolized the "spread of culture," we are told, harking back to the "college" (*biyung*) of Jou Dynasty. What it really drained was the national exchequer. In point of loud colors, it was what a country peasant would have liked to see. The barbaric festive colors had a fascination of their own.

Behind the Temple of All Creatures and standing on a higher level to the west, was the Tientang, or Hall Celestial, the Paradise of Buddhism. From its third floor one could look down over the Mingtang. The Hall Celestial housed a giant plaster Buddha stuffed with hemp. It stood fully 250 feet high. Ten men could stand on its little finger. The Empress loved all that was big and glorious. The abbot was big and glorious privately, and the giant Buddha to be housed in the Hall Celestial was big and glorious publicly. She strove for the ultimate, the prodigious, the overwhelming, the gorgeous and unprecedented.

In other words, Lady Wu was becoming a Buddhist. The monk was good, therefore Buddhism was also good. The front of the palace, usually forbidden to the public, became a temple. She sat in the Divine Temple of All Creatures and the giant Buddha sat in Paradise, while the abbot communicated with both. These two temples symbolized a spiritual adventure, sensuous, florid and lurid, the divine and the human, piety and sensuality, sex and religion combined. The Divine Temple of All Creatures was but Lady Wu's purple boudoir, glorified and magnified. She was at the peak of her power, and was enjoying all earthly bliss, with Paradise brought right into the Palace.

The prodigious fascinated both Lady Wu and the abbot. He had the head of a Buddha painted on cloth two hundred feet high, its nose the size of a boat. The image was painted with cow blood, but he would have the populace believe that he had painted it with blood taken from his own knee. (Sometimes a Buddhist devotee would paint a small "blood

Buddha" in this manner as an offering.) A wind rose and tore the cloth to pieces, but he was not disheartened, and had another made.

Both Lady Wu and her lover had their own notion of the people's credulity. Lady Wu and the abbot made a unique pair; both were giving free rein to their imagination and both were having a riotous, glorious time. The abbot was now engaged in creating the fiction that Lady Wu was Buddha Maitreya reborn, a myth in which Lady Wu gladly concurred. The choice of this particular Buddha had nothing to do with theology, but the popular image of Maitreya (*Milerfo* in Chinese) was that of a laughing Buddha in a sitting relaxed position, noted for his big, naked belly, a symbol of earthly bliss and contentment. The abbot, in his many sittings with Lady Wu, must have suddenly seen the ultimate reality of the universe, stripped naked of all illusions of color and sense. He had seen Lady Wu's naked protruding belly. In his sensuous-religious ecstasy, Lady Wu became transformed and identified with the Laughing Buddha. And he was of course worshiping the exposed belly of the Buddha on his bended knees, and Buddha was laughing. Of course if she was a Buddha reborn, it had to be the Laughing Buddha. The abbot had now ten monks engaged in the compilation of a new revelation called the *Great Cloud Sutra,* creating the myth of how Buddha Maitreya, out of his infinite compassion for mankind, had decided to be reborn again on earth in the person of Wu Tsertien. This was later solemnly promulgated by imperial decree.

Soaring ever higher in her intoxicating dream of self-glorification, Lady Wu went a step further. Following the abbot's and her nephew Chengtse's suggestion, she now assumed an audacious title, to fit in with the surroundings. In May 688, she—modesty temporarily waived—conferred upon herself the title "Holy Mother Divine Sovereign"

(*Shengmu Shenhuang*). The choice of the word *huang,* "sovereign," applicable to both sexes, was purposely ambiguous. *Huanghou* would be just a mere "empress" and she didn't want that. To be *huangdi,* "Emperor," was what she really wanted. She would come to that soon, once the people got used to it. The epithet "Holy Mother," suggesting a divinity sitting in the Temple, was the important thing now.

Lady Wu had what must be called an uncontrolled imagination. The pair—the raw, muscled masculinity of the abbot and the lusty voracity of the woman—reinforced one another. Lady Wu was happy, and more than happy—she was inspired.

If Lady Wu had had to select an animal for her pet, it would surely have been a whale.

❋ 16 ❋

It was now 688. The time was ripe for a political revolution. The skill with which Lady Wu planned its execution compels our admiration. Like a superb chessplayer, she trapped the Tang princes into a move which spelled their annihilation.

Lady Wu was now in a very fine position. She had established a perfect spy system, had packed the law courts and the censorate with her hand-picked men, had the people and the officials cowed into submission through a reign of terror, of mass arrests and executions. There was no question of legitimacy; she was unquestionably ruling on behalf of the Tang Royal House as the legitimate Empress Dowager. Any revolt against her would be revolt against the Tang "Emperor," although he was now held *incommunicado*. She had concentrated power in her Wu nephews and had eased the Tang princes out of strategic positions. After Jingyay's Rebellion, she had killed the chancellor by a fiat and a few old generals and challenged them all. It will be remembered, she had said on that occasion, "*Who* was more powerful than Bei Yen? *Who* came from a better family than Jingyay? *Who* was a better general than Cheng Wuting? I could, and did put them to death when they were disloyal to me. *Now any one of you who thinks he is an abler man than Bei Yen, or Wuting, or Jingyay, and wants to start trouble, go ahead!*" Now she would challenge the Tang princes to a revolt.

Lady Wu let it be known that all the semi-religious claptrap, and the make-believe about the Mingtang, had a political significance. She had decided that her own dynasty was to be called Jou, the Golden Period of Confucius. For the Mingtang was the classic audience hall of the Jou Emperors.

The make-believe, the political hogwash which heralded the coming of a new dynasty, were intensified about this period. Fantastic claims about the Wus and the Jou Emperors were made. Scholarship cannot find the remotest connection between Wu Tsertien and the classical Jou Emperors. However, the first emperor of Jou was Emperor "Wu" (ca. 1100 B.C.) which was an honorific title conferred upon him after his death, and not a clan-name, the Jou House being of the matriarchal clan of Ji. But it sufficed for Lady Wu. After the *coup d'état,* she actually had the spirit tablet of Emperor Wu installed in the ancestral temple as her "fortieth-generation ancestor" and worshiped as such! Her history was bad, but her histrionic sense was excellent. She would have claimed Confucius as her ancestor if she could.

Already scholars pointed to a prophecy in the Confucian Classics. There was a chapter celebrating the success of Emperor Wu in the *Book of History,* entitled "The Success of Wu" (*Wucheng*)!

The Mingtang was started in February, 688. Lady Wu went on merrily with make-believe, just in case the Tang princes missed the point. The founding of a new dynasty has always been heralded by a sign from heaven. Lady Wu wanted to make it patently clear that exactly such a sign had appeared.

The omen could be a bright star, an aurora, or a white smoke rising from the roof in the shape of a dragon where the Man of Destiny sleeps. What was a real omen and really happened was that, in July, 687, a farmer reported that his hen had changed into a cock. This was to happen again, in January and October of 689, when the same thing occurred and was reported by farmers of different districts.* The *yin* and *yang* were turned upside down, and it was truly prophetic. Lady Wu didn't want to publicize that. She thought she could do better than that.

The omen from heaven was conveniently provided by Chengtse, as the *Great Cloud Sutra,* the Buddha Reincarnate legend, was being prepared by the abbot. This forged Sutra, making Wu Tsertien the Buddha Reborn, was still under preparation. It was not yet finished, but would be published in the following year.

In April, 688, Chengtse had a faked antique stone inscription made, engraved with the eight characters.

Shengmu lin ren;
yung chang diyay.

"A *holy mother* shall appear to *rule* over *mankind,* and her *empire* shall *prosper forever.*" These words were painted with a mixture of purple marble, resin and powders, and the stone tablet was thrown into the Lo River, to be accidentally hauled up by a peasant. It is impossible not to conclude that Grandmother, Chengtse, Princess Taiping and the abbot had all this carefully planned. When the peasant came to report about this find, Lady Wu affected to be surprised and delighted. The peasant was appointed a "roving general."

However, it was discovered, the Empress Dowager never doubted that the term "Holy Mother" referred to herself, that an ancient prophecy was about to be fulfilled. The "omen" was exploited to the full. In the following year, she gave herself the title "*Holy Mother* Divine Sovereign" (*Shengmu Shenhuang*) without false modesty, and in Decem-

* See *New Tangshu* (official history), vol. 4, for the years mentioned. Because of the *Yin-yang* philosophy, all such unnatural phenomena (such as birth of quadruplets, snow in summer, etc.) were recorded along with other important political events.

ber of that year the title of the reign was changed to "Eternal Prosperity" (*Yungchang,* 689), to accord with the text of the prophecy.

During May-June, it was announced that she would worship Heaven and Earth at the "southern suburb" to offer her thanks, and that the Lo River was to be consecrated as "River of Eternal Prosperity," its god to be created the "Count of Visitation," the stone inscription to be called "Holy Script," and the place where it was found the "Holy Script Spring." Fishing was forbidden in that area, and the Sung Mountain was named "Divine Mount" and its god raised to the rank of "King of Middle Heaven." To celebrate the great occasion a general amnesty was declared. It looked almost as if Lady Wu was an honest victim of her own swindle, which she was now imposing upon the public. But she had a wonderful sense that the people wanted legends, miracles and omens to believe in.

All this mixture of religious mummery, political propaganda, fantasy and megalomania was trumpeted about that summer. According to a court announcement, a ceremony would take place at which the Empress Dowager would herself go to the Holy Script Fountain to receive formally this evidence of God's call to rule her people. It was to be a grand ceremony, and all princes of the royal house, all civil and military leaders, and ladies of rank were to congregate at the capital ten days before the ceremony.

All indications pointed to an immediate political crisis. The founding of a new dynasty looked imminent and inevitable. A strong, persistent rumor was now carefully circulated that a "revolution" was about to take place and that the convocation of the princes was a death-trap. The "Emperor" together with all the princes of the royal house would be rounded up *en masse* and wiped out or thrown in jail when they should appear at the capital. The rumor in quarters close to the court grew serious and was believed in.

Secret letters flew back and forth between the princes in the provinces and their friends in the capital. Was the rumor true? Should they, or should they not appear for the ceremony? Some princes in the capital itself did not know what to think, or what to believe. The signs were clear that something portentous was happening. But nobody really knew. The Prince of Ji heard the rumor, but chose to ignore it. Duke Yung, son of Prince Feng, wrote to ask his friend Gao Tsegung, and Gao replied, "Don't come if you want your life!"

At this time, six or seven of the elderly princes, the brothers of Taitsung and uncles of Gaotsung, still survived. Among these the most respected were Archduke Yuanjia, Prince of Han, and Grand Master Lingkwei, Prince of Lu—both born of the same mother and very close to each other. Next to these was Archduke Yuangwei, Prince of Ho, senior living uncle of Gaotsung. Much admired for his character, he was also an archer who could hit every boar in a pack with his arrow; at the same time he was a studious scholar. When he was magistrate, he delegated all routine matters to his secretaries, and enjoyed himself with his books. He hated ostentation and lived simply. Deep and quiet, his advice was much sought by Gaotsung. The latter used to send him secret letters asking for his opinion on important matters of state. Of Gaotsung's brothers (sons of Taitsung), the Prince of Ji and the Prince of Yuay, now about sixty, were reputed to be the best writers among the princes. All of them had held the highest ranks as archdukes or grand masters, but since Bei Yen's death in 684 had been sent away from the capital to serve as magistrates—Yuangwei in Shantung, Yuanjia and Lingkwei in Honan, etc., all scattered. What were the princes to do?

Grandmother and her nephews had circulated the rumor of a "death-trap" in order to provoke the princes into rash action, in the way a jailer would sometimes give a prisoner a chance to escape in order to shoot him in the back. What resources could the princes draw upon to defend themselves? Should wisdom counsel caution, against being provoked into a precipitate act of overt rebellion? But should they obediently assemble at the capital, to be herded together and slaughtered like pigs, as the rumor said? Or perhaps be subjected to indignities, humiliations and tortures by the grand executioner Jou Shing? Was it not infinitely better to go down fighting like men than to rot in jail?

Those immediately concerned were the following:

Taitsung's brothers	Yuangwei, Prince of Ho	His son Shyu, Prince of Jiangdu
	Yuanjia, Prince of Han	His son Juan, Duke of Huang
	Lingkwei, Prince of Lu	His son Ai, Prince of Fanyang
	Feng, Prince of Her (deceased)	His son Yung, Duke of Dunguan
Gaotsung's sister	Princess Changlo	Her husband, Jao Huai
Gaotsung's brothers	Tseng, Prince of Yuay	His son Tsung, Prince of Langyay
	Shen, Prince of Ji	His five sons

Yuanjia sent word by messenger to the other princes, "The Empress Dowager fully intends to massacre the princes after the ceremony. If we don't take action now, the family of Li [Tang] will be wiped out."

Juan, now posted at Tungchow (near Peking), wrote a cryptic letter to his cousin Tsung, Prince of Langyay, stationed near the capital:

My old wife is suffering from an acute illness, and requires immediate treatment. If I wait till winter, it may be too late.

As the princes were scattered about in the provinces (mostly in modern Hopei, Honan and Shantung), coordination was difficult, especially under the universal spy system. But there was no time to lose. A decision had to be made, and at once.

Grandmother had succeeded in throwing them into a real scare. She hoped they would start a precipitate, hasty revolt, and waited with her dagger in her sleeve. She would defend and protect the House of Tang even if she had to kill all the Tang princes. Or if they didn't, she could use some *agent provocateur* and create an incident, then spread the net and enmesh them all. She had the whole S.J.T. setup of Jou Shing prepared for action. She could not lose.

The Princes' Rebellion of July-August, 688, known as the Rebellion of Prince of Yuay, was really started by his son Tsung and his cousin Juan. Juan forged a letter, purporting to be written by Prince Jer (i.e., the deposed "Emperor") asking the princes to free him from his captivity in Fangchow. Tsung acted immediately. He sent letters to the different princes and asked them to raise forces and march on the capital. He would start the revolt at once from Shantung.

There had been no sufficient preparations, no coordination, no careful planning. As he was no soldier, his revolt died out in seven days, he himself killed by one of his officers. The news of his swift defeat reached the other princes, who were now paralyzed by fear. None of them took action. Only Princess Changlo and her husband responded. It will be remembered that Princess Changlo was mother of Prince Jer's wife who was starved to death, after the Princess herself had been banished from court. She said to her husband, "If the Tang princes were men, they should have done something before now." Tsung's father, the Prince of Yuay, alone decided to throw in his lot with his son, for he knew that he would be implicated anyway for his son's doings. However, he had only 2,000 troops available, and his district was not far away from the capital. The government countered with 100,000 troops under Jang Guangfu, his forces were outnumbered and overwhelmed; he took his own life.

The Empress had now caught them neatly in a trap. The princes had risen in open rebellion. She needed only her instrument Jou Shing to implicate and convict them all and exterminate their families. There was a semblance of a basis to build upon, for the letters of the Prince of Yuay to his cousins had fallen into her hands. With Jou Shing's technique of forcing confessions so well tried out in the last few years, she knew she could get any number of witnesses to testify, so that the ramifications would practically cover all the princes, their relatives and the people close to them.

Now the purges and trials began. In the normal process of justice, probably five or six princes who had participated in the revolt should be condemned. But the shadow of persecution—for these were persecutions, not regular court trials—fell over the entire royal house, including the princes' wives, children and their children's children and friends. Events show that, incredible as it seems, the forced revolt was merely an excuse for the wiping out of the entire Imperial House of Tang, which was wholly irrelevant to the punishment of the guilty. Jou Shing did what Lady Wu wanted and had full power to condemn and kill anyone. It was enough to say that so-and-so was a close associate or acquaintance of the accused to sentence him for complicity in treason. Thus for one person brought to trial, with a bare show of legality, dozens of families were destroyed. Purge followed upon purge, and wave upon wave. Executions turned into parades, glorified and made as public as possible. For the purpose of the executions was to instill terror. No longer the secret murders at the Palace with lame excuses!

The trials and arrests lasted from the summer of 688 deep into 691 with increasing ramifications, until it may be accurately said that the great majority of the royal house and all the important princes were wiped out. A look at the genealogical table (*Murder List-II,* pp. 180-181) will show that the five families of the Prince of Ho, Prince of Han, Prince of Shu, Prince of Shuh, and Prince of Yuay were completely wiped out, while a few grandchildren of the Prince of Lu, the Prince of Ji and the Prince of Shyu survived. The younger children and grandchildren were banished to the subtropical south, some as slaves, some in hiding, all branded as "Lizards."

Grandmother's mask was off. The House of Tang was the intractable horse which she had once boasted to Taitsung she could break if no one else could, and now she bared her stiletto and without batting an eyelid plunged it into the heart of her husband's family, whom she had pretended all along to love and honor and serve faithfully.

Hell now broke loose. It was a black day for the royal descendants of the great Taitsung. No mercy was shown the princes and none was intended. It is impossible to imagine the situation in those days. One saw it happen and refused to believe it possible. High ministers' heads fell; scholars in chains were herded through the streets; archdukes shut up in a convict's cage and paraded through the streets on the way to exile; whole princes' households, with their women and infants and servants, marched a thousand miles to the remote, barbarous south. I saw one of my own two brothers whipped to death, his face mangled. How I survived I do not know.

Wu Chengtse, nephew and arch-plotter, directed the murders, convictions and banishments his aunt wanted.

The first wave of persecutions took place in September-December, 688, soon after the rebellion started. Archduke Yuangwei, an old man of seventy, was placed in a convict's "cage" and sent on his way to Jienchow (border of Kweichow and Szechuan), and died of exposure on the journey at Paochi before a week was out. His son, the Prince of Jiangdu, was executed in the city. Field-Marshal Yuanjia and Grand Master Lingkwei were ordered to commit suicide at home, their property confiscated. All three sons of Yuanjia were executed. It was then found that Prince Yuanjia had a fabulous library of over 10,000 volumes, many surpassing in value those in the library of the Palace, all carefully annotated by this lover of books. Gaotsung's brother, the Prince of Ji, a cautious man as his name Shen implies, had repeatedly received the people's tributes to his administration. He had never taken part in the rebellion, had in fact tried to keep clear of it. He, too, was charged with "failure to inform" since he admitted knowing of the Prince of Yuay's letter. He was placed in a convict's cage and died, aged about sixty, on the way, after half a month of exposure. Five of his sons were executed. Grand-uncle Archduke Yuanming survived the journey to exile; since he refused to die on the way, he was sentenced to death and executed half a year later.

The pickings were not random. To forestall future comebacks, the work had to be thorough. Grandmother did a thorough job. In the whole hierarchy of government, the highest were all disposed of. The respected leaders of the Tang House were gone; it was left only to dispose of the minor figures. Would it not be a simple matter to abolish the Imperial Tang House when the imperial family had already physically disappeared?

* 17 *

The ceremony of formal reception of the Holy Script Tablet had been interrupted by the Princes' Rebellion. Soon after the rebellion had been put down and the elderly princes of Tang had been executed or marched to exile, the formal ceremony was held at the Holy Script Spring. It was one of the grandest occasions of the regime. Lady Wu appeared in her regal robe with a crown of twelve strings of pearls coming down over her face. After the ceremony, the Holy Script Tablet was placed in a tabernacle and brought back and installed in the Temple of All Creatures. On New Year's Day, 689, Lady Wu, now "Holy Mother," sat in the Temple to receive the congratulations of the courtiers.

I was looking on at the reception, with Uncle Dan's wives, Liufei and Dufei, beside me. They were still living then. Grandmother sat on the throne, holding a piece of ceremonial jade in her hand. In front of her were displayed the seven precious vessels associated with Buddha Maitreya. Except for very fine wrinkles around her chin, visible only at close range, she looked vigorous and in good condition and beatific, as happy and contented as a cobra who has just eaten a rabbit and is now curled up for a comfortable stretch of sleep. On the side stood the tabernacle with the Holy Script Tablet, with the words: *"A Holy Mother shall rise to rule over mankind, and her empire shall prosper forever."* There was the Holy Mother in flesh and blood. The reign-title was of course *Yungchang* ("prosper forever").

It was impressive and fascinating. This year's New Year truly was unusual. The Temple of All Creatures was lavishly decorated and glittered with gold, and everything was gleamingly new. The abbot had done a good job, for no expense had been spared to make this the most sumptuous building. The abbot, now made a duke, wandered about in his glittering purple cassock. Uncle Dan, for once, appeared in public, for he was to make the second offering at the worship. Grandmother's eyes, which often closed into narrow slits, now flashed, brilliant and happy, as the important ministers came up to kneel before her and offer their congratulations on the new reign of the Holy Mother. These officials knew, and Grandmother knew that they knew, that she held the power of life and death over every man, and what was of more immediate importance, that their jobs depended upon her.

Now the persecution and banishment of the lesser Tang princes continued. What really was wanted was not the tracking down of the seditionists and their accomplices, but the uprooting of all branches of the royal family and intensification of the terror before the final doom of the Tang Monarchy was pronounced.

The waves of killings led imperceptibly into one another. The second wave followed in March-April 689, when another batch of twelve princes went to their death. Hundreds of families were marched 2,000 miles to the south. The tension mounted, the third wave came. Chengtse was made Lord Secretary, with Sanse aiding and abetting; and heads of princes, generals and high ministers began to roll. In July, thirty-six princes, dukes, high ministers and generals were killed. This time the killings included many famous scholars and intellectuals. Lady Wu was as suspicious as she was autocratic. Her secret agents were at work, surveying and investigating anyone who by word or conduct showed the slightest disapproval of the trend of events, or who looked noncommittal, or undependable, or who was not ready to swear by the Holy Mother. And many there were. In those purges and trials she executed nine generals, three lord chancellors, one vice-chancellor, four lord secretaries, two vice-secretaries, two vice-premiers and six ministers (*see Murder List-III*).

All through the latter part of 689 and the first half of 690 the killings followed one another in quick succession. There was not much of the Tang House left when the fourth wave came, which turned its principal attention to the officials and generals. In July, 690, two months before the declaration of the new monarchy, the daily killings became bewildering, just to make sure that no one was going to say "No" to Heaven when it passed its mandate to Wu Tsertien. Lady Wu wanted the people to be quite convinced that there was no Tang House to save, that the Heaven-appointed Holy Mother had risen to answer and fulfill an ancient prophecy. She knew that, two months hence, thousands would beg her to abolish the Tang Monarchy, that she would modestly refuse, but that tens of thousands more would follow and insist and beg her to found a new dynasty of Jou. Then and only then would she find it hard to refuse and reluctantly consent to be made "Emperor."

Only Prince Jer and Prince Dan, whom she did not wish to destroy, still survived in captivity, like the professional gambler's last two coins, always kept in the pocket. They were, however, to be graciously granted the favor to adopt the royal surname of *Wu*.

Lady Wu had never liked her stepsons, Sujiay and Shangjin. They had long been confined. Now the long arm of the stepmother leisurely reached for them and finished them off easily. Sujiay and his nine sons and Shangjin and his seven sons were killed off; only the youngest few, among them my cousin and good friend Chiu, the present Duke of Ying, were spared, sent to Hainan and survived. This was in July, 690, just before the declaration of the new monarchy.

The purge was completed by 691, but the most grisly episode took place in 693. Wan Guojyun, one of Lai's gang, had been sent to Canton to investigate rumors of grumbling and discontent among the orphans and wives of the princes. He summoned them to his office and told them to go and hang themselves. Howling and dismay filled the court. "All right," said Wan, "come with me."

He led three hundred women and children to the brink of a river and had them slaughtered. He was thus able to come back and report that there had indeed been a serious conspiracy and disaffection for the throne, but luckily he had stopped it in time. Wan was immediately pronounced a *dafu.*

Seeing that Wan was rewarded for his services, others suggested that there might be disgruntled elements in the other places of exile. Consequently, different palace officers were appointed circuit judges and sent out to the provinces of Szechuan, Kweichow, Kwangsi and Yunnan borders (in the southwest). The grim and ghastly episodes repeated themselves. Vying with one another in showing loyalty to the throne, Liu Guangyay slaughtered about nine hundred men, women and children, Wang Dershou about seven hundred, while three other emissaries took the lives of two to five hundred each.

Isn't there something beastly in our human race? Or am I wrong? I wonder what future historians will say. Will they join issue, or will they condone and "accommodate" themselves to a situation and merely admire a great tyrant who extended China's frontiers to Korea, Nepal Kazakhstan and Southeast Asia?

Even a catalogue of these murders can be disgusting. Suffice it to say that these murders and miscarriages of justice happened, not because of Jou Shing and company, but because they were part and parcel of Lady Wu's cool and premeditated policy.

Here is a more or less complete list of the men and women who went to their death in order that one megalomaniac superwoman might realize her ambition. It must be remembered that, for one person named in the murder charts, usually a family of ten to twenty persons was exiled, to trail the dreary road to remote Hainan or the coasts of the subtropical China Sea. Also the killings of officials below the third rank are not listed.

In the midst of this orgy, Lady Wu issued an edict, in April, 692, forbidding the *butchery of pigs!* For under the influence of the abbot she had become a devout Buddhist.

MURDER LIST—I

LADY WU'S IMMEDIATE HOUSEHOLD

No.	Date	Name	Relation	Manner	Family: branded
1	Winter, 655	New-born infant	Daughter	Strangled	
2	Winter, 655	Empress Wang	Mistress	Butchered	Exiled: 'Cobra'
3	Winter, 655	Shiaofei	Rival	Butchered	Exiled: 'Vulture'
4	655	Duchess of Han	Sister	Poisoned	'Viper'
5	August, 666	Duchess of Wei	Niece	Poisoned	'Viper'
6	April, 675	Prince Hung	Son	Poisoned	
7	March, 684	Prince Shien	Son	Condemned	Two sons flogged to death
8	December, 664	Prince Jung	Stepson	Condemned	Buried as commoner
9	July, 690	Prince Shangjin	Stepson	Condemned	Seven sons killed; youngest exiled; 'Lizard'
10	July, 690	Prince Sujiay	Stepson	Condemned	Nine sons killed: youngest exiled; 'Lizard'
11	676	Beifei	Daughter-in-law	Mortification	(Prince Hung's wife)
12	April, 675	Jaofei	Daughter-in-law	Starved	(Prince Jer's wife)
13	January, 693	Liufei	Daughter-in-law	Secretly murd.	(Prince Dan's wife)
14	January, 693	Dufei	Daughter-in-law	Secretly murd.	(Prince Dan's wife)
15	656	Yuanching	Stepbrother	Condemned	'Viper'
16	656	Yuanshuang	Stepbrother	Condemned	'Viper'
17	August, 666	Weilang	Nephew	Framed	'Viper'
18	August, 666	Huaiyun	Nephew	Framed	'Viper'
19	September, 701	Prince Chunglun	Grandson	Flogged to death	
20	September, 701	Princess Yungtai	Granddaughter	Flogged to death	
21	September, 701	Yenji	Grand-nephew	Condemned	(Husband of No. 20)
22	683	Yuji's wife	Nephew's wife	Murdered	
23	September, 688	Princess Changlo	Aunt	Condemned	

MURDER LIST—II

THE TANG PRINCES (ALL BRANDED 'LIZARDS')

No.	*Date*	*Title*	*Name*	*Relation*	*Family Survival*
1	August, 688	Prince of Langyay	Tsung	Son of No. 4	Wiped out
2	September, 688	Prince of Han*	Yuanjia	Brother of Taitsung	Wiped out
3	September, 688	Prince of Lu*	Lingkwei	Brother of Taitsung	3 grandsons survived
4	September, 688	Prince of Yuay†	Tseng	Brother of Gaotsung	Wiped out
5	September, 688	Duke of Shangdang	Shen	Son of No. 2	Wiped out
6	September, 688	Duke of Huang	Juan	Son of No. 2	Wiped out
7	September, 688	Duke of Wuling	Yi	Son of No. 2	Wiped out
8	September, 688	Prince of Fanyang	Ai	Son of No. 3	3 sons survived
9	September, 688	Duke of Dungguan	Yung	Son of Prince Feng*	1 son survived
10	September, 688	Prince of Changshan	Chien	Brother of No. 4	Wiped out
11	December, 688	Prince of Ho*	Yuangwei	Brother of Taitsung	Wiped out
12	December, 688	Prince of Jiangdu	Shyu	Son of No. 11	1 son survived
13	April, 689	Prince of Lingling	Jyun	Son of Prince Tsao†	Wiped out
14	April, 689	Duke of Li	Jiay	Son of Prince Tsao†	1 son survived
15	April, 689	Prince of Runan	Wei	Son of Prince Yun†	1 son survived
16	April, 689	Duke of Boyang	Yen	Son of Prince Yuanching*	1 nephew survived
17	April, 689	Duke of Guanghan	Mi	Son of Prince Yuanching*	1 nephew survived
18	April, 689	Duke of Wenshan	Tsin	Son of Prince Yuanli*	Wiped out

MURDER LIST—II *continued*

THE TANG PRINCES (ALL BRANDED 'LIZARDS')

No.	*Date*	*Title*	*Name*	*Relation*	*Family Survival*
19	April, 689	Prince of Kuangdu	Shou	Son of Prince Yin†	Wiped out
20	April, 689	Prince of Shuh	Fan	Son of Prince Yin†	Wiped out
21	July, 689	Prince of Ji†	Shen	Brother of Gaotsung	Grandsons survived
22	September, 689	(Without title)	Chyuay	Son of Prince Chengchien†	1 survived
23	October, 689	Prince of Jeng	Jing	Son of Prince Yuanyi*	2 sons survived
24-29	October, 689	Duke of Shuay and five brothers	Shiuchi	Sons of Prince Yuanying*	Wiped out
30	December, 689	Prince of Yiyang	Tsung	Son of No. 21	2 sons survived
31	December, 689	Duke of Chu	Rui	Son of No. 21	Wiped out
32	December, 689	Duke of Siangyang	Shiu	Son of No. 21	Wiped out
33	December, 689	Prince of Liang	Shien	Son of No. 21	Wiped out
34	December, 689	Duke of Jienping	Chin	Son of No. 21	Wiped out
35	July, 690	Prince of Shu*	Yuanming	Brother of Taitsung	Wiped out
36	July, 690	Prince of Yuchang	Tan	Son of No. 35	1 son survived
37	August, 690	Prince of Nanan	Ying	Son of Prince Yuanshiao*	1 son survived
38	August, 690	Duke of Yu	Jow	Son of No. 35	Wiped out
39-50	August, 690	Twelve others	Lije, etc.	Minor distant members	

MURDER LIST—III

HIGH MINISTERS AND GENERALS

No.	*Date*	*Name*	*Office*	*Remarks*
1	November, 658	Suiliang	Vice-Premier	Exiled with 2 sons
2	July, 659	Han Yuan	Lord Secretary	Died in exile
3	April, 660	Wuji	Archduke, Field-Marshal	Sons and brothers exiled
4	December, 664	Shangguan Yi	Vice-Chancellor	Son executed, children enslaved
5	October, 684	Bei Yen	Lord Chancellor	Brothers exiled
6	October, 684	Cheng Wuting	General	Terror of the Turks
7	October, 684	Wang Fangyi	General	Empress Wang's relative
8	April, 687	Liu Weijy	Vice-Chancellor	Teacher of Prince Dan
9	December, 688	Chien Weidow	Acting Lord Chancellor	
10	April, 689	Deng Shyuanting	Minister of Civil Service	
11	August, 689	Jang Guangfu	Lord Chancellor	Suppressed rebellion, 688
12	September, 689	Wei Shyuantung	Lord Secretary	
13	September, 689	Tsuitsa	Minister of War	
14	October, 689	Heichy Changjy	General	
15	October, 689	Jao Huaijiay	General	
16	October, 689	Li Guangyi	General	
17	January, 690	Wei Fangjy	Lord Secretary	Exiled January, died October
18	February, 690	Wang Benli	Minister of Interior	
19	May, 690	Fan Lyubing	Minister of Ceremonies	

MURDER LIST—III *continued*

HIGH MINISTERS AND GENERALS

No.	*Date*	*Name*	*Office*	*Remarks*
20	May, 690	Li Shiawyi	General	Suppressed rebellion, 684
21	August, 690	Jang Chujin	Minister of Justice	
22	August, 690	Ashna Hui	General	Turkish origin
23	August, 690	Jang Shinglien	Vice-Premier	
24	August, 690	Bei Jyudow	Grand Master	Father of No. 11, List 1
25	October, 690	Tsung Tsinker	Acting Lord Chancellor	Promoted new dynasty
26	November, 690	Shy Wutse	Lord Secretary	
27	November, 690	Chiu Shenji	General	Suppressed rebellion, 688
28	August, 691	Jang Chienshyun	General	
29	September, 691	Fu Yuyi	Vice-Secretary	Promoted new dynasty
30	October, 691	Ouyang Tung	Lord Secretary	
31	October, 691	Chen Changching	Vice-Premier	
32	October, 691	Lo Syhwei	Vice-Secretary	
33	October, 691	Ger Fuyuan	Minister of Interior	
34	October, 691	Li Antsing	General	
35	October, 691	Chuan Shiencheng	General	
36	January, 697	Li Jaoder	Lord Chancellor	

❋ 18 ❋

From January to August, 690, the political storm gathered its fury; the terror mounted as the time for change of dynasty approached. The time was ripe for giving the *coup de grâce* to her husband's house; the pretense of loyalty could now be laid aside. All she needed was to seal its doom on a strip of paper. Lady Wu, her nephew Chengtse, Princess Taiping and the abbot had the plan carefully worked out.

The "revolution" was scheduled for September. Two months before that, the *Great Cloud Sutra* had been promulgated. It was the story of a special revelation given to ten priests, telling of the rebirth of Buddha Maitreya as Wu Tsertien. An edict was issued that copies should be distributed to all temples of the land. Four months later, two temples, in Changan and in Loyang, called Great Cloud Temple, were ordered to be constructed especially to house this revelation, the youngest of the Buddhist sacred texts. Priests were to give lectures expounding the passages of this text. Nine of the sacerdotal toadies who produced this were given the rank of counts, with the privilege of wearing purple cassocks and silver tortoise pendants. Lady Wu had thus publicly acknowledged that she accepted the story herself.

All was now ready. On September the third a delegation, headed by Fu (Yuyi), a citizen of Changan, representing nine hundred people, came up to the palace gate, demanding to see the Empress. They presented a request, as the will and desire of the people, that the old dynasty be abolished, the new one Jou be established, and that Prince Dan, the "imperial heir," *should be given the clan name of Wu.*

Lady Wu was cordial and smiled graciously. She was profoundly touched. But she wasn't quite sure it was the people's will. She politely declined and laid the petition aside. Fu, however, was rewarded with a post as departmental chief in the Imperial Secretariat.

But of course it was useless to test God's will. Soon afterwards, sixty thousand people, among them monks, tradesmen, officials, princes and tribal chiefs, had come up, surrounding the Palace and demonstrating noisily for the change of dynasty. They were led by the nephew, Chengtse, and a chosen delegation went in to see the Empress. They had brought along a scroll signed with sixty thousand names. Why, Chengtse must have worked on it, collecting the signatures behind her back, and had not told her about it! She was overwhelmed. She couldn't believe it. Sixty thousand people from all walks of life! The voice of the people had spoken then. As if this was not enough, Prince Dan himself had sent a letter, begging for the honor of bearing the surname of Wu. In the face of such an overwhelming expression of popular opinion, she found it hard to resist. She promised to consider, if that was truly the wish and fervent desire of the nation.

It was then said that on September the fifth hundreds of red sparrows chirped on the roof of the Temple of All Creatures. God had spoken. But, even more significant, a phoenix, that mythological bird which appeared only when a sage or prophet was born, came flying to the royal park west of the Palace, then flew away in a southwesterly direction. A few people had seen it; then a hundred; then all the courtiers had seen it with their own eyes. Only an absolute idiot would say that he hadn't.

Lady Wu was unable and unwilling either to disappoint

the nation or disobey the will of God. Modestly, on September the seventh, she finally wrote the word "approve" on the document of the petition.

On September the ninth the decree was given. Henceforth the Tang Imperial Dynasty was abolished, and the new one was to be called "Jou." The year's reign was changed to "Heaven-Appointed" (690). Lady Wu appeared at the front tower of the Palace and had the edict read and a general amnesty declared. (Lai, the executioner-judge, always took the precaution of killing the important prisoners before the order for pardon was read, for which he was greatly commended by the Empress for his thoughtfulness.)

On September the twelfth, in accordance with a predetermined scale of self-promotion, she now assumed the audacious title "Holy Spirit *Emperor*" (*Shengshen Huangdi*). It was an advance from "Holy Mother Divine Sovereign." At last her ambition was realized. She was a "female emperor," not merely an empress. The term "Holy Spirit" * constituted also an advance toward divinity, a jump from "Holy Mother" to "Holy Spirit." On the same day Prince Dan, whose royal surname Li had become a stigma, was graciously granted the surname of Wu.

On September the thirteenth the names of all princes of the Tang House were struck off the peerage list. The Wus, Chengtse, Sanse and twelve others, were created princes, while their sisters and cousins were made princesses. On that day the Wu Ancestral Temples at Loyang were formally inaugurated. Their spirit tablets had been brought from the old temples at Changan and installed here. Whereas these ancestors for five generations back had already been made "princes" in 684, they were now raised to the rank of "emperors" and "empresses" for seven generations back, and worshiped according to imperial honors. The Tang Ancestral

* *Shengshen* is the word for "the Holy Ghost" in modern Chinese.

Temples, originally called "imperial" (*taimiao*), were now degraded to "Worshiping Virtue Temple" in name. Four of the seven temples were shut down, and only the last three generations received the seasonal offerings.

The transition of dynasties was now completed. How Grandmother must have laughed!

But amidst all this pomp and celebration a great man, one greater than them all, Di Renjiay, sat and watched silently. The famed master detective and judge, whose name has passed into popular legend, and who was to undo all the work of Lady Wu and restore the Tang Dynasty, was present at these ceremonies as a Vice-Minister of the Interior. Surveying the situation with his keen, analytical mind, he knew the time was not yet, for he had a coolness which equaled that of Lady Wu. What he had in mind he told only to a few of his closest friends.

Book Three

* 19 *

THERE seems to be an inexorable law in the affairs of men that chaos must return to order, the abnormal return to the normal, and the equilibrium of things be restored, like the sequence of storms and calm at sea. A hidden mechanism, we might almost say, exists which turns the wheel of fortune so that the wicked shall be punished and justice shall prevail. I should bless the spirit of Taitsung for the invisible hand that guided the turn of events which took place. But I should nonetheless ascribe it to one greater than Taitsung, to the hand of God, whose immutable law is for the equilibrium and balance of *yin* and *yang* by which the movements of the universe and the affairs of men are regulated. As Laotse says, a storm does not last forever. Epidemics die out by themselves without any apparent external agency. Rich fortunes become bankrupt, tyrants die and dictatorships burn themselves out.

I mention this, not in idle philosophizing, but to record a remarkable fact that somewhere after the year Heaven-Appointed (690) there was a curious reversal of events; men like Jou Shing perished one by one, and by their own devices, while good men escaped death by a miracle, or rather a series of miracles. Somewhere there was an invisible hand. I am not saying that good men like Granduncles Yuangwei and Yuanjia had not suffered a cruel end. Most of them did. But many good men had been preserved, men destined to save the Imperial Tang Dynasty. A series of events now took place, each remarkable in itself, all resulting in the rise of a group of extraordinary men and shaping the course of events. The machinations of Chengtse and Lai notwithstanding, they were always foiled by men like Di Renjiay and Wei Yuanjung and Shyu Yugung. They, and not Lai and Soh and Jou Shing, dominated the situation. The morale of the ministers became strong and united; courage returned. An assistant attorney-general dared death and defied the Empress's order for him to leave the capital. A common judge would rather lay down his office than obey the Empress's order to condemn an innocent man. And Lady Wu, by her disgraceful indulgence with her lovers (by now she had established a male harem in her palace), provided a common cause for the ministers to rally around and restore the Imperial Tang Monarchy.

Power corrupts, and Lady Wu was no exception. In giving herself over to sensual pleasures, to the extent of keeping the notorious Jang brothers in her harem, Lady Wu proved once more that, strong and superhuman as she thought herself to be, she went the way of all flesh. Her debaucheries contributed to her ruin. Then it seemed all so natural. It was natural that Lady Wu, her ambition realized, should want to relax and give herself a great deal of license, and it was natural that the secret agent chiefs should be jealous of and destroy one another, and other petty politicians like Lai and Chengtse should in the end fall out with one another and severally perish.

It was like the winter solstice, the shortest day of the year, with the *yin* at the zenith. Yet on that very day the slow curve of the *yang*, now at its lowest point, begins to rise, and the days begin to lengthen. From now on, we shall see the gradual rise of Di Renjiay, the master mind that became the pivot, and his miraculous escape from death, the equally miraculous escape of Prince Dan, the dramatic end of the mad monk, the frustration of Chengtse and return of Prince

Jer, the no less dramatic end of the secret agent chief Lai, and finally the storm which blew around the Stork Institute, the harem of Lady Wu, which ended this sordid comic opera.

There was one side of Grandmother which so far we have not seen. It cannot be denied that she was a remarkable woman. Except for her power madness and egocentricity, she was perfectly sane and sober, astute and strong in character. It was the more pity, for in the last ten years of her life she showed more tolerance, while still firmly keeping the direction of things under her control. She halted the murders and recalled the good men who had variously been dismissed, degraded and exiled. While Chengtse plotted and Lai schemed, she never allowed things to get out of hand. She could have been a good ruler, better than many kings anyway, if she had not set her mind upon a grand sedition. As soon as her new dynasty was established, it became very clear that she had used men like Soh, Lai and Jou Shing to further her own end, knowing perfectly well what she was doing; but when her end was accomplished she threw these tormentors of the people overboard and called to power men whom she had secretly admired all along for their courage and ability, although she had herself banished them. In this she showed an ease and mastery and self-composure which compels a certain admiration, however impossible it is to exonerate her from brutality.

Almost none of the petty politicians who had helped her in the revolution survived a year, except her nephews. Fu, for example, the man who had led the citizens' petition to change the dynasty and who had been rapidly promoted from season to season, was killed exactly one year after the revolution on charges of corruption and misconduct. Among those who met their end now, there was no one whose death caused more merriment than that of the grand executioner, Jou Shing.

It is possible that directly after her accession to the throne, Grandmother deliberately started to dismantle the terror machine. Of the three henchmen of the grand persecution, Soh had already died. He had been accused of extortions and was handed over for trial. Now the position was reversed and Soh found himself not in the position of "extracting" confessions from others, but having it extracted from himself and by one of his own cherished devilish devices. When he refused to plead guilty, the judge, one of his former friends, had said, "All right. I will have one of your iron clamps brought in." Soh quailed at the thought of having his skull compressed and possibly cracked, out of which the "confession extract" was to flow. He at once pleaded guilty and died in prison.

The death of Jou Shing was similar, but more dramatic. His death gave birth to a phrase which is now common idiom. The story has been so often told that the phrase *"please step into the jar"* has passed into current language. It took a gangster chief to kill another gangster chief. For now the ambitious Lai, jealous of Jou's power, had secret letters of information sent to the Censorate, implicating him in a case which had cost the life of a general (Chiu Shenji). Lai had seen Lady Wu privately and had obtained from her a secret personal order for the trial of Jou Shing. Jou was in Lai's hands.

The two friends were having a cup of wine. Jou Shing was unaware that he had even been accused. He had just been made a vice-premier at the beginning of the new regime as a reward for his services.

"I have a difficult case," said his friend Lai. "No matter what I do, I cannot make the prisoner confess. He is terribly stubborn. I don't know what to do."

Jou Shing replied exuberantly, "Don't tell me that you are helpless. If you want my advice, put the prisoner in a big earthen jar and build a fire around it. I will wager you anything that before he gets really roasted, he will cry for mercy and confess anything you want out of him."

Lai's eyes brightened. "Why, what a capital idea! I have the prisoner right here in the house. We will try."

A jar was brought in and a fire was lit around it.

"Do you think it is hot enough?" asked Lai. "If so, we can send for the prisoner."

"I think it is."

Lai's expression suddenly changed. He pulled out of his sleeve a script signed by the Empress for the trial of his rival. "Now *will you please step into the jar?*"

Jou Shing's face blanched, and he seemed visibly to shrivel up and crumble. He fell on his knees, kowtowed and begged for mercy. His confession was signed and reported to Lady Wu. The Empress (now officially "Emperor") thought that his services entitled him to some consideration and had him banished to the south instead of being killed. On his way, he was fallen upon by one of the numerous men whose relatives he had killed, and so paid with his own life.

With the death of Jou Shing, the gang of illiterate judges who had been having a riotous time was broken up. Only Lai remained. Working closely under the nephew, Chengtse, he tried to create enough nuisance, but the machinations of the brash nephew were like minor ripples in a back-eddy compared to the tempest raised by Lady Wu.

Under the wing of protection of Chengtse, Lai was the most feared man now. For if Lady Wu's aim was accomplished, her nephew's was not. Prince Dan was still the heir to the throne. While the Empress had no more use for executioner-judges, Chengtse had. As the eldest grandson of Lady Wu's father, he presumed, and logically, that the throne was naturally his in the dynasty of the Wu family. Busy, active, but tactless and haughty, everywhere he invited only contempt. With the help of Lai, he was able yet to involve a few high ministers who had opposed him and have them killed. Finally, his attention was directed to the greatest man of his generation, Di Renjiay, whom he set Lai to destroy.

The fate of the Imperial Tang Dynasty now hung upon the survival and rise to power of Di Renjiay, a man of the people who had always fought for the people against the generals and high officials, but who during the persecutions had so far managed to keep his head on his shoulders. For Di's was a master mind which knew when to speak and when not to speak. Like the good lawyer that he was, he chose his time to speak as well as his points of attack, and pressed only the point that he knew would win the case. And he always did.

Of course he was loyal to Tang, and disapproved of the change of dynasty. For the time being, he kept his mouth shut and watched the Wu nephews cackling and strutting about, young upstarts that they were. Like Lady Wu in her undertaking, he knew he needed patience, planning and timing. He knew that to put the Tang princes back on the throne and abolish the new dynasty he needed a group of able, fearless men, placed in strategic positions, and the creation of a different political atmosphere and a strong official morale. In the famous Judge Di, Lady Wu had at last met her match. His task was admittedly stupendous, like reversing the course of the heavenly bodies.

He was not alone. He was a close friend of (Jang) Jienje and others who were of the same mind. Years ago, when the princes were imprisoned shortly after Gaotsung's death, Jienje was Governor of Jingchow, on the Yangtse River. Jienje and his friend Yang (Yuanyen) met. In the darkness of the night, they took a boat out to the middle of the river where they could talk without being heard. Both spoke of the treacherous imprisonment of the Tang princes. Both were enraged. There before the pale moonlit sky the friends made a solemn pledge that one day, when there was a chance, they would drive out the low usurper and restore the throne to the descendants of the great Taitsung. It would be the greatest thing they could do. Then the political situation steadily deteriorated and the reign of terror blew like a winter wind chilling everything it touched, until the House of Tang tottered and fell and the woman usurper, a daughter-in-law of the Tangs, sat on the throne. They had to keep quiet, but in their hearts they never forgot their secret pledge.

Di was now in his sixties. Some twenty years earlier, serving under Gaotsung, he was already a judge of the Supreme Court, and he had been a metropolitan judge before. It is a question whether Judge Di's fame will go down to posterity more as a master detective-judge or as the man who restored the Tang Dynasty.* Among the people he is more popularly known as the judge who invariably tracked down the criminal. As a judge who often went about in plain clothes to detect crime, he made the astounding record of always solving crime mysteries which had puzzled and frustrated other judges and magistrates. He was credited with clearing up seventeen thousand old cases, setting many innocent accused free. This may be an exaggeration, but of his talent and the basis for his reputation there was no doubt. Certainly the many cases he had disposed of as metropolitan judge were just cases which had accumulated for years by sheer bureaucratic indolence. Before anything else, he wanted efficiency and hated slipshodness of any kind. He was known not once to have convicted an innocent man, but had saved the lives of many innocents and, what was more difficult, tracked down the guilty and sent them to jail. He had helped so

* The famouse detective cases dealt by Judge Di have been popularized in Chinese as *"Digungan."* Some of these stories have been woven together and retold with good effect by Robert van Gulik.

many people and saved so many lives that when he left as governor of a place, the people always built a stone tablet in his honor. His name has thus become a popular legend.

He hated Buddhism or its practice by the wealthy established priests, and made no bones about it. His rational mind hated superstitions of all sorts. Once as inspector-general of the Ministry of Works he closed down seventeen hundred temples in the provinces devoted to sorcery and immoral practices.

He had been successively Governor of Ningchow (in Kansuh) and Vice-Minister of Works and Vice-Premier. Once, after the Princes' Rebellion, he was sent out to the district of the revolt (Junan) to investigate the cases on the spot, his rank being then a vice-premier. Six or seven hundred men were sitting in jail, awaiting trial for complicity. He knew the people well. Most of the common people were pressed into rebel service by force. He refused to do what the military commander wanted him to do and condemn the men to death. Moreover, he sharply reprimanded the commander for slaughtering soldiers who had surrendered, in an effort to claim "results" for so many killed.

"The stench of these surrendered soldiers fills the moat. If I had the royal scepter in my hand, I would kill you first and report afterwards. Do you want to drive all the people into another, greater, rebellion?"

The commander reported to the Empress on Di's rude behavior, and Di was relegated to a post as magistrate.

Now Lady Wu once more called Di to power. In an interview, Lady Wu asked Di, "You got into trouble at Junan—do you know who spoke against you?"

"No," replied Di. "And please do not tell me. I do not want to know. If I had done something wrong, I am glad to have been punished. If I had not, and Your Majesty understands, I am satisfied. The man who spoke against me must have been one of my friends."

That was Di's humor, the humor of great human understanding. The Empress could not help admiring a man like that. Incidentally he was also quite handsome.

Di was made a Vice-Minister of the Interior, with the rank of privy councilor, participating in the highest government council. Chengtse was at the height of power, flushed with success. Five or six high ministers had just been executed for obstructing his ambition to be made crown heir (Nos. 30-33, *Murder List*-III) and Di had just stepped into that dangerous position. Being promoted to a position of such prominence was like climbing up to the top of a ladder, when another step meant fall and sure death.

In January, 692, Di himself was arrested together with four or five ministers and faced with the same charge of sedition, by Chengtse's orders.

Being a master detective, Di had to use his own wits, to outplay and outmaneuver the hated and feared S.J.T. chief, Lai. Di did an unusual thing. He pleaded guilty at once. For if anybody knew the law, Di did. There was a provision that anyone who pleaded guilty outright should not only be spared tortures, but was entitled to have his death sentence converted.

"Your Honor, I plead guilty. The Great Jou Dynasty has now received Heaven's mandate, and a new era has begun. As a loyal servant of the Tang House, I am willing to die."

Lai was pleased. The other accused high ministers followed Di's example, but the stubborn Wei Yuanjung alone refused to please guilty. The accused were led back to prison.

Di had thus gained time. He needed all his ingenuity to save himself. He wrote a letter to his son, asking him to bring the matter to the Empress's direct attention and requesting to have a direct interview with her. He had the letter secreted in a quilted gown and was able to persuade a jailer to have it taken home. When the son received the quilted gown, he thought it unusual for it to be sent back, for it was winter. He suspected a message, cut up the lining and found the letter. He lost no time in seeing that the letter was properly delivered to the Empress herself.

As luck would have it, a child of nine saved Di's life. He was the son of Vice-Secretary Lo (No. 32, *Murder List*-III), who had been executed three months before. The child was turned into a slave at the disposal of the Ministry of Public Works. As a bright boy, he was sent into the Palace. The Empress saw the child's bright face, called to him and asked who he was. The child told her and said he had something to say.

"What do you have to say, child? Your father was properly tried in court and found guilty. That was why he was killed."

"No," replied the child. "Everybody is afraid of Lai's tortures. He could make anyone confess. My father was innocent."

"So?"

"If you don't believe me," continued the boy, "choose the man you trust most, and hand him over to Lai for trial for treason. Lai will come out with a confession."

The Empress was impressed. She was in a more receptive mood when Di's letter came, and kept her eye open. She had always admired Di and liked him. She sent for Lai.

"What are you doing?" asked the Empresss. "I hear you are doing all sorts of things to the prisoners. What about Di Renjiay and Wei Yunajung and the others?"

The famous Judge Di with a goatee and the towering Wei Yuanjung were among the most impressive personalities of their time.

"I beg your pardon," replied Lai. "The prisoners have pleaded guilty of their free will. They are comfortable in prison, and I have even permitted them to keep their caps and gowns."

"Have they all confessed?"

"All except Wei Yuanjung."

"They are good ministers. Question them again. Give them a fair trial."

Not quite willing to take Lai at his word, the Empress sent an officer to visit the S.J.T. prison. When the officer announced his visit, Lai quickly snatched Di's cap and gown, and put it on someone of his height, to prevent Di from having a talk with the palace officer. Lai himself came out and stood at the porch facing west, with the man in disguise by his side. The officer was facing east with the sun in his eyes. He was so terrified of Lai by his reputation that he dared not even look straight. He went back and reported that he had seen Di in good health, and apparently treated very well.

Sensing that something had gone wrong, Lai hastily had the prisoners' letters of farewell to the Empress written and sent, to convince the Empress that the prisoners were gladly going to their death. All would be over soon.

Warned by the child, the Empress was now suspicious. She at once sent for the condemned ministers and gave them an interview as Di had requested. They came, knelt before her and said they were not guilty.

"Why did you confess if you are not guilty?"

Di replied, "Your Majesty, we should be dead from torture by now if we did not. We wouldn't be here in your presence today."

"Then why did you write the letters of farewell?"

"I never wrote one," said Di, surprised. The others also denied having written such letters. The letters were produced and the handwritings checked. They were clearly forgeries.

They should have been acquitted. But Chengtse insisted that he knew they were planning a rebellion. And even if not, these men were dangerous and should be removed.

"There is no case against them," replied the Empress. It was 692, and she felt herself more secure.

Chengtse still tried to insist on his point.

"Stop it!" said Grandmother. "I have given my word. I will not go back on it."

For now there was a conflict between the Empress and her nephew. Her objective was attained, but his was not. The result was that the ministers' lives were spared, but they were sent out to the provinces as magistrates, as Chengtse had wished. Normally, Lai should have been severely punished, but he was still under the protecting wing of Chengtse, and this time his position remained secure.

Di's escape from death was not only lucky for himself, but also marked the end of the trial and persecution of the ministers. His was the last case. For one thing, the Empress's faith in Lai had been badly shaken. For another, she had no political need to keep on the reign of terror now. In June and July various officials (Yen Shanse, Ju Jingtser, Shyu Jien, and above all Jou Jyu) sent a succession of letters, suggesting variously that the normal process of law be restored, that the judges themselves be reviewed for their records and the unworthy ones eliminated, that capital punishment should, as under the laws of Taitsung, take place only after reviews and appeals to the proper authorities, that an eighth-rank prosecutor should not be permitted to kill a man on the spot, and that, politically, it was time for a more humane regime to win the hearts of the people. All of them expressed the opinion that the great majority of those who had been killed were innocent. It was then that Jou Jyu wrote his famous impeachment of July, 692, describing in detail the gruesome tortures used (quoted in Chapter 14, p. 153), and scoffing at the fantastic notion that the land swarmed with heroes all trying to mount the dragon throne.

Among those who were in the same trial and had thus escaped was another great man, important in this part of the story, the always dramatic Wei Yuanjung. Hearty, honest and stubborn as a mule, he had refused to plead guilty but had escaped harm, luckily, because of Di's strategy. Loved by everybody, he was having a checkered career, was promoted and degraded, and promoted and degraded again, and became the stormy petrel when the fight over Lady Wu's harem of handsome boys began.

The dramatic Wei was four times on the point of death or exile, and four times escaped and survived by the merest chance. This man's life seemed to have been protected by a fairy godmother. Once he was saved by a last-minute pardon, and once he outwitted his judge.

During the persecution of ministers, Wei had been sentenced to death and was already tied up, kneeling on the execution-ground with four or five high ministers. Suddenly word came that an emissary from the Palace was on his way with the Empress's pardon. The execution was held up. The others were greatly excited, but Wei was unmoved. Then the emissary appeared flashing the note from the Empress. The prisoners were untied. Some were getting up, but Wei remained on his knees. "Read the edict first," he said. "I haven't heard it yet." The edict was read, then Wei slowly and leisurely rose from his knees, drawing a deep breath, but without showing any expression on his face.

Another time, he was being tried by the illiterate pastry peddler, Hou, now a judge. He was being trailed along the ground, his head and shoulders in a rack. He saw the humor of the situation—Wei Yuanjung the great scholar being tried by a pastry peddler! He made as if he wanted to speak and the judge thought that now he was ready to confess.

"What have you to say?" shouted the judge.

"Just this, that I am so unfortunate as to be trailed along as by a donkey."

The judge was furious and cursed him in low slang.

"You shouldn't say that," answered Wei.

"How do you mean?"

"You talk with such a terrible accent. And you use such words! You have never read a book. Now that you are a judge, you should learn to talk like a judge, and you can, if you will devote some time every day to study. I can help you. You don't know how lucky you are to be talking to Wei Yuanjung himself."

The illiterate judge was greatly impressed. He had the peasant's respect for a scholar, and he knew the prisoner was Wei Yuanjung. He came to untie him and offered him a seat. Wei began to correct his accent. He was freed!

It was men like these whom Destiny had chosen to restore and perpetuate the glorious Imperial Tang Dynasty. The calm and wisdom of Di Renjiay, the unswerving strength of Wei Yuanjung, the integrity of Shyu Yugung, the courage of Sung Jing and the leadership of Jang Jienje constituted together a moral force which overthrew and defeated the evil genius of Lady Wu.

❋ 20 ❋

In the trial of Di Renjiay, Chengtse had, with the help of Lai, tried to destroy those who opposed him. He was foiled by Di, and the consequence was that Lai was clearly exposed in the presence of the Empress. But Chengtse never gave up. This time, both he and Lai overreached themselves.

The restless, ambitious Chengtse had found himself out in the cold. His aunt was made "Emperor," to whom he had contributed not a little. What about himself? Was this not to be a dynasty of the Wus, and was he not the eldest in succession? To be sure, the nephews were all placed in high positions—Yuning, Yitsung, Sanse, and all the rest of them. Some were made commanders in the metropolitan districts, some were privy councilors. Their actual power and influence were greater than their ranks and offices.

For two or three years now, the question of succession had hung fire and Grandmother was slow about it. Chengtse had tried his best to make himself declared the Crown Prince. He knew he was unpopular, and he had sent a number to death (Lo Syhwei, Chen Changching among others) for influencing the Empress against him. Officially, however, Prince Dan was now "imperial heir," whatever that meant. So long as Prince Dan's position remained unchanged, he had no prospect of becoming Emperor himself one day. He induced Lai to work with him. Lai was ambitious and looked forward to becoming the head of the government when

Chengtse should be on the throne. Lady Wu was not going to live forever.

In 693 the forces were set to work first to discredit and then to destroy Uncle Dan. First, two minor officials were executed for seeing Uncle Dan privately. We were still living in strict confinement at the Eastern Compound at the time. A secret interview with Uncle Dan suggested or implied that the "Emperor" (never crowned and never deposed) was plotting to get back to the throne. To publicize the story and discredit Prince Dan, Bei Feigung and the other official were executed by the unusual and extinct method of "quartering."

The net closed in. Next, Chengtse's attention turned to my aunts, Uncle Dan's two wives, Dufei and Liufei. Grandmother's favorite maid, Tuan-erl, induced by Chengtse, one day informed her that the young daughters-in-law had been grumbling and had been heard to curse and hope for Grandmother's death. One day shortly afterwards, my aunts accompanied Grandmother on a visit to Jiayu Hall. When Grandmother came back, they had just disappeared! They never returned to their rooms. No trace was found of them. They had been secretly murdered and the bodies disposed of. Prince Dan sensed that Chengtse was after him.

At dinner, Grandmother glanced several times at him. It was strange that she had invited him to dinner that very evening, most probably to see if he dared protest or say something impolitic as Prince Hung had once done. Dan played the docile, dutiful son, ate his dinner and said nothing. Naturally, there was no search for the bodies and no funeral. One of the murdered daughters-in-law, Dufei, was no other than the mother of the present sovereign (Minghuang), who was then only eight or nine. As I have mentioned already, when the son mounted the dragon throne, he wished to do honor to his mother and looked for her remains so as to bury them together with his father's. He could not find them, nor those of Liufei. He had to satisfy himself with having a suit of Empress's robes and insignia buried in an empty coffin, symbolically representing his mother.

All these things had happened within a month or two of each other. Lai and Chengtse were now after Uncle Dan himself. They came to our place and, without the knowledge of Grandmother, held a trial of our servants. Their object was to implicate Uncle Dan in a move to get back to the throne. What were the executed officials talking about? Didn't they hear their conversation with Prince Dan? Was not Bei Feigung suggesting a *coup d'état* within the Palace and had not Uncle Dan approved? All this took place within the Eastern Compound, for, as far as Chengtse was concerned, he was running the Palace and we were his prisoners, for him to do with as he liked.

The usual racks were displayed, and the flogging started. Vinegar was poured down the noses of some of the maids—Lai's favorite method of starting a trial. All this happened within one hundred and fifty yards, at most two hundred, of Grandmother's residence in the western part of the main Palace.

The servants, maids and eunuchs were completely terrified. They were ready to say "Yes" to whatever Lai wanted them to say.

Now another miracle happened. At this time a man, An Jintsang, was also brought in for questioning. He was not a servant of our house. Suddenly An cried out, "You can't do this! It's a lie, a lie! The imperial heir is innocent!"

Without warning, An flashed a knife, bared his belly and slashed it open, pulling out his own intestines. It was a form of protest by suicide. Soon he was lying unconscious in a pool of blood.

Chengtse's face whitened. The affair had taken a turn

which was entirely unexpected. The tortures and questioning stopped automatically and the hall was in confusion. The maids screamed and ran away in horror.

Some servant had run to inform Grandmother and she immediately came over, having no idea that all this was happening inside the Palace. Chengtse and Lai stood up respectfully, looking sheepish. She scolded her nephew severely, while she looked at the dying man on the floor. She had seldom come so close to blood, and the sight was horrible. She questioned the maids as to what was happening while Chengtse and Lai absconded. The court physician had arrived. She ordered that the man's wounds be tied up and every effort be made to save his life. Luckily he was still breathing, and the doctor was commanded to attend him every minute until he returned to consciousness. The big wound was stitched with mulberry bark fiber and bandaged, and chimney soot liberally applied against infection. Then An was removed to a bed.

Grandmother seemed unusually moved by this incident. She inquired about the man the next morning. An had slept through the night, still weak from the shock and profuse bleeding. Luckily he ran no fever and was expected to live, though he remained in a semiconscious state.

Grandmother came over again in the afternoon when she learned that An was able to say a few words.

"Thank you, An, thank you," said Grandmother. "That I should not know my own son, and you should have to risk your life to save him."

An was treated royally and not removed from the Palace until his wound had healed, and then he was sent away with liberal gifts from Grandmother as well as from Uncle Dan.

The episode left a strong impression on Grandmother. She repented once, if she ever did in her life. And she did not speak to Chengtse for several days. This was the sort of *gau-*

cherie Chengtse often committed that displeased Grandmother. She was incensed at Lai for the effrontery of trying to apply tortures at the Palace.

For the first time, Lai was degraded from his post of Assistant Attorney-General and sent away to the provinces. This incident marked the beginning of Lai's falling into disfavor and increased Lady Wu's dislike of Chengtse. Her maternal feeling toward her sons, Jer and Dan, was still dormant, as evidenced by the fact that she had not wanted to send for Jer at all. But far deep down in her a spark remained, waiting to be kindled by Di Renjiay—perhaps.

Lai was temporarily out and Wu Chengtse had fallen into disfavor, but the mad monk, no longer so young, but insolent and grown powerful, was making a lot of trouble for Grandmother. There was no question but that the monk was mad, suffering from delusions of grandeur. And since this malady was largely shared by the Empress, the results could not but be spectacular.

While the romance lasted, it was gay, it was pleasant, and the near-Godhead which Grandmother achieved was largely the abbot's work. The *Great Cloud Sutra,* creating the legend that the Empress was Buddha Reincarnate, had been published and duly circulated. Nobody questioned it and nobody took it seriously. She now espoused Buddhism ardently, since she herself was one of the Buddhas. She had ordered, in March, 691, that in all public processions the Buddhist priests and nuns should take precedence over the Taoists. In April of the following year she produced the now famous Buddhist edict forbidding the taking of pigs' lives, just before the butchery of three hundred women and children on a riverbank.

The abbot, Chengtse and her daughter Princess Taiping now conspired to give verity to her claim of Buddhahood. More and more Buddhist epithets were added to her title.

Chengtse was always heading petitions, at one time numbering twenty-six thousand signatures, piling up honorific titles on her, more or less along Buddhist lines. First, she was "*Holy Mother* Divine Sovereign"; then, at the time of the assumption of the new monarchy, "*Holy Spirit* Emperor"; then in September, 693, "*Golden Wheel, Holy Spirit* Emperor"—an occasion celebrated at the Temple of All Creatures. Then in May, 694, "The *Eternal, Golden Wheel, Holy Spirit* Emperor." She loved all of it.

The spell of religiosity lasted as long as the abbot was faithful to her. But the abbot had tired of her. However she wore her make-up, she was already seventy and her wrinkles showed. The Laughing Buddha's protruding belly was no longer as edifying as it had once been. Now rich and powerful, the abbot stayed away at the White Horse Temple, where he had other ways of amusing himself. Grandmother many times sent for him, but he made excuses. She resented this. The abbot had practically blackmailed her into allowing him to do anything he pleased. What the man was trying to do was not clear. He had shaved the heads of several hundred husky young men, among them boxers, and provided them with luxurious quarters at the temple as "monks."

The monk was of course mad to treat the Empress like a castaway mistress. Grandmother was powerless to stop this. He was the only man she feared in this world. Meanwhile, she sought a new lover, this time the imperial physician, Dr. Shen Nanchiu. The abbot heard of it and was enraged. He became more insolent than ever. His visits were perfunctory. She could not excite him anymore. He knew her, better than anybody else. But in a way he was not mad, for he knew the worst perversities of the Empress, and the price for his silence was to let him do as he pleased.

In desperation, the Empress sent him out as commander in

chief to fight the Turks up north, so as to keep him away from the capital. At this time the abbot's power was above that of any minister. As luck would have it, he arrived when the Turks, torn by internal dissensions at home, called off the invasion. The abbot therefore returned in triumph, after having a war memorial erected to commemorate his "victory."

Now the New Year holidays arrived, a stretch of fifteen days from the first to the fifteenth. (This was November, 694, but ever aspiring to greater semi-divinity, the reign was changed to *Chengsheng*—"Sainthood Confirmed"—and by a fiat, November was made the first month of the new year.) As usual, men and women flocked to temples, and the Hall Celestial was thrown open to the public, with its Buddhas and myriad lights rising from the ground. The abbot had reported to the Empress on the "successful conclusion" of his Turkish campaign, and informed her that he was giving a great celebration. He had fully expected a reward from the Empress, perhaps a rise in rank, or some other form of recognition. But the Empress was merely cordial and did nothing.

The mad monk went ahead with his celebrations. The big cloth image of Buddha, two hundred feet high, was hung outside the palace gate. The fifteenth arrived, the great Lantern Festival at which the whole town usually turned out. There was a large gathering, and coins were thrown to the spectators in the square.

The abbot fully expected the Empress to appear at the celebrations, as she used to. He had even prepared a special program for her, as one of the Buddhas. He told everybody that the Empress was coming, and waited for her appearance. He would gain so much face in the public's eye, as being still in the Empress's favor. He waited and waited. She failed to appear. So she was with her new lover, Dr. Shen! He flew into an uncontrollable rage.

That night, in a fit of insane fury, the mad monk set fire to Hall Celestial, or Paradise, which had cost millions to build. The huge Buddha almost two hundred and fifty feet high, being stuffed with hemp and coated with plaster, burned and spluttered like a giant festive bonfire, and the whole building now went up in a blaze of flame and smoke, shooting and spluttering sparks. The fire, fanned by the bleak winter wind, caught the Temple of All Creatures in front. Soon the Temple was ablaze. Tientsin Bridge was lit as by daylight. The fire was spectacular and the holiday-makers watched from a distance this great conflagration shooting up three or four hundred feet high. Sparks flew and set fire to the cloth image of Buddha, already torn to pieces and fluttering in the cold wind. "There goes the Buddha's nose!" the spectators shouted. The fire licked the nose bit by bit, to the amusement of all. The smell of paint and blood mixed with that of the crackling structures. Some sparks fell as far as the North Market. The mile-high red glow of the sky was visible from all parts of the city.

The dawn found the huge timber and hard woodwork still smoldering, crackling and bursting into flame here and there. The gold-plated phoenix on top had survived the fire, charred and twisted and inclining at a grotesque angle.

This was known as the Great Fire of January the fifteenth. It was the lesson which Embracing-Righteousness intended to teach the Empress for neglecting him. In his diseased imagination the fire, huge, powerful and like an evil red demon, was also something beautiful to see, and satisfying.

Was the Empress going to punish him? The abbot knew that she daren't. She was ashamed and embarrassed. She knew who had done it and why. To her courtiers, she explained that some workmen had been careless and a burning pile of hemp had started the fire. She ordered the Temple of All Creatures to be rebuilt, with the abbot again in charge of the construction. She felt humiliated of course, but she would not like to offend the abbot. For she knew that discretion was not one of his virtues and he could spread quite a lot of stories around, salacious and incredible, if he made up his mind to do it.

Lady Wu now hated herself for getting herself involved with such a lout, rascal and impostor. Handing over the abbot for trial would be impossible. She did not relish the prospect of a court trial of the monk, during which anything might happen. The public would be all ears for the suggestive, *risqué* details, and surely every bit would be spread by word of mouth to the whole nation. There was no telling how stories might come out during a trial, and she herself would be subjected to ridicule, even as had happened once at the execution of Ho Shiangshien (p. 20). But the abbot knew more than Shiangshien; if the whole story came out, she would be known as history's sexiest queen. Of course, gagging was impossible if the abbot was to answer questions. Outright murder would be simpler.

The prosecutor Jou Jyu, however, brought up an impeachment on the ground that the abbot had, for suspicious reasons, gathered a thousand boxers, wrestlers and other riffraff at the White Horse Temple, parading as monks. Jou Jyu was the man who had spoken against the tortures of Soh and Lai, and for the restoration of the regular system of justice (pp. 153 and 202). He spoke to the Empress and wanted the abbot handed over for trial. The Empress tried to make light of it.

"It isn't really necessary," said Lady Wu thoughtfully, a little worried.

"I have no doubt that the abbot is up to some mischief. I have many questions to ask him," insisted the prosecutor.

The Empress thought a moment and answered, "All right. You go back. I will send him over immediately."

Jou Jyu went back, not believing that she would. He had not been waiting long before the abbot really turned up, to his surprise. The husky monk tied his horse at the gate and stalked into the prosecutor's office. He threw himself upon a couch, put his feet up and laughed.

Jou Jyu called him for questioning. Suddenly, the mad monk jumped up from the couch, went out and set off on his horse.

The monk's outrageous conduct was reported to the Empress, who had probably herself directed the abbot to pretend insanity and act in the way he did.

"The monk is mad," she said to Jou Jyu. "It's not worth your while prosecuting him. You can take up the case of the others at the White Horse Temple, and I will let you do with them as you see fit."

Jou Jyu had no choice but to accept. He tried the other monks and had them banished.

Now Princess Taiping, who knew everything that was going on, came to speak with her mother. She was as thoughtful as her mother and was just as afraid of a scandal which would involve herself. She was a sexual pervert, too, and loved to dress as a boy when she was sixteen.

"Why allow that baldhead to run riot at the capital?" she said. "This can't go on. He must be taken care of definitely."

The Empress smiled a wan smile. "It is not so simple. What can I do?"

"Leave it to me," replied Taiping. "I will take care of him. It is simply intolerable."

The Empress understood. "All right, but be extremely careful."

The Princess sent word to the abbot that the Empress wanted to see him about plans for the new Mingtang. She chose two dozen strong women servants, armed with ropes and poles and broomsticks, and told them what to do. When the time for the appointment came, she went out with these women to Yaoguang Hall, where the abbot would pass on his way to see the Empress. At the same time, she instructed her Cousin Yuning to come with a selected group of palace guards, concealed and well placed for action. Keeping the women with her, she stood at the porch waiting for the mad monk. The latter usually came on horseback, accompanied by his own servants.

The abbot was hesitant when he received the Princess's note, after what had happened to his monks at the temple. However, he remembered that the Empress herself had saved him from trial and told the prosecutor to let him off. Cautiously, he came in through the north gate and looked about. A large garden separated the entrance from the residential buildings. Passing around a pond, he came near the back of the residences, connected by winding, sheltered corridors.

Looking about guardedly, he saw only the usual palace maids. Princess Taiping was standing on the porch, smiling her welcome. He alighted, and was tying his horse under a tree when all of a sudden the women rushed out, threw ropes around him, tripped him and had him fairly entangled like fish in a net. With broomsticks and poles, the women went at him. The abbot roared and screamed, but his attendants had run away. Already the guards had rushed out from their hiding place, and felled him on the spot. The monk was killed then and there by the Princess's order, and his body was sent back to be burned at the White Horse Temple.

It was a neat job, well done, and the Princess was highly commended by her mother for it. It really appeared that her daughter was a replica of herself.

So ended the episode of the monk Shuay Huaiyi, only one month after the burning of "Paradise."

With the death of the mad monk, the Empress's adventure into Buddhism was terminated. In her revulsion against the abbot, she seemed to drop her Buddhism, too. Thirteen days after the abbot's death she announced she would drop the epithets *"Most Merciful"* and *"Eternal"* from her long honorary title. Her spell was suddenly broken. She didn't like the Buddhist reign-title *"Sainthood Confirmed"* anymore.

With her Confucian lover, Dr. Shen, she turned Confucianist. The years 695-6 were the maddest of all in respect to the reign-title which was changed four times in two years. First it was changed from *Sainthood Confirmed* to *Heaven-Appointed Banzai.* Then it was called *Banzai Elevated,* and again in September, 696, to *Banzai Reaching Heaven.* For these were Confucian concepts and "Heaven" was the Confucian term for God. When the new Mingtang was completed, it, too, was called "The Hall Reaching Heaven" (*Tungtien* Hall. *Tungtien* means "in touch with Heaven" or "in direct communication with Heaven"). The god had changed; the megalomania remained.

❋ 21 ❋

A foolish, but gay and highly enjoyable drama was now closed. While Lady Wu's private life was far from above reproach, her rule became more humane. The gang of illiterate judges and ruthless hangmen had been broken up, and the terror had stopped. The only one still living, Lai, was in disgrace. Since the attempted frame-up of Prince Dan, Lady Wu was sick of her nephew, Chengtse. Whenever she saw him, her black humors stirred. Chengtse, unpopular, uncouth, aggressive without intelligence and a flatterer without tact, was the visible symbol of the failure of her dream of a House of Glorious Wus. More and more, she turned her attention to another nephew, Sanse.

The year was 696. One is tempted to say that Grandmother, a woman of seventy-one, was at last growing mature, and even a woman must outgrow her childishness and her caprices sometime. Sound in body and mind, she began to recall the good ministers she had always admired secretly, men at degraded posts in the provinces now—the upright Judge Shyu Yugung, the hearty, forthright Wei Yuanjung, and the wise Judge Di Renjiay of detective fame, elderly men now in their sixties.

Truly, she could have been a great queen if she had not that excessive ambition. She did not exactly intend to reform, and meant to go on sinning. She was yet to have more pink episodes, pinker than that of the mad monk. A long life and a wicked one, wining, feasting, and orgies with her paramours—that was what she wanted for herself. As for the government of the country, she never had much trouble thinking about it, she had been governing for so long. She wanted it in the hands of good, honest men ruling over the good, honest and entirely moral common people. What else was there?

Di became the Attorney-General, and he had picked two of the strongest and best men to help him. Shyu Yugung was back, as Assistant Attorney-General. He was the honest judge who had dared to argue with Lady Wu and refused to condemn the mother of Prince Jer's wife, Dufei, for saying prayers for the soul of her murdered daughter. The dramatic Wei Yuanjung was back like an old oak which had survived a storm—three storms to be exact. He, too, was made Lord Secretary and a member of the Privy Council.

"Why did you always get into trouble?" Lady Wu asked him.

"I was the deer," replied Wei jokingly, "and men like Lai and Jou Shing wanted to make venison soup out of me."

Di Renjiay had been Governor of Yuchow (modern Peking), where he had driven away a Kitan invasion by first establishing close contact with the farmers and boosting their morale. In 698 he was called back to become Lady Wu's right-hand man at the head of the government. It looked as though the darkness of night had passed and dawn was breaking.

Lady Wu had an eye for the right men, the ablest and the best, and put Di at the head of the government. As for being really a good judge, Lady Wu was unaware that the appointment of Di to power was her own undoing. She had forgotten perhaps that at the trial Di had said, "As a loyal minister of Tang, I am willing to die."

Di came now trailing a cloud of glory like a comet attracting the lesser lights, and Lady Wu believed implicitly in him. The master judge-detective wore a pair of down-hanging whiskers and a goatee. His voice was pleasant and he had a natural eloquence, always seizing the right point, the important point, and expressing it firmly, incisively, like a good lawyer. Everyone he recommended was accepted by Lady Wu. He had gathered around the court twenty or thirty men, some, like Yao Tsung, promoted by him, others, like Sung Jing, who were already there. A transformation of the court atmosphere took place.

Di himself became concurrently Attorney-General. Judge Du Jingjien, who shared the reputation of incorruptibility with Shyu Yugung (p. 155) in the days of Lai-Soh, was made Vice-Secretary. With Shyu and Du as Assistant Attorneys-General, and Di himself at the head, it was now impossible for Chengtse to turn the Censorate into an instrument for committing legal excesses, as was once the case.

The first thing Shyu Yugung did as prosecutor was to impeach the most hated and feared executioner of the people, Lai.

Lai had now come back, occupying a small post, no longer the all-powerful Assistant Attorney-General. As usual, petty men like Lai and Chengtse fell out with each other when out of luck. Lai even threatened to impeach Chengtse himself and—worse for him—involve Princess Taiping, too. Ever ambitious, Lai was planning to come back to power. He was still very rich, had many concubines and was now embittered and grown careless. There were any number of things which Chengtse and Princess Taiping did that were being talked about. Chengtse, for instance, had forcibly taken another man's concubine and the concubine had committed suicide, and the poem which her husband wrote on her death passed from mouth to mouth. The teahouses seethed with such gossip. It was highly impolitic of Lai to repeat such gossip, especially in matters touching the Princess. That was his great mistake. Princess Taiping was not a person to be trifled with. A good politician herself, she pulled the strings to have Lai charged with a number of crimes—extortion, bribery, miscarriage of justice, taking another man's wife, etc.

On the day Lai was arrested for trial, all Loyang rejoiced. Everybody was thirsting for his blood. This man who had murdered hundreds of innocent people and ruined several thousand families was the most hated man of all. Shyu Yugung and the other judges had no difficulty in finding him guilty of all the charges.

The verdict of the judges was submitted to the Empress for approval. For three days she let it lie on her desk while, outside, the public waited tensely every minute for the news—whether Lai was to be executed, and when. One of the Empress's attendants, Ji Shyu,* had once been nearly ruined by Lai. He was now driving the Empress's carriage around the royal park.

"Why isn't the judges' report on Lai's case approved yet?" Ji Shyu asked. "The whole town is waiting to hear the news."

"He has done so much for the government," said the Empress. "I have been considering."

"But Lai's extortions could fill a mountain, and the ghosts of his victims fill the valleys. The whole court is getting quite wrought up and waiting for Your Majesty's approval."

Lai was now gagged and marched to the execution ground. An unprecedented crowd had gathered to watch the execution of the last of the executioners. As soon as his head fell, the crowd broke loose and surged forward, going berserk, screaming a veritable thunder of unrestrained madness. The crowd would like to take a good look at this man whose name had caused so many sleepless nights in so many a home.

* Lady Wu herself told Ji Shyu about the conversation with Taitsung about how to break a horse (Chapter 1).

The mob would like to sink its teeth into his flesh. But there was no chance. There was a rush for the body. The corpse was dragged and pulled about, torn limb from limb, kicked and stamped upon until it was a mess of bones and bloody paste. Someone got hold of an eye, or a wrist, without knowing why, and then threw it down in disgust.

That night, the people of Loyang said in their homes, "Now we can sleep with our backs touching the mat!"

Only then did the Empress realize the full extent of the people's hatred for the man she had used as her instrument for years. As a fine gesture, she decreed that his whole family be wiped out "so that the people's anger may be appeased."

With the death of Lai, the court settled into a dead calm, so much so that Lady Wu once asked Yao Tsung in surprise why she didn't hear of plots of rebellion anymore. Chengtse was quiescent and the courtiers breathed more easily. There had been a time, when Lai was in power, that officials going to office in the morning would say to their wives, "I do not know whether we shall see each other again." High officials could be picked up in the street, thrown into prison, charged with treason and never heard of again.

Chengtse now stood alone. Di's first move was obviously to have the question of succession settled. Chengtse's attempt to discredit Prince Dan had been foiled by the harakiri of An Jintsang. He was in a very uncomfortable position. No one was willing to support his claim.

Di had one purpose, to restore the imperial heirs Jer and Dan to the proper line of succession. Difficult but not impossible, in Di's judgment.

For Lady Wu now found herself in a political dilemma which she had not thought of before. *How was a woman who wanted to found a dynasty and yet not have her sons as heirs, to do it?* Here was a perplexing problem, the problem of a man who has built himself an estate all his life and sees no worthy relation in sight to bequeath it to. Unfortunately, being a woman, she had married into the Lis, and her sons were Lis. The conferring of the surname "Wu" on Uncle Dan was necessarily superficial. She had not wanted to see her son Prince Jer, now shut up and separated from her for fourteen years. She had not cared to send for him. She had Prince Dan at her apronstrings, or more correctly, sewed up in her pocket like a gambler's last penny. What was she to do with Dan?

Unfortunately, too, her father had only two grandsons, Chengtse and Sanse, who were cousins. She tried her best to found a dynasty with them but as she looked at them, her heart must have sunk within her. Chengtse and Sanse went about in their slick ingratiating way, haughty to some and obsequious to others—bullies and snobs at the same time—and invited only general hatred and contempt. Yitsung, another nephew, was a tiny man looking like a scarecrow, but ambitious. No matter what Yitsung and the other nephews wore, made as ample as possible to hide their small frames, they could not look royal; they had not the stature, nor the breeding, nor her intelligence and strength. None of them was properly educated nor, what was more important, knew how to respect scholars, nor cared for books. The heir presumptive, Chengtse, was physically so repulsive that Princess Taiping would on no account consent to the proposed match with him. Princess Taiping's husband, Shuay Shao, had died during the Princes' Rebellion. She was available, but she preferred another cousin, Yuji. Yuji was a married man, but when her preference was made known, Lady Wu had arranged for Yuji's wife to die conveniently and quickly, without stirring up too much attention.

At this time the Empress was more inclined to prefer her nephew Sanse to Chengtse, and asked her ministers about it. Di and another minister strongly opposed the suggestion.

The Empress was sincerely worried and could not make up her mind. Once she told Di about a dream that she always lost at chess, and asked Di's opinion. Di told her that the dream had a profound meaning. The word "chessmen" contains a pun; *tse* also means "sons."

"Your Majesty," he told her, "you lost because you had no chessmen. Without chessmen, you are bound to lose."

To convince Lady Wu that she must abandon the Wu nephews and put back the Tang princes was not easy. It went against all her previous plans for the new dynasty. But the master detective-judge was also a convincing talker.

Di drove home an unanswerable argument which won the day. Like all great ideas, it was simple. The Empress, like every old woman, would think it horrible to die without proper seasonal offerings of food at the ancestral temple. Di really scared her.

One day the question came up again, and Di said to her, "There is no question but that Your Majesty must make one of your sons the heir. Then your spirit tablet will occupy a seat in the imperial ancestral temple, rightfully as an emperor's parent, and receive the sacrifices forever and ever. But it would be unthinkable for an emperor to place his aunt's spirit tablet in the temple.* It is unheard of, and against all rules. Besides, you must consider which relationship is closer, mother and son, or aunt and nephew? Even sons have rebelled against their parents. What assurances have you that your nephews will always remember your kindness and not ignore you or turn against you?"

The argument went home. The rules and rituals about ancestor worship are sharply defined and rigorously prescribed, and Lady Wu knew it. She hated to think of herself

* An aunt would be married and her spirit tablet would be found in her husband's ancestral temple, in this case the Lis, not in that of her nephews, the Wus.

as a starving ghost, unprayed to and uncared for. The last point, a realistic one, was fully appreciated by Lady Wu. She certainly could imagine that Chengtse or Sanse might neglect her or even dishonor her after her death. She had always admired Di's wisdom and judgment. But she was not ready to yield.

"This is my domestic affair. I will decide," she replied.

Di pressed further. "Don't forget that yours is the Royal House. There's nothing in your domestic affairs which is not the affair of the government, and nothing in the affairs of government which is not your domestic affair. The question of heirship is of concern to the imperial family, but also to all your subjects, and to me as your servant. This question affects the foundation of the state, and must be settled clearly and definitely." Di waxed eloquent and spoke with real feeling. "The great Taitsung went through the smoke and dust of battle to win this empire. He risked dangers and hardships and toiled and labored to establish this Royal House, which he bequeathed to your late husband. And now his sons are in your sacred trust. Prince Jer and Prince Dan are your own sons. From any angle, it would be the right thing to do to make Prince Jer or Prince Dan your heir."

Lady Wu had been perplexed by this question for years. Now she saw, as Di had pointed out to her, it was a choice between being the next sovereign's mother, or aunt. Which was more secure?

Lady Wu said one day again to Di, "Which shall it be? Jer or Dan?"

"Of course, Prince Jer, by seniority," said Di. His advice was always clear, definite.

Prince Jer, who had been separated from his mother for fourteen years, was now sent for together with his wife. Their return, however, was kept a secret. It was said that Prince Jer was ill and had returned for treatment. Jer's mind was already conditioned to fear and abject obedience. He still remembered how as a young emperor he had been abruptly dragged off the throne. He did not know exactly why he had been sent for or what was going to happen to him.

Di went in and spoke to the Empress again to press for a decision. Had Her Majesty not yet made up her mind? Why did she keep it a secret? The very purpose of welcoming the Prince home was to set the people's minds at rest regarding the heirship. Di was always persuasive. He always played upon the close relationship between mother and son.

At last, Lady Wu's maternal instinct was awakened, or she was strongly convinced of what was for her own good if she wanted to be fed regularly in afterlife. She called Prince Jer out from behind the curtain and said warmly to Di: "There, I return to you your Crown Prince!"

Di and the Prince went down on their knees to thank her, and Di congratulated her on having made the right decision.

"This must not be a secret," said Di.

"What would you suggest?"

"Prince Jer's return has not been seen by the people. I suggest that he and the Princess go out to be formally welcomed by Your Majesty at the Lungmen Station as if on their return. Thus the nation shall know that your son has come back."

The advice was followed, and the act of welcoming Prince Jer back was formally gone through. This was in March, 698.

Prince Jer was now proclaimed the crown heir. Chengtse saw his hopes dashed to pieces. There was hardly anyone alive to stand by him. And his aunt had turned against him. He fell ill, and died in September of the same year, a frustrated and disappointed man.

Uncle Dan had yielded to his brother's claim without any resentment. In the following year, I and Uncle Dan's children, among them the present sovereign (Minghuang), were permitted to leave the Palace and began our normal life of liberty. I was twenty-nine then, and our present Emperor was only fourteen. I felt like a bird which had been freed from a cage. I should have been greatly excited at this new freedom to see the streets and the shops and the common people's houses once more. But I remember I wasn't. Something in me had died. It took me years before I shed the attitude of caution and silence and fear and began to live a normal life again.

Di was getting old. He had done the best he could. He was treated royally by the Empress. Everywhere he went and at every public appearance he was given special honors. The Empress called him not by name or title, but addressed him as *guolao*, "elder statesman."

He saw the muddle and the feud between the Lis and the Wus which must be played out to the end, for the Wus were entrenched in power. There were things he could not know, he told himself. How would all this end? Of one thing he was sure, that the situation called for a man of action and unusual courage, capable of making great decisions. The Empress had so far accepted all his recommendations for office. It looked to him that there were enough men of sterling character to act together at a crisis. Good old Wei Yuanjung was there. And there were some good men in the younger generation, Yao Tsung and Sung Jing,* for example. Morale was high, which was the principal thing.

But he had also a far higher objective in mind, the eventual overthrow of the Jou Dynasty. There were some among his friends, men he had known for a lifetime, men he knew he could trust. He thought first of all of (Jang) Jienje, who was then only a district magistrate. He knew Jienje, a man of

* Yao Tsung and Sung Jing became the much admired great ministers under Minghuang.

few words, quiet and deep, but of unusual ability. They had one thing in common, the secret great purpose of restoring the Tang Dynasty and overthrowing the Jou.

One day, the Empress asked Di if he could recommend a man for an important post.

"How important?"

"I want a man of outstanding ability, who can act and lead and think ahead of others."

"That depends upon what you want him for."

"I want a man who some day may head the civil government or the military forces."

Di replied, "If Your Majesty just wants a scholar to carry on as royal assistant, men like Su Weidow will do. But if you want a man of force and character, a real leader, there's Jang Jienje."

What the Empress had exactly in mind when she spoke to Di was not clear. Jienje was made a magistrate in the metropolitan district. It was important enough, a post which Di himself had once occupied. Perhaps the Empress was going to try out Jienje's ability.

Another day, the Empress asked him again for a good man.

"But I have already recommended Jienje."

"I have already appointed him."

"That was not what I meant. I recommended him not for a magistrate's job, but for a prime minister!"

Jienje was promoted next a Vice-Minister of Justice. Eventually he ended up as head of the government.

Di felt his end was coming. He knew he would die happy, for he had placed his pawns well and would leave the rest to Heaven. Later events show that the men who staged a *coup d'état* to restore the Tang Monarchy (Jienje, Yao Tsung, Jing Hwei, Huan, Tsui and Yuan) were all men recommended by him. After having a long private talk with Jienje, he died, in 700, at the age of seventy-one. He knew that when the time came, Jienje would set the court on fire. He didn't have to do it himself. It was like a perfect murder, conceived by the master detective, the greatest mind of his generation.

❋ 22 ❋

Before Di died, Lady Wu had already been having affairs with two new favorites, the notorious Jang brothers, already mentioned. Di had his ways. He regarded these young men in their twenties as the Empress's "mistresses"; the Empress's affairs were her own, and he had bigger things to do. He could, like the master detective which he was, even utilize these male mistresses of the female emperor at times. As a matter of fact, he had made use of them to speak for Prince Jer and Prince Dan; a detective always had his line of persuasion. And in any case his reading of the signs of the times was correct. He had probably calculated in his analytical mind that the degeneration of the morals of the court was directly helpful to the restoration of the Tang Monarchy. The straight-talking Wei told Lady Wu that these handsome boys of her harem were going to be her ruin. Di did not have the same kindness to tell her.

Lady Wu was now not satisfied with the Confucian physician, Dr. Shen. After having had two lovers, she moved on to have three, four, or five. She was now establishing what could only be called a male harem. It is entirely easy to believe that the old woman, aged seventy-three, wanted to relax and enjoy herself. A woman who had proceeded from "Sainthood Confirmed" to "*Banzai* Reaching Heaven" could be expected to do no less. It is also entirely appropriate that, as an old king often enjoys himself with young girls, whether sexually competent or not, so a queen should enjoy the company of the opposite sex by keeping a harem of handsome young men.

The Jang boys, in their twenties, were fair-skinned and remarkably handsome—Yijy the elder, and Tsatsu (short for Tsangtsung) the younger. They were popularly called "No. 5 Bridegroom" and "No. 6 Bridegroom" ("Wulang," "Liulang") for that was their seniority at home. They came to the Palace, faces rouged, hair heavily pomaded, and keeping chicken-tongue (a spice, breath-perfumer) in their mouths. No. 6 Bridegroom was particularly handsome and it was currently said his face was "like a lotus." A certain Yang (Jyrou), a great flatterer, once said to Tsatsu that it was rather the lotus that should envy the beauty of his face. These brothers now practically lived in the Palace, although they had been given mansions and huge estates with servants and cattle. Their mother, Madame Tsang, also had a "lover by imperial decree"—that is, with the Empress's express approval—in the person of Vice-Minister of War Li Jyungshiu.

Tsatsu the younger was Princess Taiping's discovery. Unable to contain her delight, she shared the good news with her mother. The Empress found that all her daughter had said about him was true. Overnight, Tsatsu was made a "General of Flying Colors." Tsatsu then revealed to the old woman that his elder brother was even better in the art of love, being a specialist in aphrodisiacs and rejuvenation. Again Lady Wu found that what Tsatsu had said was true. Indeed, from Yijy's continued popularity with the old lady, he must have had special ways of exciting and satisfying the old rouée. Lady Wu certainly had remarkable vitality. At sixty-seven she grew a new wisdom tooth, and at seventy-four, probably as the result of Yijy's aphrodisiacs, she grew a new set of eyebrows, which was officially celebrated with a dinner.

Nobody would have been surprised if she grew a pair of whiskers.

Tsatsu was physically the more attractive, but Yijy was the more practiced lover. Choice between the two was difficult, but choice was unnecessary—she could have both. And in any case, the mother and daughter could well do with two men. Forgotten were the abbot and the elderly doctor. Here was youth, beauty, and joy. From now on till her last day, Lady Wu would not let these two men out of her sight. She could not live without them.

That it was a true sexual romance and not merely an old woman's fantasy is shown by her jealousy. There was a girl secretary who was very fond of Tsatsu. She was no other than the granddaughter of the poet Shangguan Yi. When Shangguan was condemned for trying to induce Gaotsung to depose Lady Wu (p. 91), his family were turned into slaves to work in officials' households. Miss Shangguan, whose name was Wan-erl, had practically grown up in the Palace. Moreover, she was a gifted writer. Now a lady of rank, she had been in charge of drafting edicts for Lady Wu since 696. (Later, under Jungtsung, she was once chief examiner of the scholars for civil service.) Needless to say, the attraction was probably mutual between her and Tsatsu. They had met so often at the wining and gaming tables. Their flirtations perhaps went too far. One day, in their happiness at being together, they had forgotten about Lady Wu's presence. "How dare you!" Lady Wu exclaimed and flashed a golden pocketknife at the young girl. Miss Shangguan quickly shrank away to avoid it. Worse could have happened if Tsatsu had not gone down on his knees and begged forgiveness on her behalf. The knife had scraped the girl's forehead, and later she always wore her curls on one side to cover up the scar. Miss Shangguan never tried flirting with Tsatsu again, at least not in Lady Wu's presence. She was quite a devil, and later shared her lover Sanse with the Empress of Jungtsung (Prince Jer). Between the two women, they almost turned the court upside down.

The affair of the Jang brothers soon turned into an institution. What were the two brothers doing at the Palace and what was their office? people asked. Obviously, Lady Wu did not want her lovers to be encumbered with office duties of a vice-premier or a minister, or even to be chief of an independent bureau—the Armory, the Protocol, etc. But if gossip was to be stopped and their uncastrated presence in the Palace justified, a new office should be created for them. Hence the Stork Institute. The elder brother Yijy was made President of the Institute.

The name, Stork Institute, set off that of the Unicorn Terrace (imperial library) nicely. It was appropriate also because the stork was the symbol of Taoist immortals riding on those birds to the never-never-land of eternal bliss. To make them chamberlains would be too earthly and involve real duties and to make them anything less, such as Guardian of Chamber-pots, would be too realistic. But an institute must have a purpose; Lady Wu had thought that out, too. It was to be an institute of intellectual research. Having an institute also meant having a staff of secretaries. It was decided that the best subject for research was on the three religions, and the editorial staff, headed by Yijy, was to compile an *Anthology of the Three Religions*, of Confucius's sayings, Laotse's sayings and Buddha's sayings, together with those of the saints and lesser philosophers.

The anthology was to consist of passages of an inspirational nature, rather than abstruse philosophy. In general, discourses on the vanity of life and the emptiness of all existence could lead to greater devotion and higher living. But it could also lead to a more practical epicureanism. . . . In any case, scholarly research did not appear to be the principal duty of the inmates of the Stork Institute, although there was a sprinkling of scholars and writers among them. Their work was more accurately described by their office, which was frankly *gungfeng,* or "royal attendants" to Her Majesty.

The real business going on was wining, dining and gambling. It seemed that Lady Wu had the idea of making the institute a fairy palace. It was appropriately situated around the sumptuously carved and decorated Yaoguang Hall, evoking memories of the debauchery of the Sui Emperor who had lost his throne by his love of women. At its back was the royal garden a mile long with an oblong pond and two islets, surrounded by trees, shrubs and decorative arches and winding corridors with carved and painted girders.

The fiction was now created that Tsatsu was an ancient Taoist immortal, Wang Tsetsin, in his previous incarnation. To make this Taoist dream of fairyland come true for Lady Wu, Tsatsu was dressed in the feather coat of a Taoist immortal and, playing a flute, was made to ride around the park on a wooden stork, to the admiration and envy of all.

In the end, however, the Stork Institute was filled with a number of handsome young men. It became thoroughly notorious as a homosexual center. Its notoriety produced the most amusing letter a subject ever wrote to a queen. A certain young man, Wei, had publicly claimed qualifications to be a member of the Stork Institute on the ground of his subabdominal beauty. This aroused the wrath of Ju Jingtser, an old dignified scholar of seventy who had earlier written against the judicial excesses of Lai and company (p. 202). He saw it as his duty as censor to write an official letter of protest to the Empress:

> Your Majesty, it has seemed to me that you have already your favorites in Yijy and Tsatsu. Are they not enough for

> you, but there must be more boys? The court is filled with ugly gossip. I hear that a Wei Houshiang claims to be admitted as a royal attendant on the strength of his personal excellences, and there are others beside him . . .

The Empress said to Ju, after reading the letter: "Thank you for the letter. I didn't know!"

The Confucian scholars generally looked askance at this exhibition of moral depravity. Sung Jing, a minister of fiery temper and uncompromising character, once insulted Tsatsu by calling him "Madame" to his face. And once Chancellor Wei Anshe, coming upon the gambling tables and finding that the Jang brothers had brought in common merchants from Szechuan, had the merchants thrown out.

After Ju Jingtser's letter, Grandmother was aware of the terrible reputation of the Stork Institute abroad. She thought she should change its name, and called it plainly *Fengchenfu,* or Bureau of Royal Attendants. Between her carousals, she had to spend half her time in bed.

Gossip buzzed. Prince Jer's son, now called "Crown Grandson"—another innovation of Grandmother's—was thoroughly disgusted. He was a young man just about twenty, and his sister had newly married Chengtse's son, Yenji. The brother and sister could not help discussing between themselves the disgraceful conduct of their grandmother. When Grandmother heard this, she thought it lack of respect for the elders. Old age had not softened her, but made her harder and coarser and more temperamental. She had her own grandson and granddaughter whipped to death, and then asked the granddaughter's husband Yenji to hang himself.

* 23 *

Such scandals did not stop the gossip, but increased it. Opposition to Lady Wu increased as her morals degenerated. The ministers at court were now solidly arrayed against the Jang brothers, whose cousins had steadily grown more arrogant and were running riot in the capital, just as the mad monk had behaved a decade ago. So long as these boys kept to their harem to amuse the Empress, they would shut their eyes to it. But Tsatsu's other brothers and Tsatsu himself were getting ambitious and in many ways interfered with the running of a decent administration. The scholars took it as a personal insult to allow such a state of things to go on. Already there were posted bills against these inmates of the Stork Institute, against No. 5 Bridegroom and No. 6 Bridegroom. Their scandals had traveled faster than an edict sent by the imperial courier system; every teahouse and every wineshop was a relay station for the "doings at the Stork Institute" which later became the title of a book.

In particular, the forceful Wei Yuanjung would permit no nonsense. When Tsatsu's household servants committed breaches of the peace, he had them flogged publicly. One of the brothers, Tsachi, was a sub-prefect of the metropolis under him. Tsachi ordered people about and was taking liberties upsetting all office rules and regulations; on the strength of his brothers' influence, he was running the office as if he owned it. Wei reprimanded him before his staff and blocked his appointment to a well-paid post he was seeking. In addition, he wrote to the Empress, "I am ashamed that as Your Majesty's servant I have not been able to carry out my duty and have permitted disreputable characters to attend upon you." The phrase "disreputable characters" (*shiaoren*) clearly referred to the favorites of the Empress.

The feud was in the open now. As far as Wei Yuanjung was concerned, his purpose was to clean out the government and rid it of the handsome boys. He was not in the inner ring of Jienje and Yao Tsung. Tsatsu opened the first attack. He accused Wei before the Empress of having said that she was getting old and they should all rally to the support of Prince Jer. This was exactly the kind of accusation to inflame Lady Wu. Return the throne to her son? Not so long as she was alive!

The affair became a big fight between Lady Wu's favorites on the one hand, and the ministers solidly behind Wei Yuanjung on the other. The Empress regarded it as a very serious charge and ordered a court session of the high ministers, at which Prince Jer and Prince Dan were also present. Wei was to be questioned and defend himself.

Tsatsu had induced a (Jang) Yuay to testify that he had heard Wei say the thing he was accused of. Yuay, a poet, was at that time a fifth-rank official and Tsatsu had promised him a quick promotion. The cunning Yuay had probably given his promise that he would.

The ministers were assembled in the antechamber, ready to go in. Now there was the fiery Sung Jing, Assistant Attorney-General, who said to Yuay:

"I should regret it very much, Yuay, if you should lend yourself to do harm to the Lord Secretary. What are you afraid of? Those *mesdames* brothers? This is our fight, for all of us. Fight like a man and public opinion will be behind you. I will back you up. It will be an honor to be dismissed or exiled for fighting those girls."

There were a number of scholars present, among them the famous historian, or rather philosopher of history, Liu Jyji.*

"Death with honor, or promotion with dishonor. Make your choice," said Liu. Others also urged him to turn against Tsatsu. There was such an atmosphere of general belligerence that Yuay changed his mind, if he had ever promised Tsatsu to cooperate.

Wei now came in, his face angry. Seeing Yuay, he said, "So you are testifying against Wei Yuanjung, you rascal!" Wei was always dramatic.

Yuay replied, "Why, Your Excellency, such language! You can trust me."

The bell had sounded. There was no time to continue the discussion. The ministers filed in.

Now it was an amusing contest between the pretty half-educated favorite and the learned scholars. Her Majesty opened the meeting and asked Yuay what he had heard. While Yuay was preparing to reply, thinking what to say, Tsatsu gave him a nudge.

"Come on, speak!"

"Your Majesty," said Yuay, "here in the very presence of Your Majesty, Tsatsu is pressing me to say what he wants. You can imagine what he does outside. Now in front of all Their Royal Highnesses and Their Excellencies, I must tell the full court that I never heard the Lord Secretary say that we should support the Crown Prince against Your Majesty. That was what Tsatsu wanted me to testify, but I am sorry, it is not true."

Tsatsu was aghast, furious. He forgot himself and shouted, "Yuay and Wei are in a conspiracy together!"

"This is a very grave charge," said Lady Wu. "You should not make such a charge unless you could prove it."

"I have the facts."

* Author of *Shytung,* one of the best books on the writing of history.

"What facts?"

"I once heard Yuay say to Yuanjung [Wei] that he should try to be Duke Jou."

The ministers were really relieved, and could not conceal their laughter. Why, Duke Jou was the sage, the ideal gentleman of Confucius, the man Confucius dreamed about. Tsatsu had meant that Wei's ambition was to be like the all-powerful Duke Jou, but there had never been a more loyal minister in history. To compare a man to Duke Jou was the highest form of flattery.

"I am sorry," replied Yuay. "Tsatsu should know his elementary history better. It is true that when His Excellency came back, I went to offer my congratulations on his promotion. I expressed the hope that His Excellency would be a Duke Jou. Whom else should he hold as his model if not Duke Jou?"

The court laughed. Tsatsu was discomfited and whispered something in Lady Wu's ears. Lady Wu was angry. "You double-crosser!" she said to Yuay, and had him and Wei ushered out of her presence pending further hearing.

The next day, under questioning, Yuay stuck to his story. It became necessary for the princes and all privy councilors to try Yuay and Wei in open session. Lady Wu's nephew, Yitsung, was also among the judges.

Wei's case became a hot public issue. The ministers all rallied to the support of Wei. Wei was the stormy petrel, always the center of some attack. On his recall from exile, all officials and people had acclaimed his triumphant return and given the Empress credit for "being a good judge of men." Now a score of officials deluged the Empress with letters, and Huan (Yenfan), a man recommended by Di Renjiay, offered to guarantee Wei's loyalty with his own life.

However, a word whispered at the pillow was always more

effective than a prosecutor's harangue in court. Lady Wu liked Wei and always had. But she could not make her favorite boy lose face. Proved guilty or not, she sent Wei once more to exile.

Wei came to say good-bye to Her Majesty.

"Your servant is old, and there is but one chance in ten that I may come back alive. But take my advice. There will be a time when you will think of Wei Yuanjung and remember his words."

"Why?" asked Lady Wu kindly.

Pointing to Tsatsu and Yijy, who were in the room, Wei said, "Those two young men will be the ruin of you!"

Wei said farewell and left.

"So Yuanjung is gone!" said Lady Wu regretfully after Wei had departed.

But the matter did not end there. It was an obvious travesty of justice. Wei had been dismissed from court for no discoverable reason at all, except that he had run against the Empress's favorite. But Tsatsu was not satisfied. It was the custom for friends to give a farewell dinner at the suburb when an official was going far away. Eight friends had seen Wei off and given such a dinner. Tsatsu had a "letter of secret information" sent under the forged name of "Tsaiming" alleging that Wei and his friends were plotting rebellion on that day at the suburb.

These friends were only minor officials, and Lady Wu appointed a judge to try the eight men. She, or Tsatsu, asked a palace officer to send word to the judge, "Her Majesty says this is a simple case. Just give a questioning and report quickly."

The judge, Huaisu, did not think it so simple. He did not want to be a party to the destruction of Wei Yuanjung, whom he admired greatly. For if the charge was true, Wei

Yuanjung could easily be granted death at his place of exile, and nobody would be able to stop it. Lady Wu, or rather Tsatsu, again sent word: "The facts are clear. What is causing the delay? Her Majesty is getting impatient."

Judge Huaisu was compelled to see the Empress. He just could not find the accuser, the person called "Tsaiming" or what his address and profession were.

"How do I know where is Tsaiming? The letter is enough," said Lady Wu.

"I am sorry, Your Majesty. I cannot give a decision unless I have a chance to question the accuser."

"Just go on the basis of the letter of information. It is not necessary to produce the accuser."

"But it is," said the judge. "I cannot go upon a paper witness. For all I know, there may be no such person. I cannot judge a case without plaintiff and without witness, just on the strength of a letter from an anonymous informer whose identity and whereabouts are not even known."

"So you mean to let the accused traitors free?"

"How dare I?" replied the judge. "But Wei was Lord Secretary to Your Majesty. His friends were obviously giving him a farewell dinner before his long journey. I cannot in my conscience believe that Wei Yuanjung is a rebel. Your Majesty has the power to put him to death if you want to. Just give an order to that effect. But if you want me to condemn him at court as a judge, I cannot do otherwise than proceed according to law."

"Do you mean that, according to law, these men shall go free?"

"I am a stupid man, Your Majesty," said Huaisu. "But I just don't see what those eight men are guilty of."

The facts were so triumphantly clear that it would be embarrassing even for the Empress to punish the judge. She allowed the case to drop, and consoled Tsatsu by some other form of her favor.

Wei went down a third time, to come up again, more loved and honored than ever.

❋ 24 ❋

The sorry mess which Lady Wu and her lover had made in the arbitrary persecution of Wei made a bad impression on the minds of all the court officials. The ministers and secretaries, men recommended by Di and others, closed ranks. Public sentiment was bitter, even rebellious, so unlike the days when Lai was in power. The names of the handsome boys now appeared in placards, were celebrated in songs and ditties, and provided refreshing titbits to go with tea and melon seeds in the wineshops, as naughty and entertaining as the exploits of the mad monk. It was very embarrassing for Lady Wu. Her prosecutors were not doing their duty, she thought. Tsachi, brother of Tsatsu, had become fabulously rich, living in a great mansion. The more money these brothers had made, the more ambitious they became, and the more ambitious they were, the greater their unpopularity. An anonymous person used to chalk words on Tsachi's gate at night: *How long is this going to last?* They were wiped out the next morning, but the words appeared the next night and the next, for six or seven successive days, always repeating the same question: *How long is this going to last?* At last, desperate and growing impatient, Tsachi himself chalked a reply haughtily: *One day of enjoyment is enough!*

Now the two causes of destroying the unpopular Tsatsu and Yijy, and of rebellion and forcing the Empress to abdicate, became merged into one. Some fifteen persons in the inner ring, led by Jienje, kept the plan to themselves. They were men who could keep a secret. These were the leaders placed in position by Di Renjiay: Jienje, Yang (Yuanyen), Jing Hwei, Huan (Yenfan), Yuan (Shuji) and Tsui (Shyuanwei). The general hostility against the Jang brothers included a wider range of officials who were not let into the secret, but who fought zealously for the purge of the Empress's favorites. It was a good cause to rally the support of all, and provided the best pretext for a *coup d'état.*

The Stork Institute could stink, for all the ministers cared, so long as its orgies were confined to the queen's private chambers. But their influence was growing, and it was an upsetting one. The ministers decided to strike back. They were never in better form. Thus the officials sought some means to entangle Tsatsu legally, while Jienje said not a word to others except his own men.

Years before, Jienje had made a secret pledge with his friend Yang (Yuanyen) to restore the Tang Dynasty and drive out Lady Wu (p. 196). One of the first acts of Jienje on coming to power was to appoint Yang commander of one of the units of the palace guards.

"I have not made this appointment without a purpose," said Jienje. "Do you remember what we said in a boat on the Yangtse one moonlight night?"

Yang understood. Yao Tsung, another appointee of Di Renjiay, was also an important link in the inner circle. It was Yao Tsung who had urged Lady Wu to appoint Jienje Lord Chancellor.

Matters quickly came to a head. Wei Yuanjung's dismissal was in 703. In the following year Lady Wu was constantly ill. For months she was confined to her room with her two lovers at her side. Even privy councilors could not see her. The lovers were worried. What would happen if their Lady Protector was gone? Lady Wu was already seventy-eight. The best beaver's male glands and other rejuvenators in the world could not stay the march of the years. The lovers, seeing that they were hated all around, began to maneuver and make allies and consolidate their power. Already posters appeared in the streets saying that the brothers were plotting to put themselves on the throne.

In July the officials found a chance to prosecute Tsatsu for depriving a farmer of his land. Jienje let them do it, knowing that a legal prosecution would only further damage the brothers' reputation and intensify public hatred against them. It would also put Lady Wu in a very awkward situation. Whether Tsatsu was condemned, or justice was thwarted again as in the case of Wei's dismissal, it would be bad publicity for Lady Wu and her lovers. Jienje could not lose.

A case of an official depriving a poor farmer of his land by pressure was a crime punishable by a fine of twenty pounds of copper and dismissal. The prosecutors recommended that Tsatsu be deprived of all his rank and offices. Lady Wu sensed the political atmosphere. Her favorites were unpopular, she knew. But she felt that in attacking Tsatsu they were challenging herself and closing in on her.

At the meeting of the ministers, Lady Wu said: "I know you people do not like him. The people under him may have used pressure to take land from a farmer. However, Tsatsu has done so much for me as your sovereign. For the sake of his past, let him keep his post."

"What has he done?" asked Sung Jing.

Lady Wu turned to Yang (Jyrou), a close follower of Tsatsu, celebrated in a poem "The Two-Legged Fox."

"He has, hasn't he?" she asked Yang.

"Yes, indeed, Your Majesty. He has secured the most rare medicine for your rejuvenation and longevity."

Yang had meant this seriously. But the ministers smirked.

"Well," said Lady Wu. "Tsatsu shall retain his post."

The ministers did not relax. Wei Anshe and another minister sent in formal impeachments of Tsatsu, and two judges were appointed to examine his case. When it was clear that the judges meant business, Lady Wu resorted to the subterfuge of suddenly appointing Wei Anshe and the other judge to some post away from the capital. The prosecutions were shelved.

In December of that year, however, Tsatsu was faced with a graver charge, that of having consulted a fortuneteller about his chances of becoming Emperor. The divination-sticks indicated a pure, homogeneous *yang,* a sign that Tsatsu was to become Emperor. The fortuneteller Li Hungtai told him so, and furthermore advised him to build a temple at Dingchow for good luck.

The fortuneteller was arrested and questioned. Li confessed that indeed the divination-sticks had shown a pure *yang,* and confirmed the interview with Tsatsu about the chances of his becoming Emperor. The case was formally presented to Lady Wu, and Tsatsu lost no time in writing a formal letter informing her of the fortuneteller's words. He would thus be able to say that he had reported the matter fully to Her Majesty. That was his defense. Furthermore, he arranged for Lady Wu to appoint two of his own men as judges. The judges returned the verdict that indeed he was guilty, but in view of the fact that he had reported the information to Her Majesty and had not kept it from her, he should be pardoned.

Assistant Attorney-General Sung Jing stood his ground. It was a grievous offense, involving clear intentions of treason, he wrote to the Empress. Why had Tsatsu failed to report before and did so only after the case had been brought to court? He demanded the arrest and handing over of Tsatsu for trial.

Lady Wu did not like it at all and shelved the letter. But

Sung Jing wrote again. "What will the public say if such a crime goes without investigation?"

Lady Wu now tried to delay the case.

"The case will be properly dealt with," said Lady Wu. "Wait a while. I want to take a look at the documents myself."

Lady Wu was not prepared to throw her lover to the dogs. They wanted his blood, she knew. Sung Jing was as stubborn as a mule, as difficult to bring around as Wei Yuangjung. She issued an order for Sung Jing to investigate a case at Yangchow in the south, resorting to the same subterfuge by which she had sent away Wei Anshe. Sung Jing refused to move, on the ground of his official duty at the capital. Then she had him appointed to investigate a case at Yuchow (Peking). Sung Jing refused again.

"I am sorry. My duty prevents me from obeying Your Majesty's order. According to the regulations, an assistant prosecutor is sent out to investigate cases where local officials of higher ranks are involved, and a curcuit judge, if of lower rank. As an assistant attorney-general, I cannot leave my post unless it is a case of the first importance."

The case hung fire. Lady Wu refused to hand over Tsatsu, who was safe and secure in her palace. The ministers made a concentrated attack. Huan (Yenfan) wrote to the Empress:

> Tsatsu has twice violated the criminal law. But he is still at large. If he is not arrested for trial, why not let all the criminals go free? This strikes at the foundation of law and order in the state.

Unable to get at the accused, the Attorney-General's Office went upon the basis of the fortuneteller's affidavits and Tsatsu's own admission to the Empress, and recommended that Tsatsu's acts constituted treasonable conduct, subject to the supreme penalty. With this report in hand, Sung Jing went in once more to the Palace to demand the immediate handing over of the accused.

"Here is the decision of the judges," said Sung Jing. "I request Your Majesty to let the criminal be tried."

"But he has reported the incident to me. That shows he is not disloyal at heart."

"He did so only after the case was brought to the Prosecutor's Office. He would have kept quiet, if it wasn't. Nor is this a crime which can be pardoned merely by the defendant's admission. The admission was not voluntary. What will remain of respect for the law if exception is made of a man who is in Your Majesty's favor?"

Lady Wu now tried to pacify Sung Jing. Her only concern was to save her lover who was in trouble, and the Assistant Attorney-General might be persuaded to let him go.

"Would you please consider?"

"I know that I have offended Your Majesty. But duty is duty, and I am prepared to die at my post."

It became an impasse between the stubborn queen and the equally stubborn minister. To save the situation, the Two-Legged Fox, who was at the Empress's side, said, "Her Majesty will make the decision. You are permitted to retire."

Lady Wu was in a dilemma. She could not flout the law too openly. The only thing she could do would be to repeat what she had done to save the abbot from trial.

Tsatsu was sent over to the Prosecutor's Office. Sung Jing thought he had succeeded at last. He proceeded with the questioning, which was properly taken down. Before he got very far, an emissary from the Palace brought a note from the Empress summoning Tsatsu to go back to the Palace immediately.

"Damnation!" cursed Sung Jing under his breath. "I should have flogged the rascal to death at the first instance. Now he is gone!"

So justice was once more thwarted. The Empress's favorite had escaped the law through the shameless intervention of the old, infatuated woman! Her perverse protection of one guilty under the law had now been ruthlessly exposed. The Jang brothers had done enough to hang, and many high ministers had been hanged for less.

The officials' patience was exhausted. The Jang brothers must be eliminated, by fair means or foul. Jienje took action.

* 25 *

Lady Wu was very ill all through December, when the case was on. The turn of the year found her still worse. She was eighty. No royal assistant or privy councilor was admitted to her presence, not even her own sons. Only the two brothers were constantly by her bedside.

Jienje decided to strike. The general contempt for the notorious Bridegroom No. 5 and Bridegroom No. 6 made it easy to find a common cause to support. He had already appointed his friend Yang a general of the palace guards. There were several units of palace guards and metropolitan gendarmes, both cavalry and infantry. Roughly, the so-called South Guards were the police force responsible for maintaining peace and order in the capital, while the North Guards were charged with the duty of protecting the Forbidden City, where all the government bureaus, besides the Palace, were situated. These were divided again into various units, under six commanders of a general's rank. The most important one was the commander-in-chief (Li Duotsa). Jienje proceeded secretly and cautiously to win over the commander-in-chief. Duotsa was reminded of his debt of gratitude to the Tang Emperors. He was an honest man and they took an oath before Heaven in the privacy of Jienje's house.

Next Jienje appointed another three of his own men to the posts of commanders. Yao Tsung, one of the inner circle, had been sent for, and he had just arrived from his post about a hundred miles away.

"That's perfect," he said when he heard of Yao Tsung's arrival. He informed Yao of the plan.

The *coup d'état* was set for January the twenty-second, a month after Lady Wu's intervention for Tsatsu. Every detail had been carefully worked out. Simultaneous action was to be taken by the South and North Guards. While the metropolitan police rounded up Tsatsu's brothers and took over their properties in the city, the North Guards, a force of one thousand cavalry and five hundred soldiers, were to surround the Palace and force the abdication of Lady Wu.

On the morning of January the twenty-second, 705, the palace guards were gathered at the North Gate of the Palace. Jienje, Huan, Duotsa, and the other leaders were all there. Among these was a son-in-law of Prince Jer.

Commander Duotsa went in with the son-in-law to see Prince Jer. His presence was necessary because the *coup d'état* was staged in his name, to put him on the throne. He had not been aware of it. Perplexed and a little frightened, he did not know what to do or what to say.

Duotsa lost patience. "This is a great day. Do you know what we are doing? Restoring the Tang Monarchy, the monarchy of your grandfather, Taitsung! We and the officers are ready to risk our lives for the great cause. The least you can do is to appear and lead them."

Prince Jer was still hesitant, quivering inside. "I know that the Jang brothers deserve this. But my mother is so ill . . . And this is so unexpected . . ."

"All right, you go out and tell the officers yourself that you don't care. If this does not come off, our families will be wiped out." If Prince Jer had refused, they would have had to escort him and put him on the throne by force.

The son-in-law (Wag Tungjao) put in his plea. "You've got to do it. No time must be lost. The guards are outside the gate, ready to march in and support you as Emperor. You yourself will not be safe if today's venture does not come off."

Rather hesitantly Prince Jer was assisted on to his horse, not knowing whether he was going to his throne or to his death.

The Crown Prince's compound was connected with the Northern Gate by a long garden. Jienje and the others breathed an audible relief when the Prince appeared.

At once the men entered the palace gate and set off in different directions according to a previous order, Duotsa's own unit going straight toward Lady Wu's quarters at the Welcome Fairies Court.

Hearing the commotion, Tsatsu and Yijy came out, sensing something unusual. All over the place, the guards were pouring in around the pond and marching in full uniform. A strong detachment was coming straight toward Lady Wu's quarters. Now they had come around the pond and were pouring down the corridors. Tsatsu and Yijy were spotted and instantly recognized. They scampered back, knowing that this was the end. Order was given to chase them. With a shout, the guards bared their knives and rushed forward. Too quickly they surrounded and seized the painted boys and neatly slashed their heads off.

Over two hundred yards away was the Welcome Fairies * Court, half-hidden by trees and entered from the south by a decorative arch, the Welcome Fairies Gate. Inside the Welcome Fairies Court, at the Gather Fairies Hall, Lady Wu was sleeping in her bed.

Commander Duotsa went into the court and ordered all attendants to get out. Jienje and the other leaders went in.

"What is all this noise?" asked Lady Wu, still authoritatively. "How dare you people come here?"

* "Fairies" is the original Chinese word. Its English connotation here is a pure coincidence.

"We beg Your Majesty's pardon," said Jienje. "Tsatsu and his brother are guilty of treason and we have come to get rid of them. They are dead. I am sorry we could not have informed you beforehand."

Lady Wu's eyes rested on her son.

"You!" she exclaimed. "Quickly go home, now that they are killed and you are satisfied."

Huan stepped forward. "I am sorry. The Crown Prince is not going back. His father the late Gaotsung entrusted him to your care as his heir. It is high time that the throne be given back to him. We humbly request that Your Majesty abdicate in your son's favor."

Lady Wu took it rather calmly. Her eyes traveled across the leaders who had come in and lined up before her.

"Why, Lijan, you too! I showed you and your father [Li Yifu] so many favors. And you [Tsui] Shyuanwei. I promoted you myself. I can't believe it!" She was as sure of herself as ever. "Rebels! Swine! All of you!"

"We are grateful, Your Majesty," replied Tsui. "But perhaps Your Majesty will understand that we are doing this as a measure of true gratitude."

The operation took no more than half an hour, thanks to the careful planning of Jienje. The leaders left, leaving Lijan to keep guard over Lady Wu, the officers taking with them the heads of the two Jang brothers.

Tsatsu's gang had been quietly rounded up in different parts of the city, and their relatives had been arrested. The heads of Tsatsu and Yije were prominently displayed at the Tientsin Bridge and a vast crowd gathered to witness the execution of the brothers and cousins of the hated Jangs.

On January the twenty-third, the following day, Prince Jer was declared Regent for the interim period, and on January the twenty-fourth Lady Wu formally abdicated. Prince Dan was made Archduke. All the royal descendants of the Tang

House were pardoned and restored to their former ranks. All exiled persons and their families condemned by Lai and Jou Shing were pardoned and allowed to return to their homes—except the children of the executioners themselves.

By January the twenty-sixth, Lady Wu was removed under guard to the royal park residence in the west of the city. The new Regent, as respectful to his mother as ever, dutifully reported to her once every ten days to pay his respects. She was kept under detention. But as the days passed, she felt she would have been happier if they had killed her at once.

The autocratic Lady Wu felt for the first time in her life that she was powerless—and defeated. Lijan still stood guard over her, virtually holding her prisoner. Her pride was terribly hurt. She was alone. Her lovers were dead. She could not even see her darling daughter, Princess Taiping, who had as a matter of fact deserted her and gone over to the side of Prince Jer. Worse, the dutiful Regent came to report a series of new orders which sounded to her like news of defeat in battle. It all came to this, that her Dynasty of Jou was abolished and all her plans and labors had come to naught. If she were only young and vigorous and could get out of bed, she would know how to deal with these ingrates whom she had fed with her own hands but had now turned against her.

The personal blows came, in rapid succession. On February the first the Dynasty of Tang was officially restored. All colors, insignia and titles and names of offices were restored to what they had been at the beginning of Gaotsung's reign. The "Northern Capital," Bingchow, Lady Wu's home district in Shansi, was abolished. The name for Loyang, "God's Dwelling Place," was dropped and Loyang became the Eastern Capital once more.

Wei Yuanjung, the man Tsatsu had driven to exile, had returned by popular demand to become Lord Secretary, and then Lord Chancellor. Lady Wu remembered what Wei had said on his departure: "Those two young men will one day be the ruin of Your Majesty. There will come a time when you will think of Wei Yuanjung and remember his words!"

But the worst news was yet to come. In March the descendants and relatives of Empress Wang and Shiaofei were given back their clan names, and the punitive names "Cobra" and "Vulture" were removed from them. And, worse still, in May the Wu ancestral temples were no longer imperial in name, and her ancestors were deprived of their ranks! This was "present-day retribution" (in one's own lifetime). Buddha Almighty! That she should live to see this day!

In November, Lady Wu finally yielded up the ghost in her luxurious confinement, aged eighty. Ever mindful of her offerings of food in afterlife, she had said in her will that she would now be contented to be worshiped as "Empress" and not "Emperor," as dutiful wife of her beloved husband Gaotsung (who, I think, was trembling at the thought of their reunion). In her last testament she had "pardoned" Wuji, Suiliang, Han Yuan and Empress Wang's uncle, Liu Shy, to make her way through Hell easier and pleasanter.

She had "pardoned" Empress Wang and Shiaofei, too. The news about Empress Wang's and Shiaofei's families sent her mind wandering back to old memories, memories of her youth. Those ghosts came back once more and sat on her conscience. Should she make peace with them so that she could say *she* had forgiven them and they were friends once more when they should meet in Hell? But she was Buddha Maitreya! She had the *Great Cloud Sutra* read to her and felt better as she heard the sweet flow of words which was music to her ears. It reminded her of the days of the abbot. She could truly say that she had enjoyed life fully, more than any other woman that ever lived. How she had fooled them all! She laughed. She was sure she was the most wonderful and the most powerful woman ever born on this earth, and she was going to do bigger things still in Hell or Heaven, whichever it was. She was sure of one thing, that Wu Tsertien's name would never be forgotten.

All the last arrangements had been made. Her son Jer, now Emperor, would be sure to take care of the seasonal offerings as due to the Emperor's own mother. Di Renjiay had been right in his advice. Her passage through Hell should be quite easy, she thought. Poor old Gaotsung would be there to meet her, she was quite sure. Since she had "pardoned" Empress Wang and Shiaofei, it was not impossible that they would be there among the welcoming delegation, including Suiliang, Wuji, Han Yuan, her sister the Duchess of Han and her daughter Sansan. She had not officially "pardoned" the mad monk, but if she should meet him, she would be quite willing to make up, for old times' sake. Then of course Wu Tsertien would go to Heaven, riding in a jewel-studded carriage in her regal pomp and splendor, where Buddha, Laotse and Confucius must all have heard of her. She would be surprised if they hadn't read the *Great Cloud Sutra.* There, too, would be the first king of Jou Dynasty, Emperor Wu, whom she had once honored as her "fortieth-generation ancestor" and who must be pleased and honored to meet the founder of the second Jou Dynasty. Laotse would be a special friend, whom she had specially honored on the return trip from *fengshan,* and he should be very appreciative that she had suggested (in 674) that all government officials should read Laotse. In her choice of mansions in Heaven, she would be glad to live as a neighbor to the Western Queen-Mother of Heaven. Thus, Wu Tsertien passed happily away, her spirit in peace.

The present life is only a preparation for the next. Does one's character change in the next life? I am sure it does not.